Man with a Miracle

MURIEL JENSEN

SILHOUETTE®
SUPERROMANCE™

*First published in Great Britain 2003
Silhouette Books, Eton House, 18-24 Paradise Road,
Richmond, Surrey TW9 1SR*

© Muriel Jensen 2002

ISBN 0 373 71093 3

38-1203

*Printed and bound in Spain
by Litografia Rosés S.A., Barcelona*

'What are you doing?'

He grabbed her under the arms and tried to haul her up. She struggled against him and they both went down. This time her head collided with his arm as she fell, dislodging her watch cap. What he saw in the glow of the headlights made him stare in shock and anger.

Her luxurious red hair had been cut off so that it was barely longer than his, and it was… purple.

'I'm leaving!' she said, swinging at him with her plastic bag.

'Beazie!' Her name escaped him in a kind of gasp. He couldn't believe she'd done it, though he realised it was probably her most recognisable feature.

He forced his attention away from the atrocity perpetrated against her hair, handed her the hat so she could put it back on and made himself focus on the more important issue.

'To go *where*?'

'Anywhere a taxi will take me!' she replied. 'I got the tape to you, so my job is done.'

'Beazie, your life is in danger.'

'Not any more. Now *you* have the tape…'

Dear Reader,

Happy Holidays from Astoria, Oregon, where it rains at Christmas rather than snows. Still, the Christmas spirit is alive in our hearts and visible everywhere. Though Astoria does not have a town square, it resembles my description of Maple Hill, with Christmas lights, garlands stretched across the main street from pavement to pavement and wreaths circling the old-fashioned globe streetlights. One Christmas bonus Astoria has that's missing in Maple Hill is a parade of boats strung with lights from stem to stern.

In the light of day, Astoria is a very different setting from Maple Hill. We're positioned at the mouth of the Columbia River, on a fairly steep slope that runs down to the water. Many artists and writers live here, claiming the river to be a creative source.

I love it here. Rain never drowns out our enthusiasm. In fact, we have umbrella parades to honour it. For the most part, people are warm and loving, and because we're a small town, we're a community of friends. That warmth supports and sustains me every day, and makes it easy to sit in my second-floor office in the middle of a monsooning February and create a Christmas atmosphere.

I wish you all the blessings of the season, and your own personal Astoria.

Muriel

MEN OF MAPLE HILL
by Muriel Jensen

Man with a Mission
Man with a Message
Man with a Miracle

PROLOGUE

June 10, 2001

EVAN BRAGA WIPED HIS FACE with a towel as he hurried into the locker room of the Hatfield Gym, remembering belatedly that he'd promised to trade shifts with Halloran tonight. Someone else would have to host the Sunday-night poker game of the Boston PD's Cambridge Division. He went to the bench where he'd left his gym bag and stopped in confusion when he found nothing there. Then he spotted the bag under the bench and yanked it out. Ripping open the zipper, he pushed his sweatshirt aside and reached in for his cell phone.

His hand stopped. His heart stopped. His brain stopped. He was paralyzed.

Only his eyes seemed to be working, and he couldn't believe what he was seeing. Cash. Lots of it, neatly bundled in banded packets. One-hundred dollar bundles. Five-hundred dollar bundles.

He felt his mouth open, but no sound came out.

He was alone in the quiet room. He could hear the ticking clock, the sound of someone in the showers on the other side of the wall, shouts and laughter from the gym floor.

He had zipped the bag closed and was trying to figure out what in the hell was going on, when he saw the plastic tag looped around the handle of the bag. New England Insurance, it read. This was Blaine's bag. Their parents had given them identical gym bags and matching sweatshirts last Christmas, but his younger brother was the one usually mixing them up—not Evan.

His heart lurched uncomfortably. He knew Blaine and Sheila had been having financial problems, but what was his brother doing with banded bills in large denominations, in his insurance business?

He felt a sort of fraternal panic, and the only thought in his head that made sense told him to get the bag and Blaine out of there as fast as he could.

Jerking open his locker, he threw on a pair of blue sweats, grasped the handle of the bag firmly and headed for the gym.

Blaine was chasing across the court in a pickup basketball game, then leaped to block a shot. In an instant of detachment, Evan noticed that Blaine was leaner than he was, his body more artfully graceful than simply strong. Even as a kid, he'd had the looks, the charm, the charisma that drew people to him. He'd always been the golden child, but unfortunately had never realized it and had taken the easy way out of everything.

Watching out for Blaine had been Evan's job since he was six years old, and it had taken a lot of his time. But he'd done it well. Apparently the fact that his brother had a wife, two little sons and an insurance franchise didn't mean Evan could stop watching Blaine. Not if that bag of money was any indication.

While another player shot from the free-throw line, Blaine caught Evan's eye and tossed him a grin. Then he noticed the bag in Evan's hand and went deathly pale.

Evan started for the door. Blaine ran in his wake, his friends calling after him to come back.

"Sorry, guys," Blaine shouted over his shoulder. "Uh...family dinner. See you Wednesday." He chased Evan out of the building and across the parking lot to Evan's old Austin-Healy convertible.

"You have to put the bag back!" Blaine said urgently, standing by the passenger side door as Evan leaped over his door and into the car.

"Get in!" Evan commanded, stuffing the bag into the narrow area behind the seat.

"Listen to me."

"Get in!"

"Evan, that money—"

"That money's going to be returned," Evan said, starting the engine, prepared to leave whether Blaine climbed in or not. "I don't even want to know what you're doing with it—I'm just sure it can't be good. Now, get in or I'm turning it in to the closest police station. You'll go away for a long time."

Blaine swung his legs over the door and slid down into the seat. "You're always so sure you know everything."

Evan eased out of the parking lot, then roared away down the long country road. "Tell me I'm wrong," he said. "I'd be happy to hear that."

"You're wrong. It isn't stolen, as I'm sure you suspect. It's...it's borrowed."

Evan gave him a quick side-glance. "From whom?"

Blaine sighed and ran a hand over his face. "From my holding account," he said finally. "I'm going to put it back."

"Blaine—" Evan began.

"Oh, relax!" Blaine shouted at him. "It's a gray area, okay? It's the insurance company's account, but it's under my control. As long as I put the money back—"

"How are you going to do that, when you had to borrow it in the first place?" Evan slowed as he came to an intersection with a narrow side road, then picked up speed again, feeling an urgent need to return the money before someone found out there was trouble—for Blaine, his wife, his kids, their parents...

"That's none of your business." Blaine tried to reach behind him for the bag. "*This* is none of your business."

"No, it's *your* business!" Evan accused. "Sheila and the boys are *your* business! Did you give them any thought when you did this? What's it for? The boat's not big enough? You need a second summer home to attract more clients? Another classic Jag? Sheila seems perfectly happy..."

"Yeah, well, my girlfriend's expensive." Grabbing the bag with both hands, Blaine swung it onto his lap. "Now stop the car. I've got to go back! The bag *has* to be where I left it or I'm—"

"We're not going back. You're going to redeposit the money and I'll help you find another—"

As they approached another intersection, Blaine reached for the steering wheel. Evan tried to push him away, and caught sight of a big black Dodge Ram coming quickly down the side road. Completely unaware, Blaine pulled at the wheel, and with a screech of tires, the Austin-Healy headed straight toward the truck.

Evan shouted, but the squeal of brakes drowned out the sound. There was a bone-shattering impact, the grinding whine of tearing metal, then blackness.

January 4, 2002

"I DON'T UNDERSTAND why you feel you have to go." Alice Turner, Evan's mother, followed him from the kitchen to the driveway, where he packed two suitcases into the back of a brand-new white Safari already loaded with boxes, an apartment-size refrigerator and a television. She'd said that several times a day for the two weeks since he'd made the decision.

He couldn't tell her the truth. "I just have to, Mom," he said, taking a plastic-wrapped stack of blankets and a pillow from his stepfather, who'd followed them out. "I appreciate all you and Dad and Sheila have done for me since I got out of the hospital, but…"

"You think we blame you," his mother accused, tears spilling from her grieving brown eyes. She folded her arms pugnaciously.

"No." He avoided her eyes as he found a place for the blankets on top of a box. They didn't blame him, and Sheila didn't blame him. In fact, they'd sat with him every day for the long three months it took to heal his broken legs, his right arm, his pelvis that resulted from his ejection from the car upon impact. They'd helped with his physical therapy, then brought him home to complete his recovery at his parents' place. His sister-in-law, Sheila, and his two nephews, Mark, 6, and Matthew, 4, had visited often, bringing him cookies, and crayon artwork for his room.

But Evan saw the grief they tried to hide from him, the loss in their eyes even when they smiled and encouraged him. Their suffering compounded his own sense of failure as a brother and a son, until he felt he couldn't stay another moment. He had to spare all of them the constant reminder that he survived the crash and Blaine died, and he had to find another way to go on, before despair overtook him.

The only good thing to come out of the accident was that it put an end to the issue of the borrowed money. The car had been incinerated and the money burned up. Blaine must have sufficiently hidden his "loan" in the books, because when the franchise was purchased in August, an audit revealed nothing untoward. Or maybe Blaine had some fail-safe method of payback that he hadn't had a chance to explain before the accident.

Whatever the reason, Evan was grateful that neither his parents nor Sheila had any idea Blaine had done anything criminal.

"I just have to get my life together again, Mom,"
he explained, hugging her, "and I can't do it here.
A company in Maple Hill advertised for a housepainter. I love that kind of work and I'm pretty good
at it. Maple Hill is close enough that I can come
home regularly to visit, and you can come and see
me."

"Are you going to be happy painting houses?"
his stepfather, Barney, asked as he wrapped his arms
around Evan. "You were such a good cop."

"I'll be fine, Dad," Evan assured him. Barney
Turner had been his father since he was four, and
he'd never made Evan feel less important or less
loved than Blaine.

"You know who to call if you aren't."

"I do."

"Mark and Mattie will miss you," his mother
prodded as they followed him around to the driver's
side.

"Alice, don't torture the boy," Barney chided.
"He knows they'll miss him. He spent all day with
them yesterday, explaining things. They'll be fine,
and he'll be fine."

His mother gave his father a reproachful look.
"Men are always fine because they're the ones off
on adventures. Women are the ones who stay behind
and worry."

Barney squeezed her shoulders. "He's going to
Maple Hill, Allie, not to war. Good luck, son."

Evan hugged his mother again, climbed in behind
the wheel and drove away.

CHAPTER ONE

December 9, 2002

EVAN IGNORED THE PAIN in his right leg as he ran around the track of Maple Hill High with three of his friends. He and Hank Whitcomb, Bart Megrath and Cameron Trent formed an irregular line across the lanes as snow fell steadily in large flakes.

"What? Are we training for the Winter Olympics?" Bart asked Hank, his breath puffing out ahead of him. Bart was a lawyer, and much preferred the comforts of his home or office to the uncompromising cold of western Massachusetts in the winter.

"Can't be," Cam put in, pulling a blue wool watch cap a little lower over his ears. "Track-and-field is a summer event. Hank just likes to torture us because he's our boss. Thank God it was icy at the lake, or he'd have us running there, with the wind-chill factor making it even colder than it is here."

"Hank's not *my* boss," Bart corrected.

"No, but he's your brother-in-law," Evan put in. After eleven months on the job with Hank and Cam, and working on community projects with the two of them and Bart, he was comfortable in their company. He considered himself fortunate to have their friendship, and thought often how much brighter his life had become in the past year. "If you don't get your exercise, he'll report you to Haley like he did last time, and she'll tell the ladies at Perk Avenue not to serve you those double mochas and cream horns anymore."

"That was a joke," Bart said.

"You didn't think it was funny."

Haley was Bart's wife, Hank's sister, and the publisher of the *Maple Hill Mirror*.

Bart laughed. "You're just being superior, Evan," he said, "because you're still a bachelor. Wait till my mother-in-law fixes you up with some pretty young thing who makes you lose your senses and forget your backbone. You won't be able to laugh at us anymore."

Addie Whitcomb was a confirmed matchmaker. Evan had skillfully avoided her machinations so far, but she was growing more determined all the time.

"I'm not laughing," he insisted, even as he tamped his amusement. "I just think it's interesting that the town's leading attorney—" he pointed a gloved finger at Bart "—the head of the much-acclaimed Whitcomb's Wonders—" he indicated Hank, who modestly inclined his head "—and Cam, the Wonders' brilliant plumber and my inspired partner in land development, can be so cowed by three of the town's most beautiful and talented, but very small, women. Guys, come on. You're whipped!"

His friends looked at one another, laughed and ran on, dragging him with them, apparently not offended.

"It'll happen to you," Cam warned.

"No," he denied affably.

"That's what I used to think," Hank said with a knowing glance at him from beneath the bill of a Boston Red Sox baseball cap. "And look at me now."

Hank's wife, Jackie, was mayor of Maple Hill and the mother of four children, whom Hank had adopted.

"I like my privacy," Evan insisted.

Cam laughed. "That's what we all said. Prepare to kiss it goodbye, dude. You're ripe."

"Ripe?"

"Almost forty. Addie won't be able to stand it. Even Haley, Jackie and Mariah are starting to plot."

Cam's wife, Mariah, a former dorm mother at the Maple Hill Manor Private School just outside of town, had charmed Cam into marrying her to provide a home for two of the school's boarders, who suddenly had been without families. Five months later it had proven to be a good move for all of them.

"It's not going to happen to me," Evan said, seriousness creeping into his tone. He ignored the speculative looks his friends exchanged with one another. He hadn't shared much about his past with his friends, though he trusted them all implicitly. It was just still too hard to give words to what had happened.

He'd told them he'd been a cop, and that he'd come to Maple Hill after an automobile accident that had almost disabled him. He said he'd come to rebuild his body in the fresh air, and to restore his spirit with the more relaxed pace of small-town life.

He'd joined St. Anthony's Church, because after a month here, he still had too many memories and ghosts and needed desperately to be reminded that a power beyond his feeble abilities had charge of the world. And the Men's Club gave him somewhere to go on weekends when his friends were involved with their families.

The church group was always raising money for the school, repairing or repainting it, or helping with some community project or other. Many of the men in the club were much older than he, but he liked their old-fashioned, curiously heroic way of thinking and their incisive senses of humor. They reminded him of Barney and eased his loneliness.

"Next year at this time," Hank said, "when you're married and expecting a baby, we're going to remind you that you said that. Want to take bets on it, guys? Pick the month you think Evan bites the dust. Ten bucks. Winner buys everybody breakfast at the Barn."

Evan ran in place, while the others stopped to exchange money and make their bets. "You'll all owe me a meal when I remain a bachelor. Wait and see."

They ignored him and conducted their business. Hank, who had faith in his mother, said she'd have Evan hooked by Valentine's Day. Cam had been claimed in June and thought Evan would, too. Bart said that hurricane weather was powerful stuff and bet on August.

Evan put out his hand. "I'll hold the money."

Cam clutched the bills to his chest. "You're one

of the principals of the bet. You can't hold the money."

"I'll give it to Jackie," Hank said. "She can put it in the safe at City Hall."

Evan shrugged nonchalantly as he continued to run in place. His leg was going to seize up if he didn't. He needed a Jacuzzi and a Coffee Nudge. "You're all going to be so embarrassed."

They laughed in unison as they headed back to their cars. In five minutes they would reconvene at the Minuteman Bakery.

Evan stayed in his car an extra moment to massage his screaming thigh muscle, then joined his friends in the bakery's corner booth. Someone had already poured his coffee and ordered his daily caramel-nut roll.

When he slipped in against the wall beside Cam, they were talking about the homeless shelter being built. As mayor, Jackie had helped solicit funds for the project and directed the construction.

The members of Whitcomb's Wonders, a pool of craftsmen who could be hired at a moment's notice for an hour or a year, had each worked on it at some point.

Evan had been painting and wallpapering at the shelter for weeks. All that remained to be done was the kitchen, and a second coat of paint applied to the common room. Jackie was hoping to see the shelter open on December twenty-third. With the advent of frigid weather, Father Chabot was sheltering the homeless in the basement of the church. There were several families, and everyone wanted to see them in more comfortable surroundings by Christmas.

"So, you're okay to finish up by next week?" Hank asked Evan. Though they conducted their business over coffee and doughnuts, it was still business, and everyone's attitude was a little more serious than earlier.

"Yes," Evan replied. "Sooner if I can."

"Don't you and Cam have to get that office in your building finished this week?"

Evan nodded. "I'm doing that today and tomorrow. Unless you need me somewhere."

"No. Nothing today. Some work at the Heritage Museum after the holidays."

Evan and Cam's first project together as Trent and Braga Development had been the purchase of the old Chandler Mill on the edge of town. Someone had made a halfhearted attempt to turn it into offices at one time, but the work was shoddy, clearly done by amateurs. Hank had once housed the offices of Whitcomb's Wonders there, but had since moved the business into City Hall's basement. Evan and Cam had torn down the old walls of the mill and hired Whitcomb's Wonders to section off the first and second floors into eight large offices, and the third floor into two small apartments and two large ones.

The slow, easy approach they'd intended to take in readying the building for occupancy had gained momentum when a previous tenant, an accounting office, was happy about the renovation and eager to return—preferably between Christmas and the new year. Cam had promised the premises could be occupied on January second.

They had three more tenants eager to move in downstairs, and one waiting for a second-floor spot. It seemed that their development company was off to a good start.

Evan smiled to himself as he thought about how different his life was now from what it had been eighteen months ago. Then, he'd had morning coffee and pastries with scores of other cops in a squad room. He'd patrolled the city in a pattern that was often fairly routine, but could explode into periods of stress and danger that were sometimes energizing, sometimes terrifying. And he'd loved it.

Then he'd killed Blaine, and everything had changed. Well, over the past year he'd managed to accept that he hadn't really killed him; Blaine had been struggling for the wheel at the time of impact. But that didn't completely absolve Evan of blame. It was his fault Blaine had been in the car in the first place.

But he didn't want to think about that right now. What he had here was good. Good friends, good coffee, rewarding work waiting for him. He missed his parents and Sheila and the boys, but he wasn't up to seeing them yet. His mother had invited him for Thanksgiving, but he'd told her he had to work on the accountant's office to have it ready in time. She'd sounded disappointed, but said merely that he had to plan to come home for Christmas.

He wasn't sure how he was going to get out of that yet, but he intended to.

"You're coming to the Wonders' Christmas party?" Hank asked Evan as he consulted his watch. It was almost eight a.m., time for them to get to work. "Sunday afternoon. And since we'll all be together, Jackie's planning to hold a meeting about preparations for opening the shelter." Jackie had found a willing group of volunteers in her husband's friends.

"I've got to work on the—" Evan began.

"No, you don't," Cam interrupted. "We've got a couple of weeks before Harvey starts moving things in."

"But the carpet's got to go down."

"That'll take all of two hours. You're just trying to get out of joining us."

He was. Their warmth and camaraderie, while great on the job, was a little tough to take in their homes. It was a reminder of the family he just couldn't bring himself to see again, and the family he'd never be able to build for himself.

"I told Brian you were coming," Cam said, shamelessly forcing his hand. "The kid's looking forward to seeing you."

"And Mike was looking forward to talking to you about the Sox," Bart told him. "Nobody else has the stats at his fingertips like you do."

Hank slipped out of the booth. "Jackie wants you to bring salad. We'll expect you at two o'clock."

He conceded with a nod. "Okay. I'll be there."

The group dispersed. Evan bought a refill on his coffee and a few more doughnuts, then went out to

the red Jeep the garage had lent him while they replaced the alternator on his van.

He missed his big vehicle. EVAN BRAGA,
PAINTING, PART OF WHITCOMB'S WONDERS
was now painted in red letters on its side. He felt a
certain pride every time he looked at it. He'd managed to pull himself together in a year, and though
he still had a lot of issues to deal with, he was making progress. Life was good.

He climbed into the Jeep, grateful to have wheels
at all, put the coffee cup in the console, tossed the
bag of doughnuts onto the passenger seat and headed
for the mill.

His parking spot was around the back, where he
and Cam kept an office that also served as a storage
shed for tools and equipment. There was a lumpy old
love seat in it that Bart and Haley had donated when
they bought new furniture, and Evan wanted nothing
more than to sit on it, drink his coffee and have another doughnut, before he applied the second coat of
paint to the window frames and doors of the accounting office, then wallpapered the women's bathroom.

Balancing doughnuts, coffee and the new roller
handles he'd bought, he unlocked the door and
pushed it open.

What he saw shocked him into stillness. He experienced a playback of that moment, a year and a
half ago, when he'd opened the gym bag and found
bundles of cash.

Only, this moment was potentially more dangerous. He was looking at the business end of the Louis-
ville Slugger he kept on top of the bookshelf. Ready

to swing it was a very disheveled young woman in a torn and dusty navy-blue suit and jacket and dress shoes. Dark red hair was piled in a messy bundle atop her head, and she looked pale and obviously terrified.

He assessed her calmly as his old training kicked in. She was average in height and slender, and even with a gun would have posed a negligible threat—if she'd been calm.

But she wasn't. She looked exhausted, and her red-rimmed blue eyes said more clearly than words that she was on the brink of destruction—her own or someone else's.

His presence seemed about to push her over the edge.

"Hi," he said calmly, and stayed right where he was.

HI? BEAZIE DEADHAM thought hysterically. He'd killed her boss and chased her across the commonwealth of Massachusetts, and all he could say when they finally stood face-to-face, was *Hi?*

She was going to lose it. She could feel it happening. She was shaking so hard she could hear her own teeth chattering.

Things were beginning to reel around her. She'd been up all night with nothing to eat or drink. She'd tried to close her eyes during the four-hour drive in the back of the moving van, but each time, she'd seen her boss's broken body crumpled on the concrete floor of the parking structure, life ebbing out of him

as she ran and knelt beside him. She'd seen the red
SUV with the gunman in it rev its motor.

"Beazie," Gordon had gasped, and clutched her
hand. "Evans…" Blood trickled out of the corner of
his mouth. "Take it to…Evans. Maple Hill… No
police."

Barely able to hear him, she leaned over him, her
ear to his lips.

"No one…else," he said in a barely audible
croak. "Evans…Maple Hill."

It was only then that she noticed he'd pressed
something into her hand: a miniature tape cassette
like the kind in an answering machine.

This wasn't happening to her, she thought in a
panic now, dragging herself back to the moment and
the man who stood across from her. Although her
arms were aching from holding the bat, she didn't
dare lower the weapon. This guy had killed her boss,
Gordon Hathaway. Gentle Gordon, the man who'd
given her an advance on her paycheck when she'd
hired on, because she'd explained she was really
broke; who'd given her a bonus when she'd reorgan-
ized the filing system; who'd been kind and funny
and more of a friend than an employer.

"Do you want to tell me what you're doing
here?" the man asked in a quiet, rumbly voice from
across the room. In his large hands were two long
poles, a paper bag and a cup of coffee. His white
pants and sweatshirt were both covered with flecks
of paint in assorted colors, and a red scarf patterned
with black moose and bears was wrapped around
his neck.

It encouraged her that she could see so clearly, considering the way her eyes burned. Spots had been floating in and out of her vision, but they were gone now. Still, she felt vaguely nauseated.

The man's hair was dark blond and slightly curly, his eyes brown and calm. He apparently didn't consider her a threat. Well, she'd show him! Nobody killed people she knew and got away with it.

But what did she do with him, now that she had him at bay? Gordon had said no police. She could only conclude that meant someone in the police department was involved in his death. But did he mean in Boston or in Maple Hill? Oh God.

"You murdered Gordon Hathaway!" she accused sternly, hoping she looked like a controlled woman with a plan, even though she didn't have one. "Did you think you'd get away with that?"

Those calm brown eyes looked blank, then he blinked and said, "Pardon me?"

"You killed Gordon Hathaway!" she shrieked at him. The spots were back and she was starting to feel as though she was about to explode. All effort to remain calm disintegrated. "And you've been after me ever since!"

"Why do you think that?" he asked.

"Because I *saw* you! I saw your red SUV in the parking garage when that guy leaned out and shot Gordon! I saw you come into my apartment building, looking for me!"

"You didn't see *me*."

"I did! And just now, I watched you pull up here!"

"Look," he said in that patronizing tone. "I'm just going to put this stuff down, okay?"

"Don't think I won't smash you."

"It's okay," he said, easing the poles into the corner near the door.

She watched him as he placed the small bag and cup of coffee on the edge of the desk beside him. He looked up at her and noticed her licking her dry lips. "Are you hungry?" he asked.

He reached slowly for the bag and tossed it to the love seat near where she stood. "There's a maple bar, a cinnamon twist and a caramel-nut roll in there. Help yourself."

Without moving her eyes from him, she pointed the bat with one hand and unrolled the top of the bag with the other. She reached inside and withdrew the first thing her fingers touched. It was the maple bar. With a shaky hand she brought it to her mouth and took a large bite.

It tasted like ambrosia.

Fortified by that single bite, she indicated the coffee cup with the bat, which was getting heavy. "Move the coffee to the edge of the desk."

Certain she had him at least concerned, if not intimidated, she was surprised and dismayed when he grinned.

"Sorry. That's only my second cup this morning, and I've got a big day ahead of me. If you want it, you have to take it from me."

Beazie figured she must have looked disappointed, because his grin widened and he said, "Oh, all right." Reaching for a pottery cup on the desk, he poured half of the coffee into it, then held the paper cup out to her. "Here you go."

She'd never wanted anything more in her life, but she didn't trust him. Apparently aware of that, he put it on the edge of the desk nearest her and took several steps back.

She put the maple bar down, reached for the cup and took a careful swallow. The coffee was hot, rich and absolutely delicious.

"I'm driving a Jeep on loan from the garage that's fixing my van," he said, sitting on the desk and drinking from his pottery cup. "Not an SUV."

As she lowered her own cup, she felt an instant's uncertainty.

"Where did this murder take place?" he asked.

She sidled toward the window near his desk, so that she could see the parking area. "In Boston," she replied.

"Well, I haven't been to Boston in almost a year. In fact, I've hardly left Maple Hill. So you have me confused with someone else."

Rising up on tiptoe, she spotted the top of the red car, but couldn't see enough to be sure it was the SUV. She'd watched him pull in, she reminded herself, and she'd been sure then. Of course, she'd been dealing with those spots.

He took a cordless phone from the top of the desk and tried to hand it to her. "Call the police," he said. "They can tell you who I am."

"You'd like that, wouldn't you," she said with new resolve, polishing off the last of the coffee. "Gordon told me no police. Did you buy them off?"

He put a hand to his face and took a deep breath. "Why don't we call you a doctor?" he asked finally, preparing to stab out a telephone number. "You look as though you're on the verge of collapse. Sit down and I'll—"

She made a desperate grab for the phone, thinking that he'd probably just get a doctor to sedate her or something, then they'd throw her in that beautiful lake behind the...

She couldn't quite round out the thought.

Everything went red. Not black, but a sort of rosy red. She felt hot suddenly, as though a prickly woollen blanket were inching up her body. With a strange sort of detachment, she watched as the coffee cup fell out of her hands and the bat dangled from her fingers.

The man sprang off the desk to take the bat from her, and as she sank into a warm, fuzzy stupor, she expected him to hit her with it.

But he put it aside and reached out for her as her knees buckled. She expected a collision with the floor, but the last thing she knew was the cradle of a strong pair of arms.

CHAPTER TWO

EVAN CARRIED THE YOUNG WOMAN to the love seat, put two fingertips to her throat, and felt great relief when he sensed the tap of a steady pulse. He retrieved a ratty but clean blanket he kept in the closet. Her skin was icy to the touch. It certainly lent credence to her story that she'd been on the run all night.

Then he reached for the phone to dial 911. But remembering her fear, and her odd remark about the police being in collusion with the killer, he changed his mind.

He couldn't imagine what had happened to her, but she seemed more genuinely fearful than crazy. Something or someone had driven her to this state. Someone with a red SUV.

He called Randy Sanford, who was an EMT and worked on Whitcomb's Wonders' janitorial crew in his spare time. Evan explained briefly about not wanting to call an ambulance.

"My bag's at Medics Rescue," Randy said. "You should call—"

"Just come!" Evan demanded. He'd pressed the speaker button so that he had his hands free to make a pot of coffee for the woman. "I don't think it's life or death, but please. Just get over here."

"On my way," Randy promised.

Once the coffee was dripping, Evan went to see what else he could do to make the woman comfortable. He noticed that her head rested at an odd angle on the pillow he'd propped under her, and tried to readjust it. Then he realized that the problem was a dirty, tattered piece of elasticized fabric wrapped around her hair. He worked gently to remove it, and combed his fingers through the dark burnished mass.

As he wrapped the blanket more tightly around her, he wondered once again what had happened to her. She had a pretty oval face, though even in her unconscious state, she frowned. Her nose was small, her chin slightly pointed, and her long eyelashes were a shade darker than her hair. If she wore makeup, it had worn off in her ordeal, and a spray of freckles stood out on the bridge of her nose and across her cheekbones.

When she stirred fitfully, he put a hand to her shoulder, telling her it was all right, she was safe.

She moaned in response, but her eyes remained closed.

BEAZIE WAS LEANING OVER Gordon in horrified disbelief as his life drained away.

She heard the door of the SUV open. The driver, a young man in a fleece-lined jacket, was about to step out, but the elevator doors parted and a throng of laughing, talking commuters spilled out. As soon as they noticed her sheltering Gordon's supine body, they hurried toward her, one of them already on his cell phone. A young woman pushed Beazie aside, telling her she was a nurse.

The door closed on the red SUV and it sped away.

The ambulance arrived first, and the paramedics covered Gordon with a sheet. As soon as Beazie saw the police car pull up, she panicked and slipped away unnoticed in the crowd of onlookers that had gathered. Gordon had pleaded ''No police!'' She couldn't risk them finding the tape on her.

Once she was out on the main street, she hailed a cab and headed straight for her apartment. Everything there was just as she'd left it that morning, and she experienced a strange feeling of unreality. She had to have imagined the murder of her boss. That kind of thing didn't happen to a nice, middle-class girl from Buffalo.

Then she found the tape, still clutched so tightly in her hand it left marks. She walked to the window to examine it more closely and see if it was labeled.

Instead, her attention was caught by the bright red SUV parking in front of her building. Three men got out. One stayed with the car while the other two hurried inside.

Her flight-or-fight response kicked in and adrenaline raged through her body as she raced out of her apartment and scrambled down the fire escape. Once on the ground, she fled down an alley to the next block, and kept running as darkness fell.

She was cold, she was hungry. In her panic, she hadn't thought to grab her purse. How was she going to get to Maple Hill without cash or credit cards?

Then she came upon the gaping rear doors of a moving van and heard the driver and his assistant talking about their next stop in Springfield. She remembered from visiting a friend there and antiquing through the area that it was just a short distance from Maple Hill, a quaint little town at the foot of the Berkshires. Without a second's thought, she climbed into the truck.

For several hours she huddled in the cold darkness of the moving van, wedged between a mattress and an easy chair. When at last they stopped, the assistant opened the doors, and she got ready to do some fast explaining. But the driver shouted a question and the assistant headed back to the cab.

Her body stiff with cold, Beazie struggled down from the van and headed toward the well-lit main street, wondering how on earth she would get to Maple Hill. Down a little side lane she noticed the shipping and receiving doors of a bakery wide-open, so she slipped inside, drawn by the warmth and the light. Beyond a wall of windows, big ovens were being filled with racks of something she couldn't quite identify.

The aroma was torturous. She'd skipped breakfast, had been too busy for lunch and was now feeling weak and dizzy. Unfortunately, all of the bakery's product seemed to be on the other side of the window.

She shrank back into the shadows as a tall boy in a white uniform and headphones came out another door carrying a large rack. He walked out in to the lane, headed for a truck with Palermo Bakery emblazoned on the side. After sliding the rack of bread in the back of the truck, he went to the driver's door and climbed in. Taking her courage in hand, Beazie raced over and asked if he was going anywhere near Maple Hill.

He yanked off the headphones. "What's that?"

"Are you going anywhere near Maple Hill?" she asked again.

He looked her over and smiled. "Sure am, du-dette," he said. "That's my first stop. You need a ride?"

She nodded, grateful that he was friendly and ame-nable, if not the brightest light on the field. She wanted to add, *Yes, and a dozen doughnuts, please,* but she said instead, "I'm looking for someone named Evans there. Do you know anyone by that name?"

He nodded. "I do. Hop in, time's a-wastin'."

She couldn't believe her good fortune. She closed her eyes against a thumping headache and was mer-cifully ignored while the young man sang loudly to the tunes from his Walkman. Within half an hour, he pulled off the road and into the parking lot of what looked like an old mill. It was now about four a.m.

"You'll find him in that office," he said, pointing to the far end of the building. "But probably not for a couple of hours."

Beazie was also grateful that the driver's youth and "duh-ness" prevented him from arguing about leaving her on what was now a dark and lonely road.

"I'll be fine," she assured him, and with a heartfelt "thank you" leaped out onto the parking lot and headed straight for a garden bench under a floodlight.

The sign on the building said Trent and Braga Development. *Trent and Braga.* Beazie turned to the truck, but the driver was already back on the road and almost out of sight.

She hoped this wasn't simply the boy's idea of a joke on a disheveled "dudette" and that there really was someone named Evans here.

Tired as she was, she decided to try the windows and was deliriously relieved to find one slightly open. She pushed it open even farther and climbed inside. The smell of sealant was strong, and she imagined that was why the window had been left ajar.

In the glow of the floodlight, the room appeared to be large and empty, and she made her way carefully to a door, which led to a hallway. Every other room along the hallway was also empty, except for one at the end that appeared to be a sort of office-storage area. And it had a sofa!

The room wobbled as she stumbled to the lumpy couch. She would lie down for a minute; then, as soon as the world straightened again, she'd look for something to eat. If this place was used as an office, there might be cookies or chips stashed in a drawer. She closed her eyes, quickly reviewed all the horrible things that had happened to her over the past sixteen hours, and reaffirmed her determination to grant Gordon his dying wish. He'd been a good friend to her, and she felt bound to help him in the only way she had left. She fell asleep with tears on her cheek.

THE WOMAN WAS STILL UNCONSCIOUS five minutes later when Randy arrived, ripping off his jacket. He was tall and dark-featured, with what Evan had heard the Wonders Women, his wife and his friends' wives, refer to as heartthrob good looks. Randy never seemed to be aware of them himself.

Evan pointed him to the sofa and Randy sat on the edge of it and leaned over the woman, putting his cheek to her mouth and nose to check for breathing.

"What's her name?" he asked Evan as he straightened up. He put his index and second fingers to the pulse at her throat.

"I don't know," Evan replied.

"Pulse is a little thready." Randy shook her lightly. "Hey, pretty lady. Can you hear me?" he asked loudly. "Hello! Can you hear me? Can you talk?" He gave her another gentle shake. "What did you say happened to her?"

Evan went to the cupboard for coffee cups. "I'm not sure. She said something about seeing her boss killed, then being chased all night long. She started out in Boston."

"How'd she get here?"

"Don't know. I unlocked my door to find her threatening me with a bat. She looked pretty desperate."

"No purse?"

"Uh...don't think so." He left the small table with the coffeepot, to check the corners of the office. He searched behind a stack of boxes, then under the love seat. Nothing. "No purse," he confirmed.

"No coat, either?"

"No."

The woman stirred as though uncomfortable, then moaned.

Randy lightly placed his hand above her waist. "It's all right," he said. "Can you hear me?"

When she didn't respond, he took one of her hands and rubbed it. "She's breathing a little fast, but that would be consistent with being frightened. And her pulse isn't really strong but it's definitely there."

He put her hand back under the blanket and rubbed her arms through it. "She wasn't dressed for a winter night. That coffee ready? That'll do her the most good. She's probably just cold and hungry. Not to mention scared and exhausted."

The woman opened her eyes then, and at the sight of them, tried to propel herself backward on the sofa, looking desperate to escape.

"Whoa," Randy said, catching her hands. "It's okay. I'm an emergency medical technician."

"He's okay." Evan came forward and handed her a cup of coffee. "I called him when you fainted. You're safe. I'm driving a red Jeep, remember, not an SUV. This is Randy Sanford, a friend of mine."

She studied Randy suspiciously, then looked up at Evan, her suspicion obviously deepening. But she took a sip of the coffee and seemed to relax a little.

"I'd like to take you to the hospital," Randy said, "just to make sure you're all right and that you fainted because you're cold and hungry, not because of something more serious."

BEAZIE MADE A QUICK DECISION. She could not go to the hospital. Someone would have to take down a lot of information, create a file that could be traced.

"No, thank you," she said firmly. "I'm fine."

"You fainted," the first man reminded her. "Fine people don't faint."

"Hungry people do," she replied. "You don't have another doughnut, do you?"

He reached for the bag he'd given her earlier and offered it to her. She pulled out the cinnamon twist. "You should go to the hospital."

She took a big bite of the doughnut, then glanced at him apologetically. "No, thank you. This will put me back on my feet."

"What are you going to do then?" he asked. "You have no purse or coat."

Many times during the cold night she had wished she'd handled her escape with more thought, but when she'd seen the red SUV on the street below her apartment, she'd panicked.

It didn't matter, though. Somehow she was going to find this Evans person and give him the tape Gordon had passed to her with his last breath. He hadn't deserved to die the way he did.

"I'll do what I came to do," she replied with far more conviction than she felt. "I'm looking for a man named Evans. Either of you know him?"

Randy Sanford pointed to his friend. "Your host is Evan Braga. But I don't know anyone with the last name Evans. What's your name, by the way?"

She hesitated a moment, then replied, "Beazie Deadham." There was little point in withholding her name. If the men in the red SUV had been able to find out where she lived, she was sure they also knew her name.

Now that she was seeing more clearly and was more coherent, she realized Evan Braga wasn't one of the men from the SUV. But Gordon had warned her not to trust anyone, and had directed her to give the tape to someone named Evans, not Evan. At least, she thought he had. His voice had been frail, and the sound in the underground parking lot less than ideal.

"That's an unusual name," Randy said.

"My grandmothers were Beatrice and Zoe," she explained. "I'm Beatrice Zoe. Beazie."

"Ah." Randy stood. "I don't think you need me anymore," he said, patting her hand.

Evan Braga walked him across the room to the door, where they disappeared behind a stack of boxes.

"Thanks for coming so quickly," the man named Evan said.

"Sure. Does this square us for last night's poker game?" Randy asked.

"No, it doesn't," Evan replied. "You owe me thirty bucks and you damn well better pay up or I'll sic my attorney on you."

Randy laughed. "Bart is into *me* for forty bucks for hospital benefit tickets. Why don't you just pay me ten and we'll call it even?"

She heard a quiet groan. "Did you really think I'd fall for that?"

"It was worth a shot."

"Randy, listen. Keep this to yourself, okay? If this

woman is in danger from whoever's following her, I don't want anyone to know how she got here."

"Sure. I was never here."

"Thanks."

Beazie thought that a surprisingly thoughtful request of her host.

There was the sound of a door closing.

When Evan returned, he went to his desk and picked up a small telephone book. "I know a Millie Evans," he said, handing her the book, "but she's ninety-three and in a convalescent home."

She felt an instant's hope. "Does she have a son? A brother-in-law?"

He shook his head. "Single lady. She used to have a little house on the lake before she had a fall and couldn't see to herself anymore. I painted it for her."

Hope died, but her interest in Evan Braga stirred. "You're a housepainter?"

He nodded.

He couldn't be the Evans she was after. Why would Gordon want her to take a tape that had cost him his life to a housepainter?

"The man who dropped me here said you owned a development company."

He nodded. "I do, in partnership with a friend. I used to sell real estate, too, but gave that up when this turned out to be more fun. There's one more doughnut, and you can have a refill on the coffee."

"No doughnut, thank you. But the coffee would be nice."

"This mill is our first project," he explained as he poured her another cup. "We both work for a business called Whitcomb's Wonders. It's a sort of temp agency, but for craftsmen who can't work full-time because they have other things going in their lives. My friend's a plumber and getting an MBA from Amherst in his spare time. I paint and wallpaper.''

''And what do you do in your spare time?''

''I'm getting my life together.''

She wondered what that meant. Why wouldn't a man who appeared to be in his late thirties have his life together? A broken marriage? A financial loss?

As a rule, she found people endlessly fascinating, but she didn't have time right now for anything more than her own pressing problems.

She flipped open the book and found the *E*'s. Eaton, Eckert, Egan, Emanuel, Evans... Her heart gave one eager thump, then she read, ''Evans, Millie— 221 Lake Front Road.''

She closed the book in exasperation. Evan topped up his own cup, then sat on the edge of his desk. ''You said someone dropped you here?'' he asked.

With a sigh she sank into a corner of the couch and took a sip of the fresh brew. He did make good coffee. ''I got a ride on a bakery truck in Springfield,'' she explained. ''I told the driver I was looking for someone named Evans in Maple Hill.'' She smiled wryly. ''Apparently, he doesn't know Millie. He drove me here on his way into town.''

''And why do you want this Evans?''

''I have something for him.'' Still uncertain of everyone and everything, she thought it best to keep the tape she'd hidden in her bra a secret.

He looked her over from head to toe. ''What

would that be?'' he asked. ''You don't even have a purse.''

''It's…a message.''

There'd been something about the once-over he'd given her that was…professional. She didn't know how else to express it. The same thought had struck her earlier when she'd watched him move around the small office with a curious tension about him, a sharpness in his eyes, a quickness in his tall, powerful body that suggested formal training.

Just so he wouldn't have the upper hand in this odd encounter, she had to let him know that she had powers of perception, too. Putting down the phone book on the seat beside her, she looked up and met his eyes. She remembered gazing into their soft brown depths as she was passing out.

''Before you were a housepainter,'' she said, ''you were a soldier.''

He arched an eyebrow. ''Close. I was a cop.''

She might have felt apprehensive over that. Gordon had warned her away from the police. But this Braga wasn't a cop now.

He must have noted her wary expression.

''You asked me not to call the police,'' he said. ''Are you afraid of them for some reason? Had a bad experience?''

''Gordon told me not to trust them,'' she replied. ''I can only guess it's because there's one involved in his murder.''

''Well, you can relax,'' he said. ''It wasn't me.''

She might be naive to believe him, but there was

something solid and comforting about him, despite those watchful eyes.

As she studied them now, she thought she saw a sadness behind the vigilance. She was good at reading people. What, she wondered idly, could happen to a cop to make him give up the work for house painting? And had Gordon said *Evan,* not Evans?

It might take a little time to determine whether this really was the man Gordon meant. And how could she do so, with no place to stay and no money to find one?

"Were you a cop in Maple Hill?" she asked.

He shook his head. "You broke into my place," he reminded her. "I'm the one with the right to ask questions."

She had to give him that. "I'm sorry." But there was a limit to what she could tell him, when she wasn't sure he was the Evans she was looking for, and she wasn't entirely sure what had happened herself. Or, at least, what it all meant.

"Someone's chasing you," he prodded, when she took a moment to organize her thoughts.

"Yes," she admitted.

"The person who killed your boss."

She didn't quite remember having told him that. She remembered the spots and the way the room had undulated when she wielded her bat at him. "Yes."

"You know who it is? I mean, by name?"

She shook her head. "There was more than one. I can identify faces, but I don't know their names."

"And this happened in Boston."

"Yes."

He frowned over that. "How'd you get away?"

She touched briefly on her escape from her apartment and the long, cold night in the back of the moving van.

For the first time, she noticed the condition of her clothes, and could only imagine what her face and hair looked like. She sagged a little into her corner. Things would certainly be simplified for her if he *was* the Evans she was looking for. Then she could turn over the tape and go back to Boston.

No, she couldn't go back. Gordon had owned the insurance franchise. A sickening thought struck her. She had been a witness to Gordon's murder. Until his killers were behind bars, it wouldn't be safe to return home.

"Now that I've answered your questions," she said, leaning slightly toward him, "can I ask again where you served as a policeman?"

He considered her, evidently as suspicious of her as she was of him. "Boston," he replied.

She straightened. Could there be some connection between him and Gordon? "Did you know...Gordon Hathaway?"

He frowned again. "I ran across a lot of people, perps and victims, in twelve years. But that name doesn't mean anything special."

She sagged against the couch again, suddenly very aware of her exhaustion. But where could she go? All she could think to ask was, "Is there a homeless shelter in town?"

"There's a new one opening December twenty-third," he said, putting his cup aside.

A familiar bleak despair threatened to overwhelm her. That always happened when something reminded her of how absolutely alone she was in this world. "But...none now?"

"There are some homeless families staying on cots in the basement of the Catholic church."

She angled her chin and asked, "Would you take me there?"

He studied her, those eyes roving her completely disreputable appearance, then lingering on her face. It was impossible to tell what he thought, until he leaned forward to take her cup from her and drop it with a bang on his desk.

"No," he said simply.

EVAN LOOKED into a pair of blue eyes rimmed with exhaustion, and suspected he would hate himself later, but he couldn't take her to the basement of the church and still live with himself.

He knew many homeless people had once lived productive lives and were victims of fate and circumstance, but there were always those few among them who preyed upon each other and anyone else small or weak enough to be vulnerable.

"I live in a cottage on the other side of town." He reached toward a wooden coat rack in the corner and grabbed an old down jacket he wore when working outside. It was smeared with paint, but warm. "It has a spare bedroom and a reliable furnace." He held the jacket out to her. "You can stay with me until you find this Evans guy."

She stared at him, evaluating the offer. She was desperate for shelter, but not sure she could trust him.

"I have no money," she said finally, and took the jacket.

"The offer doesn't require money."

There was a moment's silence. Then she asked quietly, carefully, "What does it require?"

He understood her reluctance, but gave her a scolding look, anyway. "Trust," he replied. "And I can use another hand on a paint roller."

Her eyes widened slightly, and he guessed he'd surprised her. "Never painted anything?" he asked.

She smiled for the first time since he'd opened the door and found her wielding a bat at him. "My bedroom, a couple of times when I was a teenager, and my friend Horie's first apartment. Does that count?"

He ignored her question. "Horie?"

She smiled again. It made her even prettier, despite her disheveled appearance. Her teeth were square and very white, the top right one overlapping the front tooth slightly.

"Horatia Metcalf. Her father teaches Greek in a divinity school, hence her name. She's a little off-the-wall herself. We painted every room a different bright color."

"Did you do a good job?"

"We thought so. Her landlord wasn't quite as pleased."

"Then, you're hired," he said. "But I'll take you home. You can have a couple of days to catch up on your sleep before I put you to work. I, however, have to get with it."

The suggestion that she was holding up his working day galvanized her into action. She got to her feet and let him help her into the jacket.

As she snapped it closed, he remembered the watch cap in the side pocket and reached in to hand it to her. She pulled it on and stuffed her hair into it.

He looked down worriedly at her holey stockings and low-heeled dress shoes. "Wish I had a spare pair of socks, but I'll get you some at home."

"I'll be fine," she said, then wrapped her arms around herself and closed her eyes. "I can't tell you how nice it is to be warm."

He stood the collar up for her. "The lesson to be learned here is, never run away in December without your coat."

She nodded wryly. "Or your purse." She smiled again as he pulled the door open for her. "Of course, that lesson doesn't apply to you, does it?"

He concentrated on locking the door behind him, afraid of getting hooked on that smile. "No," he said, pretending to be serious. "It's hard to decide what color purse to wear with coveralls."

She laughed as he pointed toward the Jeep. Her smile...with sound. Intriguing. "It's easy. Just remember that they should match your shoes."

By the time they reached his cottage on the other side of Maple Hill, he was grateful that he had to leave her for the day. It was as though something had turned her on and she'd acquired a sparkle he hadn't noticed when they'd interrogated each other over coffee.

A long, tree-lined drive led to his cottage. Snow covered the trees and crunched under the tires as he drove up to the porch. He parked and came around to help her out, sure that the height of the van and dress shoes would make it difficult for her to get down onto the packed and slippery snow.

She'd swung her legs over the side and appeared to be considering how best to approach the leap, when he bracketed her waist and lifted her to the ground. He felt the smallness of her waist even under the thickness of his jacket, and wondered why that should impress itself upon him. He'd known small-waisted women before.

Of course, they weren't coming to live with him.

"Thank you," she said cheerfully. "What a pretty place. What grows on that arbor by the garden?" She pointed to a square-topped pergola at the side of the house.

"Clematis," he replied.

"Pink?"

"Purple."

"Ah." She sighed, smiling as though she could envision it. "I love purple. We painted Horie's kitchen a sort of pale grape color."

He wondered what that did for guests' digestion, as he led the way up the porch steps and unlocked the door.

THE FIRST THING Evan did was crank up the thermostat.

Beazie listened attentively as he showed her how

to turn it up or down, explaining that he usually lowered it when he left for work.

"I don't want to waste your oil," she protested,
trying to think about the numbers rather than the
herbal fragrance of his cologne. "The thermostat
says sixty-two, but that's still warmer than the back
of the moving truck."

He ignored her and bumped it up to seventy.

"Kitchen's in here."

She followed as he led the way through the soft,
coffee-with-cream color of the living room and its
dark blue and red furniture to an old-fashioned
kitchen painted yellow. The appliances were old, but
new butcher-block counters had been installed, and
a small nook that looked out onto the front of the
house had yellow-and-blue curtains patterned with
teapots and cups.

"I've been slowly buffing up the house," he said
with a disparaging wave at the curtains, "but I
haven't gotten to this room yet. I don't eat at home
that much, so I've left it to last."

She nodded affably, but was secretly happy he
hadn't taken down the curtains. They reminded her
of those cozy fifties commercials where women
cooked in shirtwaists, high heels and jewelry, while
an adoring family awaited mother's masterpiece.

He opened the door of a very small refrigerator.
"Not a lot in here, I'm afraid, unless you like cheese,
cola or…" He opened the freezer to reveal one box
of frozen Buffalo wings.

She took it from him. "I love these."

"Good." He pointed to cupboards across the

room. "Crackers, cereal, a few other things in there. Help yourself to whatever you want. I'll bring some things home tonight."

"Please don't go to any trouble. If you usually have dinner out, go ahead. I'll probably sleep until Monday." She put the wings back in the freezer, then hurried to follow him as he led the way upstairs.

A small corridor with ivy-patterned wallpaper led into a very large room on the left that was comfortably cluttered. A large blob of multicolored fur lay in the middle of a dark green bedspread.

"That's Lucinda."

At the sound of Evan's voice, the blob rolled onto its back and put four feet up in the air, toes curled in contentment. It was a cat.

"Really." Beazie took one step toward it, then thought better of walking into Evan's room. She stayed where she was and commented simply, "Very elegant name."

"She arrived named," he said, walking over to ruffle the furry stomach. The cat took it as her due, made a small sound of approval, then curled up again. "She belonged to Millie Evans. She can't have a cat at the care center, but I take Lucinda to visit every once in a while."

Beazie entertained that image as he led her across the hall to another large room, this one pink, with a window seat in a bay window and an eclectic collection of furniture. The temperature was chilly, but the warm atmosphere drew her inside.

He went to a heating vent in the floor and kicked it open with his foot. "It'll take a little while to warm up here. Maybe you want to fix yourself the Buffalo wings first.''

She fell onto the edge of the bed, seduced by the thick soft mattress and the wonderful ambience of the room. All tension and energy escaped her like water down a drain.

''I think I'll just go right to bed,'' she said, the words requiring effort.

He studied her curiously for one moment. She expected him to tell her he'd suddenly changed his mind, but instead he went to the closet, pulled out an extra blanket and dropped it at the foot of the bed. Then he crossed the hall to his room and returned with a pair of thick socks.

''Sleep well,'' he said. ''See you tonight.'' He left the room in an apparent hurry to get to work.

''Evan!'' she called.

He reappeared in the doorway. ''Yeah?''

''Thank you.''

''Sure.''

He left again, and this time she toed off her shoes, pulled on the socks and got under the blankets, still wearing the coat and hat. She felt her muscles relax one by one as she drifted off to sleep, strangely secure in the unfamiliar surroundings.

CHAPTER THREE

EVAN HAD THE FIRST COAT of trim on the accounting office's doors and windows and was sitting in the middle of the hardwood floor with a tepid cup of coffee, when Cameron Trent appeared in the doorway. He was carrying two cups from Perk Avenue.

"So, what's going on?" Cam asked, walking in and handing Evan a cup, then doing a slow circuit of the room, inspecting his progress.

Evan suspected this was not just a friendly visit. Cam never checked on him.

"Letting the first coat of trim dry," he replied, sipping at the contents of the cup. Double-shot mocha. Best high-energy boost in the whole world. "Mmm, thanks. Good stuff."

Cam turned away from his inspection and faced him across the room, his expression amused. "Who's the girl?" he asked.

Evan shook his head at him. "They're not girls, they're women. Someday the political-correctness cops are going to come and take you away."

Cam ignored all that. "I understand she arrived naked."

Evan rolled his eyes. "She did not arrive naked. God, is there no such thing as privacy?"

"No. If she didn't arrive naked, why did you call Mariah and ask her if there was anything in her size in the clothes she's collecting for the homeless?"

"Because Mariah's the same size. I thought she'd be able to find something."

"For the naked woman?"

"She wasn't naked!" Evan said impatiently. "She just...doesn't have a change of clothes."

When Cam looked confused, Evan lied in an attempt to protect Beazie, and possibly Cam and his family. Until Evan understood completely what was involved here, it was better to keep the truth to himself. "She left home in a hurry. We used to have a thing for each other, and that's all I'm going to tell you."

Cam frowned and came to sit cross-legged on the floor, a small distance from him. "Why did she come to you?"

"She missed me. I told you. We used to be lovers." The lie came so easily off his lips. He hoped he wasn't going to hate himself for it later.

"She missed you so much that she came in search of you without packing a bag?"

When Evan ignored that, Cam regarded him with concern. "Where is she now?"

"I took her home to rest." Then he added firmly, "Butt out, Cam."

Cam raised his hands in a self-protective gesture. "I'm just looking out for you, Evan. You'd help anybody, anytime. I just wondered if she was the reason you came here with a dark burden. If so, I was going to warn you to be careful."

Evan drew a deep breath for patience. "You know, if you hadn't arrived with a double mocha, you'd be out on your keister by now. She's not the reason I left Boston, but she wouldn't come with me at the time, and now she's decided she can't live without me."

"Really."

"Really."

"Yeah, well, if you're happy, we're happy. Just wanted to remind you to be careful."

Evan had to appreciate the sincerity of Cam's concern, if not his determination to protect him. "You know, I'm five years older than you are, and I was a cop. I think I'm equipped to handle whatever happens."

"Just reminding you that nobody's invincible." As Evan grinned, Cam went on intrepidly. "I know you've got this lone warrior thing going and you don't share much, and that's okay. I used to be that way, too, until I let a woman and children and friends into my life. Now I don't even have a thought to myself—"

Evan wasn't sure where Cam was going with this, but it was entertaining to listen.

"Anyway, we know something major happened to you because of that accident, and it makes life difficult for you. We don't even want to know what it is, or if and how this girl—woman—relates to that, just that you'll call us if you need us."

There was something oddly touching and seriously annoying in the knowledge that his friends had read his situation so clearly. They didn't have details, but they'd certainly grasped the basics.

"She has nothing to do with that."

Cam said, "I'm talking in generalities."

"You're crazy."

His friend toasted him with his empty cup and got to his feet. "Who else would go into partnership with you? See you."

Evan followed him to the door. "You know anybody around here named Evans?"

"Yeah," Cam replied. "Millie. The woman you bought your house—"

Evan shook his head. "Yeah. Thanks."

"Why?"

"Never mind. Thanks. And thanks for the mocha."

"Sure. See you Sunday. Bring the woman."

Evan accepted that his friends were intent on providing backup, whether he needed it or not. He glanced at his watch. Almost five. He'd better get moving if he was going to stop for groceries on the way home. It was a little unsettling to think that someone was there waiting for him.

BEAZIE SLEPT until midafternoon and awoke feeling a little like she was in a sauna. The house had warmed up considerably, and she was still wearing the coat and hat Evan had lent her. She was also wearing Lucinda.

The cat opened big yellow eyes as Beazie stirred, then meowed a protest and dug into the front of the jacket when Beazie tried to sit up.

Beazie laughed and stroked the cat, then tried to lift her off. Lucinda meowed peevishly and leaped down, clearly affronted at being disturbed.

Sitting up in the middle of the bed, Beazie peeled off the coat and hat, then looked around her, captivated anew by the coziness of the simple room. The furniture was trendily mismatched—an oak highboy, a white wardrobe in the distressed cottage style, a small, square shelf that served as a bedside table, and a cut-shade lamp. The bed itself was brass and quite ornate.

And the pieces had the feel of things handed down, kept because they were loved or had precious memories attached.

As a child she'd had a room something like this. She'd felt loved and...attached. Then her father, a commercial airline's pilot, had died in a crash, and her mother had remarried three times in quick succession, trying to recapture the love she'd lost. She had divorced as quickly, and died six years ago of complications from surgery. Beazie personally thought she'd simply given up on love and life.

Determined that wasn't going to happen to her, Beazie pushed herself out of bed. She was going to find this Evans person, turn over the tape, then take off for parts unknown and start all over. It wasn't as though she had loved ones in Boston. Well, there was Horie, but she could keep in touch with her no matter where she was.

She went to the window and looked out. All she could see were the tops of trees, the sawtoothlike arrangement of evergreens, and the lacy bareness of

oak, maple and sycamore. She spotted the top of a
church spire and the wrought-iron widow's walk of
what must be an old colonial home.

Or maybe, she thought with a wistful sigh, *I'll just
stay here.* She felt a little as though she were safely
tucked in a tree house in the woods, as far removed
from the threats that had plagued her last night as it
was possible to be.

Then she came to her senses and realized that was
a foolish thought. She wanted the life in that fifties
commercial, and it didn't exist. She wanted someone
to give her back her childhood, and that wasn't going
to happen. The men in the red SUV had lost her trail
but were certainly still chasing her. She had to focus
on finding Evans and getting rid of the tape.

Her eyes lingered on the view and she expelled a
little sigh of longing. Maybe she could just hold on
to that dream and tuck it away. It would never come
true, but she could still draw comfort from it in a
small way.

She found the bathroom across the hall and a stack
of dark blue towels on a wicker stand. Lucinda followed her in and curled up on the dark blue carpet.

Remembering that she'd need clothes or something to wear when she stepped out of the shower,
Beazie stood uncertainly in the middle of the room,
then, suddenly inspired, looked on the back of the
bathroom door. A brown velour robe hung on the
hook there.

Buoyed by that piece of good fortune, she peeled
off her clothes and stepped into the shower.

Fifteen minutes later she was belting the robe, a

towel wrapped around her hair, when she heard the faint sound of activity downstairs. She stood still, her heart lurching with fear that the red SUV had found her, after all.

That was ridiculous, she told herself briskly, quietly opening the door. It was probably just Evan returning home. That possibility was still a little scary, but not in the same way.

He didn't like her, didn't trust her, and had invited her to stay with him out of Christian charity. That should be good enough for her, but somehow it wasn't.

Lucinda raced out the door past her, meowing.

Beazie tossed the towel aside, combed her fingers through her hair, then stepped quietly into the hall. Pausing at the top of the stairs, she heard the sound of female laughter from the direction of the kitchen.

A surprising thought hit her. Evan was married! And maybe had a daughter. She could hear two voices.

That possibility both relieved and distressed her, but she was too curious to analyze why. Then she heard a baby cry, and ran lightly down the stairs.

She arrived at the kitchen doorway and saw a baby carrier on the table and two women unloading what appeared to be casserole dishes and…clothing.

A small, dark-haired woman went to lift the crying baby out of the carrier and spotted Beazie. She smiled apologetically.

"I'm sorry we woke you!" she said, holding the baby to her with one hand and coming toward Beazie with the other outstretched. "I'm Haley Megrath."

She indicated the squalling baby. "This is Henrietta—Henri for short."

Beazie shook her hand and duly admired the baby, then the woman indicated her friend, another dark-haired woman with a friendly smile. "And this is Mariah Trent. We're friends of Evan's. Mariah's husband is his partner, Cam Trent, and my husband, Bart, is their lawyer."

"Hi, I'm Beazie Deadham. I was already up and in the shower. What…?" She pointed to the clothing draped over chairs.

"Oh, right." Haley took a bottle out of her purse on the table and put the nipple in the baby's mouth. Henrietta stopped crying instantly and made urgent, sucking sounds. "Mariah and I are heading up a committee to supply the food and clothing bank for a new homeless shelter."

Beazie nodded, remembering that Evan had mentioned the shelter.

"So, we've been gathering clothes. I've personally contributed a lot because I needed some new things after the baby came." She rolled her eyes. "Thickening waist, bigger hips. You know."

Beazie didn't, but she couldn't imagine what this woman had looked like before, if the figure she sported now in jeans and a simple sweater was thicker than it had been.

"Anyway, he told Mariah about your arrival here with no change of clothes and wondered if we had anything you could use, since you and she are about the same size."

Beazie picked up a rich-blue sweatsuit draped over

the back of a chair. Then a softer-blue turtleneck sweater. She uttered a grateful gasp, feeling as though she'd just been given carte blanche at Filene's.

Mariah held up a pair of blue jeans. "Think these will fit? They're Haley's. Sometimes men are wrong about sizes."

Beazie shook her head regretfully. "I'm flattered to be thought the same size as Haley—" she smiled apologetically "—but I'm solid peasant stock. I'm a ten."

Mariah folded up the jeans and dug into another bag. "Good. You are my size." She smiled conspiratorially. "It's the chocolate. And Haley's always running around chasing news stories, so she gets more exercise. She's publisher of the *Maple Hill Mirror.* I just drive children around and wait for them to finish ballet lessons, tai chi lessons, swimming lessons, soccer games, baseball games, basketball—"

"She gets the point," Haley interrupted, then said to Beazie, "Why don't you just look through what we've brought and take what you want. My sweaters would fit you."

Beazie clutched the sweats and sweater to her and took the jeans Mariah held out. "Two changes of clothes will see me through. I feel guilty taking from the homeless."

"We've collected lots of things," Haley insisted. "Help yourself with a clear conscience. And Mariah made a couple of casseroles so you won't have to cook for a few days. I don't think Evan cooks at all."

Beazie felt called upon to come to his defense. "He does make good coffee, though."

Haley moved the baby to her shoulder and patted her back. "He's great, and we all love him, though he's pretty private. He's always the first one to offer help if one of us needs it, so it's nice to be able to help him in a small way."

Mariah turned from putting the last of the casseroles in the refrigerator and dusted off her hands. "Just about filled that up." Then she reached to the floor for another paper bag. "These are toiletries and some makeup samples I got at a house party and never used." She put the bag on the table and pulled out a few things. "We thought if you needed clothes, you might need some other things, too. Shampoo and conditioner, moisturizer, a sample bottle of perfume." Then she put it all back. "So you don't have to use guy stuff."

Beazie was overwhelmed, and couldn't help wondering what Evan had told them. "I don't know how to thank you."

Haley waved away the necessity for thanks. "The only thing we couldn't find was shoes. What size do you wear?"

"Eights."

Mariah shook her head regretfully. "Haley's are too small and mine are too big. But there is…" She rummaged in several bags and emerged triumphantly with a pair of pink chenille slip-on slippers. "Here. At least you can be comfy around the house."

Beazie sat down and put the slippers on. They were perfect.

The baby burped loudly and Haley laughed. "Well. Our work here is done." She stood to go.

Mariah began collecting empty bags and pushed those still full of clothes against the cupboards and out of the way. "Pick through those and just return what you can't use."

"Can you stay for coffee?" Beazie asked, remembering belatedly her good manners.

"Thanks," Mariah said, "but I have kids to pick up, and Haley has to get to a Traffic Safety Committee meeting. We have lunch with Jackie every Friday, though. Would you like to join us?"

"Jackie's the mayor of Maple Hill," Haley explained. "My sister-in-law."

Beazie nodded, following them as they moved toward the door. "Evan told me about that. Your brother has a company of tradesmen temps."

"Yes. Turned out to be a brilliant idea. They're so busy, though, the jobs are hardly temporary anymore."

"We're all in the phone book," Mariah said, opening the door for Haley and the baby. "If you can't remember names, just call Whitcomb's Wonders—that's the company—and Haley's mom is usually taking calls. She can reach any one of us."

"Thank you again."

"Sure. You take care."

Beazie watched as Haley fastened the baby seat in the back of a green sedan and Mariah climbed into the passenger seat. Haley tapped the horn as she drove away.

Beazie closed the kitchen door behind her, then,

noting the late-afternoon shadows, flipped on the light. Silence fell on her like a blanket. The sudden arrival of the two women and the baby had been like a cheerful tornado in the quiet house, and now that they were gone it seemed even more silent than before. While she could acknowledge that solitude was preferable to being chased, she'd spent most of the past six years trying to chase away the silence.

That was the worst part of loneliness, she'd often thought. A single person had only the sounds of the clock, the refrigerator, and the television, which she usually put on the moment she arrived home and turned off just before she went to sleep.

But a house should have the cheerful noise of projects under way. The hum of a sewing machine, the whine of a saw, the discordant but encouraging music of a child learning an instrument, the bark of a dog.

This house had the look of what she wanted, she thought, turning in a tight circle to take in the kitchen, but none of the sounds. She experienced one brief moment of utter and complete loneliness, then forced herself to bury it and move on. She knew how to do that. She'd done it many times.

She took the bags of clothes upstairs and spent the next half hour trying things on. She kept two pairs of Mariah's jeans, a blue and a black, a simple black skirt and sweater, and a green fleece top patterned with red poinsettias. Christmas was just around the corner. She put on the blue sweats, hung the things she was keeping in the wardrobe, then packed everything else back into the bags and stashed them to return tomorrow.

Then she padded downstairs in the slippers and checked out the casseroles. There was ham, potato and broccoli casserole in a square dish, lasagna in an oblong one, and chicken and noodles in a round bowl, each thoughtfully labeled with cooking time and temperature.

She took out the square casserole and preheated the oven. Mariah had also left a bowl of salad and a bag of dinner rolls on the counter.

When she searched the cupboards for plates, Beazie was surprised to find a four-place setting of fine china, patterned on the rim with red and yellow flowers and a gold trim. She took down two plates and stared at them. She'd expected a bachelor to have pottery or plastic.

After setting the table, she made a pot of coffee, put a small fern she'd found in the living room in the middle of the table and waited for Evan to come home.

EVAN HAD NOT BEEN GREETED at the door in— Well, he couldn't remember how long it had been. Probably since his mother welcomed him home when he was in high school.

And it had been that long since he'd walked in the door to the aroma of dinner in the oven, coffee brewing and a woman fussing around him, a floral perfume wafting in her wake.

Well, Beazie wasn't fussing, but she'd come to

take one of the two grocery bags he carried. And when he saw her, for a moment he couldn't move.

She'd showered and shampooed her hair and tied it up with a piece of twine into a fat, glossy ponytail. The blue sweatshirt she was wearing intensified the blue of her eyes, and when he looked for her freckles, he couldn't find them. She had a finished, almost glamorous look—despite the sweats. And she was giving him that smile.

He felt himself wanting to go back outside and drive away. He knew this woman could be dangerous, and not just because she was being chased. Still, he'd sometimes been stupid, but he'd never been a coward. And she needed help.

"Hi," he made himself say with an answering smile as he went to the counter with the other bag of groceries. "Mariah must have been here."

"She was." She pulled canned soups and vegetables out of the bag and lined them up on the counter. "Thank you. It was thoughtful of you to scrounge a wardrobe for me. And she brought me shampoo and makeup."

He nodded. "I noticed the freckles were gone."

"Not gone, just undercover. Mariah and Haley also brought three casseroles so I wouldn't have to cook—because everyone seems to know that you don't."

"That's because every time we have a gathering and I have to bring something, I get it from the deli. Dead giveaway."

"You're lucky to have friends who want your company." She folded the now-empty paper bag.

"Anyplace in particular you'd like these things?"
She opened a cupboard and analyzed its meager contents. "Is there a system?"

"No. There's seldom anything in there. Just put it wherever you like."

"Okay." She began putting things away with a swift confidence that spoke of experience. She paused to grin as she held up a jar of peanut butter and a box of grape Kool-Aid that were already in the shelf. "Do you like your peanut butter with jelly or marshmallow cream?"

He put the bags in a recycling bin at the edge of the counter and pulled off his jacket. "I don't like it at all," he answered. "I baby-sat for Cam and Mariah one night at the last minute, and Mariah, knowing how I am, sent those things with the kids so they'd have something to snack on. We went out for pizza, instead."

"I love peanut butter," she said, placing it back on the shelf and collecting canned goods around it. "I practically lived on it when I was first on my own because it's so economical and nutritious."

He thought it strange that they were talking about peanut butter and groceries, when just this morning she'd been bedraggled and hunted and holding a bat on him. Tonight she seemed like any well-adjusted young woman performing the simple domestic duty of stocking her shelves.

Only they were *his* shelves. And neither one of them should forget that.

The timer rang and she closed the doors on a very orderly cupboard, picked up two kitchen towels to use as pot holders and pulled the casserole out of the oven. It smelled wonderful.

He poured water and coffee, and they sat across from each other at the table. For the first time since he'd walked in the door, he felt tension. He ignored it, sure it must be just his own reaction to having a strange woman in his home after a year of comfortable solitude.

"Where's your family?" she asked companionably, passing him the basket of rolls. "Were you born in Boston?"

His family. He missed them, but he'd tried hard not to think about them since leaving home. He'd dealt with and accepted what had happened, but he couldn't find his place in their circle anymore. It was easier to put them out of his mind.

"I was born in the Midwest," he replied. "We still have a lot of family there. But my mother moved us to Boston when she married my stepfather."

"I love Boston," she said chattily as she buttered a roll. "I was born in Buffalo. We moved to Boston when my mother remarried after my father died." She took a dainty bite of the roll. "But that didn't work out and she married a third time, then a fourth. The last husband was a banker, an older man who seemed very steady and solid, but she got sick, and I guess that wasn't what he'd planned for his golden years, so…" She made an awkward little movement with her hand. "He left, she died, and I…stayed in Boston."

"How old were you?"

"Eighteen. Old enough to be on my own."

He remembered himself at eighteen, mouthy and brash and confident in his mind and his body. Until he went to college and met better minds, stronger bodies, and felt all his confidence shrivel. He wondered if she'd had to take the few steps back that eventually brought maturity.

"At least, I thought I was," she admitted after a moment, as though she'd read his mind. "Then I discovered how much parents do for you that you're unaware of until you have to do it for yourself. And that supporting yourself has a million hidden expenses that keep you too broke to have lunch out, or meet your friends after work for a drink." She sighed and gave him a frail smile. "And that being alone 24/7 is not the way I want to spend the rest of my life. To remedy that, I spent the year I was twenty-one on a determined search to find a soul mate. I went to a lot of parties, but was selective about whom I dated. But I still managed to get it wrong.

"I had narrowed my choices to two men I really liked. Turned out one was already engaged to a girl in California, and the other got arrested for insider trading."

He had to smile. "Tough luck."

She nodded with an answering grin. "True. So I gave up on the search, but I need company, noise, activity. I get so tired of the silence."

"I came here to find silence," he said. "After being a cop for twelve years, my head is full of noises I'd rather not hear again." And after he'd been here for a while, he'd stopped hearing the crash in his head.

She studied him worriedly, and he stopped with a bite of casserole halfway to his mouth. "What?" he asked.

"Is it going to be hard for you to have me here? I mean, I know you invited me to be kind, but you're beginning to regret it, aren't you. I can see it in your face. When you walked in the door tonight, I could almost hear your thoughts. *Oh, that's right! She's here. Well, I'll have to make the best of it.*"

Guilt made him defensive. She was absolutely right. "I thought nothing of the kind," he denied, "so just relax."

"I shouldn't be here long at all."

"I know that."

"And I'll work for my keep."

"Yes."

"And I'll try not to pollute your space—but I sing when I'm working, and sometimes I talk to myself, and I like to have the radio—"

"You're making a lot of noise," he interrupted, "promising not to make a lot of noise."

She sat back in her chair and folded her arms. "So you're not the sweetheart you pretend to be, are you."

Sweetheart? "I never pretended to be any—"

"No, I guess it's not pretense," she amended, leaning forward again to pick up her fork. "It just seems to come with the chromosome in some of you. You're all concerned and protective, you offer reassurances in that voice every woman dreams of, then when we begin to believe it, you pull back. Or you're on to other things."

That assessment was so brutal, he didn't know what to say.

"My mother fell for it three times," she went on between bites, her manner curiously detached considering the intensity of the subject. "We could have gotten along when my father died if we'd leaned on each other, but she kept trying to find the magic he'd put into her life—and it just wasn't there without him."

He was beginning to see something here, a possible explanation for her softly spoken assault on the male character. "So…your life was probably difficult," he guessed, "while she dragged you with her through three marriages and three stepfathers."

She shrugged one shoulder, as though it didn't matter. "The second marriage was nothing, really. He was a tennis pro who turned out to be a flake. He was never real enough for me to take seriously. It only lasted five months."

"And the third one?"

"Almost a year. He drank too much." She grew quiet.

"But the fourth marriage was different?" he guessed.

A line appeared between her eyebrows as she talked on, clearly lost in memories of her third stepfather.

"I was sixteen and beginning to feel lost because I knew my mother was. Hal was gray-haired and cheerful, and for a whole year things were perfect. They sailed and skied, and we took weekend trips to Buck's County or the Poconos. He was easy to talk to and seemed to really care about us." She took a few sips of coffee, leaned her forearms on the table and looked into his eyes. "Then he retired, my mother got sick, and it was clear from the beginning that it would be a long, debilitating illness. I got home from school, eager to share with him that I'd been accepted at Southern Massachusetts University, and he was gone. My mother said he'd told her that he'd worked hard all his life and looked forward to traveling and doing all the things there hadn't been time for before."

"That's rotten," he said, angry that a man could do that. "I'm sorry."

She shrugged again. "My mother could have lived a long time. I'd gladly have taken care of her, but she gave up. She couldn't find what she'd had with Daddy, and it just didn't occur to her that she had the ability to make her own life worth living." She added bleakly, "Or that I was still there."

Now he got the picture. She hadn't just been young and alone, she'd been betrayed and abandoned—several times.

"And on the strength of the hour you spent with me this morning," he said, "and the half hour tonight, you're assuming that I'm the same?"

She pushed her plate away. "You have that look," she said, "that says you'd really rather not have to deal with me."

Fueled by annoyance now, as well as guilt, he was vocal in his own defense. "First of all," he replied, "you're here, aren't you? And you wouldn't be if I didn't want to deal with you. And secondly, you broke into my office, held me at *bat*point, and told me some of your story, but not all of it, because you aren't willing to trust me completely. And since that story involves a murder and a ruthless chase, you're surprised that I'm a little wary of you?''

"You *offered* me shelter," she pointed out. "I asked you to take me to the—"

"Further proof," he cut in, "that I'm trying to help. I think what's bothering you isn't 'that look' I'm supposed to be wearing, but your own insecurities.''

Okay, that had been harsh. He wasn't entirely surprised when her eyes brimmed with tears and she got up from the table with a wounded look—one that would keep him awake for hours—and ran upstairs.

Some sweetheart he was.

CHAPTER FOUR

BEAZIE WAS FROZEN, and she couldn't determine where she was. It felt like she was in deep freeze. She was cold inside as well as out.

She must be dying. Tremors racked her, and she wondered if it was possible to rattle apart, for cold limbs to simply break off—the way pieces of your life sometimes did.

Darkness permeated everything, and she swore she could feel her life slipping away. She tried to remember the warmth of love, of belonging, of being needed, but it had been gone for so long.

She began to weep for it. Longing was cold, too, and only served to worsen her situation.

Then she heard the sounds of a car engine, saw headlights in her frigid darkness, then men with guns drawn, coming for her.

She couldn't escape them because she was frozen in place, a victim of her own past and her cold present.

When she opened her mouth to scream, she heard the sound reverberate around her.

The men with guns drew closer, and she tried desperately to move, to run, but her feet were planted in stone.

She shrieked as they closed in, and reached out blindly for help. "Please!" she heard herself cry. "Please!"

Someone tried to pull her free, but her feet wouldn't budge. She struggled with him, holding on tightly to arms that tried to break her from the paralysis of the cold. But it was too painful, and finally she had to give up and push him away.

They were going to get her, after all, and it was just as well. There was nothing here for her, anyway.

"No!" she shouted, pushing against the hands trying to rescue her. "Leave me! No!"

"Beazie!"

She stopped struggling, surprised to hear her name shouted.

"Beatrice!"

The man trying to free her wrapped his arms around her. "Come on!" he encouraged. "Come on, Beazie!"

His embrace was so strong, so determined that she tried to comply. Then she heard the gunshots—three fired in rapid succession. She felt their impact on the man who held her, because the two of them were chest to chest. Then she heard his gasp as life went out of him and he fell over her, tumbling them both to the ground.

"No!" she wept. "Oh, no!"

"Beazie, if you don't wake up, I'm putting you in the shower!"

A light went on suddenly, banishing the darkness, and she found herself on her back in the bed, Evan's weight holding her there with her hands pinned to the pillow on either side of her head. She was gasping for air and shaking with cold. She was also naked.

"God!" Evan said with a sigh of relief. He scrambled off her and reached to the floor, where all her blankets seemed to be, to grab a coverlet to wrap around her.

The cotton-lined blanket felt cool, and she flinched against it, but he tightened his arms around her to keep it in place. He rubbed her back vigorously.

Still snared by the horror of her dream, she leaned into him. "They shot you," she said, her voice raspy from screaming. "Three times."

He rubbed her arm, then reached down to cover the toes of one foot, which was exposed at the bottom of the blanket. "Who did?"

"The men in the red car."

"Did they get me?" His voice was light, amused.

But she wasn't. The dream had been terrifying. "You collapsed on me."

He looked into her eyes and seemed to realize that she didn't find it funny. "Beazie, you were dreaming. I'm fine. It's probably because I had to push you back to the pillows to stop you from fighting me."

Was her dream a portent? she wondered. Some people put stock in such things. She never had, but then, she'd never been chased by killers before.

It was clear he was not going to take her concern seriously, so she simply let herself absorb the comfort and security of his arms.

"What are you doing sleeping naked in December?" he asked, his voice taking on a teasing note.

MURIEL JENSEN

75

"Especially if you have a tendency to kick your blankets off."

"There was no nightgown in the bag," she replied.

"What about the sweats you were wearing?"

"I have four changes of clothes," she replied practically. "I'm not about to sleep in one of them."

"I've got a pair of pajamas you can have." He stood, and she clutched the blankets to her.

"Won't you need them?"

He'd gotten as far as the door and turned to grin. "I never wear them."

"You mean, it's all right for *you* to sleep naked in December?"

"Of course. I don't kick the blankets off. I'll be right back."

Beazie tightened her cocoon around her and sank into her own humiliation. Her host, who wasn't wild about her being here, anyway, and who seemed to see beyond the cheerful facade she presented to everyone and recognize her as needy, had been awakened by her screams, had run to her rescue, and had found her naked in bed.

He must consider her the houseguest from hell.

EVAN WAS BACK IN SECONDS, ripping open a plastic-wrapped package containing blue-gray-and-white-striped flannel pajamas. They'd been a gift from someone and had sat ignored in a bottom drawer of his dresser.

"You'll have to cuff them a few times, but they should keep you warm."

Even to his own ear he sounded convincingly casual about having run into the bedroom to grab her screaming, writhing form, only to discover she was naked. The shock of it had run right through him, and it had taken him a moment to focus on her obvious distress rather than her elegant body, its ivory curves highlighted in the darkness.

His hands were steady as he put down the pajamas.

"You put these on," he directed, "and I'll get you a cup of tea laced with brandy. That should help you get back to sleep."

She didn't look as though she wanted to close her eyes again. Though he'd been sympathetic to her plight all along, now that he'd held her in his arms, he was more aware of her desperation. It must be terrifying to be in danger when you were alone in the world and trusted no one.

She extended him a measure of trust, but her own past experience obviously made her doubt he could live up to it.

He went into the kitchen and put the kettle on, then built a fire in the living room's simple brick fireplace. It was after four and he had to be up at five-thirty, so he might as well stay down here and work on the bid Hank had asked him to submit for the Elks' Hall.

When the kettle whistled, he tossed his record book and a pen at the overstuffed chair and went to the kitchen. Minutes later, he turned around with the tea mug in hand, intending to take it upstairs, and found Beazie in the doorway behind him, wearing the pajamas and the socks he'd lent her. She had the waist of the pajama bottoms bunched in one hand.

But what claimed his full attention was her hair. It billowed about her like a scriptural fiery cloud, long and wavy and burnished with gold from the overhead light.

"Do you have a safety pin?" she asked. And when he didn't answer immediately, she added, "Evan?"

"Uh...sure." He put the mug on the counter and dug in a small junk drawer for the pin.

She turned around to make the adjustment, then turned back again, her manner quiet and apologetic. "I'm sorry I woke you."

"Not a problem," he assured her. "I was going to get up early and do some paperwork, anyway."

"You're staying up?" She asked the question almost hopefully. "I saw that you made a fire."

He guessed she was afraid of going to sleep again and having the same dream.

"Yes. Want to sit up and have your tea? There's a quilt on the back of the sofa."

"I would, thank you."

He cranked the thermostat up, poked the fire into life, then pretended to ignore her as he settled in the chair and went to work on the bid.

She spent a few minutes staring into the fire as she sipped the tea. Then she put the cup on the coffee table and was asleep almost before she could lean back. She'd draped the quilt over her legs, and he waited until he was ready to go upstairs and shower before easing a pillow under her head and pulling the quilt up to her chin.

She moved her head, and silky hair fell over his hand. It was the most amazing color, like cherry wood. He couldn't resist running his palm gently over the crown of it as he tucked it back out of her face.

She stirred fitfully, and he was happy for the excuse to touch her hair again as he shushed her. At last she settled into the pillow with a sigh.

Evan hurried upstairs, aware of a stirring in his chest he wanted nothing to do with at this point in time. Romance would be too complicated here.

He'd always enjoyed relationships that were straightforward and for mutual pleasure. But since Blaine's death, nothing seemed straightforward anymore. He'd killed his brother, but he hadn't. And it had all happened because Blaine had stolen a small fortune, but there'd been no evidence of that when the franchise had been audited for resale. His family loved him, but he saw the flicker of doubt in their eyes. Nothing in his life was whole or firm. It would be selfish to succumb to the temptation to entangle his life with anyone else's, when he wasn't sure of his past, much less his future.

He was in his running gear with a change of clothes over his arm in half an hour. When he slipped quietly out of the house, Beazie was still asleep on the sofa.

SHE NEEDED BOOTS. Beazie wandered around the kitchen in Evan's pajamas and socks shortly after nine a.m., thinking that she could get out and look for the mysterious "Evans" if she had something to put on her feet besides slippers or her battered pumps.

Finding an orange in a fruit bowl and fresh coffee in the pot, she settled down in the little nook to have breakfast. There, propped between two serviceable green-and-white glass salt and pepper shakers, was a one-hundred-dollar bill. She stared at it in disbelief. Then, seeing that a note was attached with a paper clip, she picked it up.

"Good morning," it read. "I'll be by to pick you up at ten and take you downtown so you can buy shoes. Am checking around for Evans, and might have something to report by then. English muffins in the freezer. Help yourself to the fruit. Evan."

It sounded like him, she thought, tucking the note in the pocket of the pajamas. Simple, concise and full of instructions. It was nice of him to help look for Evans, but she was sure it was because he was eager to get her out of his house.

"So, what did you expect?" she asked herself. He was a happy bachelor, and she was being pursued by killers. Hardly the ingredients for a match made in heaven.

She ate the orange quickly, taking in the wonderful kitchen as she did so and committing it to memory. She couldn't imagine how she would survive her situation, much less what direction her life would take afterward. But she wanted to remember this—a cold, overcast morning in a bright, cheerful kitchen where that fifties family might have gathered.

Finished with the orange, she carried her coffee upstairs, showered quickly and changed into the blue sweater and jeans, then put the socks and slippers back on and shrugged into the paint-dappled coat.

She was ready and waiting in the kitchen, studying the various colors of paint on the jacket, when the door opened suddenly and Evan appeared.

He was wearing a camel-colored parka over working overalls, and there were flecks of white paint in his hair. "You're ready," he said, looking surprised.

She glanced at the kitchen clock. "You said ten o'clock."

He held the door open for her. "I thought women were supposed to be late all the time."

She frowned teasingly at him as they walked out to a big white van with red lettering on the side. "That's a myth," she said. "We have too much to do. You got your van back."

"Picked it up last night on my way home. If you have so much to do, what are you going to tackle first after you buy shoes?"

"See if I can find Evans. Your note said you were doing some checking?"

He opened the door to the passenger side and helped her in, then walked around to climb in behind the wheel. "I'm working on that for you, and put a few people on it. Addie—that's Hank's mother—has been here all her life and knows everybody. And Rita Robidoux, who works at the Breakfast Barn—she's an old-timer, too, and sees everybody in town come or go through the restaurant at one time or another."

When she looked at him worriedly, he added quickly, "Don't worry. I didn't tell them why. But even if I had, their dual purpose in life is to marry off every single man in town, and be true to their friends. You're safe.''

She accepted that with a nod. ''I just don't want anyone else endangered.''

''There's one road in and out of town. If a red SUV shows up, we'll see it and be prepared. Come on. If you can make a quick decision on the shoes, I'll take you to coffee before I have to go back to work.''

Beazie felt as though they'd driven straight into a colonial Christmas. Garlands strung with white lights were draped from one side of the main street to the other at twenty-foot intervals throughout the two-block downtown area. A star hung from the middle of each garland, and the globes of the streetlights were framed in light-trimmed wreaths.

In the center of town, the common stood surrounded by shops that looked as they must have when Washington wintered in Valley Forge. Every shop was also strung with lights, and there were windows filled with Christmas gifts and goodies.

Beazie spotted two bronze statues on the common, a man and a woman, and pointed. ''Who are they?''

''We'll get your shoes first,'' Evan said, ''then you can get a closer look at Caleb and Elizabeth.''

She bought a sturdy pair of walking boots, and he encouraged her to find another pair for dress-up, since her own were ruined. They sat side by side in red vinyl chairs in a corner of the room while she put the brown leather boots back in the box. The clerk had gone to greet a newcomer with two small children.

"Dress-up?" she asked in confusion.

Their faces were mere inches apart, and she got a whiff of that herbal cologne.

"We're going to Hank and Jackie's for the Christmas party, along with most of the other guys and their families. Day after tomorrow. I don't think you'll have found Evans by then."

"But...I don't have to go. I mean, just because I'm staying with you..."

"Well, that's it right there," he said with a surreptitious glance in the clerk's direction. She was measuring the children's feet and they were giggling. "They think you're living with me and not just staying with me."

She repeated the words dumbly, searching for the significance. "Living with you, not stay—?" And then it occurred to her. "You mean...girlfriend?"

He nodded. "I didn't know how else to explain you without giving you away. You just suddenly appeared, and unless you're willing to tell more than you want people to know, I think we're stuck with it."

Frankly, she didn't find the scenario all that unappealing. Except that she was a terrible liar and tended to look guilty whenever she tried.

"What, exactly, did you tell them?"

"That you are an old girlfriend from my days as a cop."

"Define 'old.'"

"Old in respect to the amount of time we've been together rather than age."

"And how long is that?"

He shook his head. "Guys don't question that kind of detail. Make up whatever works for you—" He grinned suddenly.

She loved the way he did that. It made her feel the same way she did when the sun broke out from behind a cloud.

"I did suggest that we parted when I left the force because you didn't want to leave Boston, but you decided you couldn't live without me, after all, and just showed up at the mill yesterday."

"But...Randy knows that isn't true."

"I swore him to secrecy."

She sighed, realizing that her fate, for the next few days, at least, was sealed. "So, you're telling me that I have to act lovesick at the party?"

"Nah. Mildly adoring and sweetly amenable will do it."

She looked him in the eyes. "For that, I'll require more than a pair of boots."

He nodded knowingly. "You're going to hit me up for jewelry?"

"No." She pointed to a discount rack of purses. "I need something to put my makeup in. And a hanky. Right now, the money you left me is in my bra."

A predatory glint that was more playful than threatening sparkled in his eyes. "Can I borrow twenty bucks?"

She elbowed him, and he laughed as he followed her to the purse rack.

EVAN COULD NOT BELIEVE it took this long to select a purse. She'd decided on two pairs of shoes in a matter of five minutes. She'd chosen them, tried them on and, when they fit, given the clerk a nod of approval.

But he'd now been standing with the boxes of shoes for a full twenty minutes and she was still undecided, taking one purse down after another, exploring pockets, checking inside, slinging them over her shoulder one by one and taking a few steps.

She finally opted for one that resembled a backpack. It was brown and serviceable looking. She slung it over her shoulder and they headed for the counter.

He started to write a check.

"But you gave me money," she whispered to him as the clerk reached under the counter for a shopping bag.

He leaned down to her and whispered back, "I'd just as soon you didn't retrieve it from your bra at this moment."

She laughed. He felt a burst of warm breath in his ear that affected him in places not even remotely connected.

"I was teasing. It's in the pocket of my jeans."

It took Evan a few seconds to collect himself. "Save it," he said. "You shouldn't be without some money."

Suddenly she grew serious. "I never had this much money in my pocket at home."

He handed the check to the clerk, who handed over the shoes, a six-pack of white socks and the purse. "But you're not home, are you? Come on. We just have time for coffee. I have to be at the homeless shelter at eleven-thirty.''

She put on socks and the boots in the van, while he drove to Perk Avenue, one of the shops that bordered the downtown common.

''Wow!'' she said, going toward the square when she leapt out of the van rather than toward the coffee bar. ''Every other town square in Massachusetts has a Minuteman statue, but you never see one with a woman.'' She pointed to the Christmas tree near the statue and the lights strung around the Minuteman and his lady.

''She's his wife?'' she asked, going right up to the bronze statue.

''Yes. Just as the plaque says, they protected Maple Hill from the British army.'' He'd always liked the two of them there and appreciated Beazie's fascination with them. ''Jackie probably knows more about them. She has details of Maple Hill history since it was founded in the early 1700s. I think her family's been here that long. And her former husband's family, too.''

Beazie wrapped the paint-dappled jacket around her and focused on the plaque at the base of the statue. '''Caleb and Elizabeth Drake,''' she read, '''who defended Maple Hill in the War of Independence.' Wow!'' she said again, looking up at the statue. ''I'll bet their love made them invincible.''

He studied the statue as a light snow began to fall. ''How can you tell? They're not even touching.''

''Somebody once said that love isn't created by looking into each other's eyes, but by looking out in the same direction." She put a hand to the bronze hem of Elizabeth's dress. "They're focused on the same spot. They fought together, united by love, and that probably gave them four times the strength each would have had alone."

"That's quite a claim," he said, taking her arm and leading her back toward the coffee bar. "You've been in love?"

"No. But I thought I was a couple of times, and it gives you this raging energy." She slipped as they crossed the slushy street, and he firmed his grip on her. "You've never felt that?"

"I don't think so."

"But you're...what? Mid-thirties?"

"Thirty-eight," he replied.

"And you've *never* had a serious girlfriend?" she asked as he pulled open the door of Perk Avenue. The question sounded loud in the quiet room, but fortunately there was no one to hear.

"*You're* supposed to be her, remember?" he whispered.

She made a self-deprecating face. "Sorry."

"No harm done. What's your poison? Chocolate? Whipped cream? Cream cheese?"

He led her to a display case filled with the most beautiful pastries. She pointed to an elegantly decorated Napoleon.

"Mocha?"

"Please. Double shot."

She chose a table by the window, while he ordered at the counter. Looking out through the small panes at Caleb and Elizabeth, she smiled at the thought that two people had once loved like that. It had set a course for this town, which was now filled with closely connected people working hard for the common good of Maple Hill.

An inexplicable little breath of peace filled her being.

Evan had been wrong when he'd told her why she should keep the one hundred dollars. She felt as though she *was* home.

CHAPTER FIVE

EVAN HAD JUST SETTLED DOWN at the table opposite Beazie, when the door opened, admitting a group of older women who were laughing like teenage girls.

"Evan!" one of them shouted. "Rita, look! It's Evan!"

His back to them, Evan closed his eyes and said quietly, feelingly, "Oh, no."

"Who are they?" Beazie whispered, but two of the women had left their friends and were upon Evan and Beazie before he could answer.

He stood and smiled as he pulled out chairs for them. Beazie admired how well he masked his reluctance to see them.

"Beazie," he said, sitting down once he'd seated the older women, "this is Addie Whitcomb, Hank and Haley's mother, and Rita Robidoux, Addie's friend. Ladies, Beatrice Deadham."

The women leaned eagerly toward Beazie. Addie was gray-haired and chic in pale blue slacks and matching sweater under a pink parka. Rita, whose hair was an unusual shade of burgundy, wore denim with a red bandana tied around her neck. Beazie remembered that Evan had said they considered themselves Dolly Levi-quality matchmakers. And if they were looking for this man named Evans for her, she doubted very much that he—or anything else— would escape their notice.

If she and Evan were going to pass themselves off as lovers, she thought, these were the hands to play into.

"You're new to Maple Hill!" Addie observed, smiling warmly. "Welcome."

Beazie returned her smile, clearing her throat to try out their story for the first time. "Thank you so much. It's beautiful here."

"What brings you here at Christmas?" Rita asked, awaiting an answer with aggressive interest.

Beazie turned an adoring smile on Evan, who was watching her warily. "Evan and I were...close when he was still in Boston. He wanted to leave and I didn't, so he came to Maple Hill without me. But..." She shrugged a shoulder to indicate a powerful fate at work. "I tried, but I couldn't live without him. So, here I am."

Addie punched Evan's shoulder. "He is pretty irresistible, isn't he. Painted my living room in a day and a half. And that includes the border above the picture rail."

Beazie nodded gravely in agreement. "I've always thought so. It just took a separation to make me realize what I was taking for granted." She glanced his way just in time to see the roll of his eyes, obscured from the ladies by a quick sip of coffee.

"So, you're joining us at Jackie's for the Christmas party on Sunday?" Addie asked.

"Yes, I understand we are."

"I'm in charge of the menu, since Jackie's so busy," she said, digging into her purse and retrieving a list.

"You told me to bring salads," Evan said, "because you knew I could get them at the deli. And you were a little smart about it, as I recall."

Addie put a hand to her chest and looked at him in wide-eyed innocence. "I? Surely not." She consulted her list, then said finally, "Right. Salads."

"What kind would you prefer?" Beazie asked.

"Evan always brings potato and macaroni," Addie replied. "That's fine."

"Would you prefer carrot and raisin, and maybe a seven-layer salad?"

Addie's eyes widened in pleased surprise. "Can you do that? That'd be wonderful." She patted Evan's hand apologetically. "Not that your deli salads aren't always appreciated."

"Uh-huh," he said, drawing his hand away in pretended affront. "Don't try to backpedal on me, Addie. You don't have to hit me with a brick to make it clear that I'm not appreciated. But don't worry about me. I'll be fine." His forehead furrowed, showing just the right amount of distress. "Just because I drop everything whenever you have a painting or a wallpaper emergency—or any other kind, for that matter—is no reason for you to think you have to spare my feelings."

Addie got out of her chair and wrapped her arms around him. "Evan, sweetheart," she cajoled, "you know that of all the Wonders, you're my favorite."

He sat implacably in her embrace. "You told Cam

he was your favorite just the other day. He bragged to everybody.''

''Well, he just needed a little extra encouragement. He was having a bad day. But you're *really* my favorite.'' She squeezed him. He coughed.

''Addie!'' one of her friends shouted from the counter across the room. ''A praline muffin, as usual?''

''Tell them I'll have a chocolate croissant.'' Addie dispatched Rita with the message. ''And a small pot of Earl Grey.''

Rita patted Beazie's shoulder as she left the table. ''Welcome, honey,'' she said.

''Thank you, Rita.'' Beazie smiled a goodbye, then turned her attention to Addie and Evan, whose conversation had suddenly become serious.

''Well, I'll have no one to work on but Randy,'' Addie was saying. ''And I don't know where that boy's head is. He's the one that seems to most value my services, but every girl he takes out never hears from him again.''

''Be patient,'' he advised. ''His fiancée died last year. He seems to think that means he can date and enjoy the company of a nice woman, but that he'll never find anyone to love the way he loved her.''

''That's silly.'' She slapped his shoulder gently, as though he were responsible for that philosophy.

He shrugged it off. ''We're all silly deep down.'' He took the hand she rested on his shoulder and kissed it. ''Have a good day. We'll see you Sunday. With a couple of very elegant salads, apparently.''

Addie kissed the top of his head, then hugged Beazie. "I'm glad you came back to him, sweetie," she said with quiet sincerity. "He's one special Wonder."

Beazie was beginning to believe that.

"So, now I have to take you grocery shopping," he said, after Addie joined her friends.

"No." She took a sip of the mocha he'd brought her earlier. It was drizzled with chocolate syrup and colorful sprinkles, and topped with an animal cracker. "Just point me to the market. I have money in my pocket, and I saw a bus running when we left the house. It goes right by your place."

He studied her as though assessing her ability to navigate Maple Hill all by herself. Then he finally asked with a cocked eyebrow, "You're sure you can get at your money without being arrested?"

She tapped the side pocket of her jeans. "Absolutely. Anything you want me to pick up that you didn't get yesterday?"

He held a fork in his right hand and pointed in her direction with his little finger. "You might buy yourself a jacket so you don't have to wear that everywhere. I've got an account at Maple Hill Mercantile across the street. I'll walk you over before I leave, so you don't have trouble charging."

"I don't mind wearing this," she said, then teased with a light laugh. "It proves I'm yours, if that's our story. Everything you own has paint all over it."

"Now that Addie and Rita have the 'news,'" he said, glancing toward the two women gathered around a large table with their friends, "it'll be all over town. You won't have to wear a paint-spattered jacket for people to know we're together.''

They were leaving the shop half an hour later to head for the mercantile when he grabbed her by the fabric of the jacket and yanked her back into the doorway. He stood in front of her, leaning a shoulder on the side of the building, effectively blocking her from view.

"What's the matter?" she asked, her heartbeat quickening.

"Red SUV coming up the street," he said without turning around. "Stay behind me.''

The thought that she might have been found already kept her huddled behind him, against the side of the building. And it reminded her that she'd been enjoying Maple Hill and its people too much, and not attending to business.

"Did it have Connecticut plates?" he asked, his head turning as the vehicle drove past.

"New York," she replied. "Something, something, something, HAR. I didn't stick around long enough to get the numbers.''

He straightened finally and drew her out beside him. "Sorry," he said. "I saw it coming a block away and thought it might be yours. But there was a woman driving it, with a baby in a carrier in the second seat.''

She put a hand to her heart as her pulse dribbled back to normal.

Noting her relief, he slipped an arm around her shoulders and squeezed gently. "Didn't mean to scare you.''

"It's okay," she said, as flustered by his touch as she had been by the possibility she'd been found. "I'm okay."

"Good. I'll take you to the mercantile, then I'll wait for you at the market."

"But you have work to do."

"You'll come with me tomorrow and we'll get twice as much done."

That was all right with her. The fear she'd conquered because she'd begun to feel safe in this pretty little town had surfaced again, reminding her that she was foolish to think about anything but finding Evans. Family hunting would have to wait.

IT OCCURRED TO EVAN to wonder what he was doing, but he had no idea, so it seemed pointless to ask himself. He'd been awake most of the night, trying to determine what he was feeling, precisely what had changed in the quiet life he was rebuilding here.

Well, it was easy to see what had changed. There was a woman in his life with dangerous problems. But those problems were in her life, not his. And he'd always considered himself not quite worthy of total involvement with a woman. He was the son of a father who'd walked away, after all. He had the same genes as the man who'd left a weeping wife and a little boy who'd adored him, and never looked back.

Evan had always considered himself a good person and he knew he'd been a good cop. But he wasn't sure he could be a family man. Curious genetic details were hereditary.

That concern about himself had deepened when he'd had to leave Boston after Blaine's death. He'd had reasons he had thought validated his departure, but his mother had wept, anyway, and he knew his stepfather had been hurt.

But despite his best efforts, his life was becoming dangerously entwined with Beazie's. He felt mildly anxious, but he knew the best thing to do was simply coast until he could figure out how to handle it.

She worked across the room from him in the homeless shelter, in what would eventually be a common room. They were applying the second coat of a soft green chosen by the decorator who'd volunteered for the project. Beazie worked in an old coverall of his, after cutting several inches off the sleeves and legs, and her hair into a paper hat that advertised a paint company.

He'd felt a surge of adrenaline yesterday morning when he'd spotted the red SUV. He hadn't experienced that fierce determination to stand in harm's way since his days on the force. The possibility that she could be hurt, or worse, had become very real, and he'd been surprised by the intensity of his protective response.

This was getting serious.

And he didn't mean the threat of the red SUV.

"When are you going home for Christmas?" she asked, applying paint with a roller in a long, even stroke.

"I'm not," he replied.

"Why not?"

He heard the surprise in her voice.

"Too busy," he replied. "You don't have to be that particular. You can roll up and down in smaller strokes. It'll go faster and still cover evenly."

She stopped working and turned to him. He kept working, pretending not to notice.

"Why just maybe? Don't you get along?"

"My family's wonderful," he said briskly, hoping to make it clear he didn't want to talk about it. "I just have a lot going on here."

He heard the squishy slap of roller against wall as she started painting again.

"I know it's none of my business," she said. "It just surprises me because I have no one to be with on holidays, and I can't imagine having a family to go home to and not going. It seems all wrong."

He remained quiet.

"Do you have brothers and sisters?"

He could say it easily, then maybe she'd leave the subject alone. "I had a brother, but he died in a car wreck."

There was a moment's silence, just the sound of his roller on the wall.

"I'm sorry," she finally said. "Was it recently? Is that what makes it hard to go home?"

"A year and a half ago. And yes."

"Well...think about how hard that must be for your parents," she said gently, "to know that he can't come home, but that you aren't sure you want to."

He turned angrily in her direction, the roller balanced on the pan on the floor. She had no right to be so...right.

"That's true," she said, reading his expression. She turned back to her work. "Your eyes are telling me it's none of my business. I went too far."

Relieved that he'd put an end to the conversation, he recoated the roller with paint.

Then, after a moment, she added, "It's just that I feel sorry for them, you know, because I don't know what he was like, but you're such a sweetheart. I'll bet they really miss you."

That was more than he could take. He dropped the roller into the pan again and propped the handle against the window frame.

"I've been a cop," he said emphatically when she turned in surprise, roller still pointing upward. "I've chased criminals down, I've knelt on their backs to cuff them, I've even punched a few. I drink beer and sometimes don't shave for days. I am *not* a sweetheart."

She was trying to hold back a smile, and that really annoyed him. Realizing the roller was dripping, she finally put it down in the pan and came to meet him in the middle of the room.

"Yeah, you are," she insisted. "It has nothing to do with being tough or what you drink, and whether you do or don't shave. Some gorgeous, apparently refined men can turn out to be bastards. Sweethearts are few and far between, and often a surprise—apparently, even to themselves."

He couldn't believe his ears. He often felt as though his soul was black, that he'd failed everyone, himself included, and she thought…

She took two steps to cover the small space that

separated them and put her hands to his chest, a look in her eyes that caused the weird stirring of warmth inside him that she'd made him experience once before.

"Why are you surprised that I find you to be a sweetheart?" she asked, rubbing unconsciously up to his shoulders. "You didn't get all physical when I held a bat on you, you called a doctor for me..."

"An EMT," he corrected absently, his brain focused on her hands on his chest.

"You gave me a place to stay, saw that I had clothes, gave me a—"

He just didn't want to hear any more. He couldn't stand to watch that soft, mobile mouth move another instant without kissing it. It was time to straighten her out on that sweetheart notion.

SHE'D SEEN THE KISS COMING. She'd seen it in his eyes and was a little worried because it seemed to be fueled by anger rather than desire or even simple affection.

But she felt the anger only for an instant, and only in the hands that grabbed her shoulders and held her still. The moment his lips touched hers, a tenderness surfaced and took control.

The hands that held her in place relaxed their hold and slipped around her, one hand drawing her to him while the other pulled her hat off and delved into her hair. Gooseflesh rose along her scalp in the wake of his fingers, and followed down her spine as his hand moved, tracing the line of her back, vertebra by vertebra.

Forgetting their unconventional circumstances, she wrapped her arms around his neck and leaned into him, feeling life come back to her after the dark hours of her escape and the tedious loneliness of her world before that.

Feeling surged in her, entangled her, enveloped her. She was caught in it, deliciously trapped by the man who held her.

This, she thought drunkenly as his lips wandered down her throat, then up again, branding her mouth with the tender intensity of his emotions, *is falling in love.*

He seemed to have to tear himself free of her. When he took her arms, a trace of anger was back in his touch, and he pushed her away from him, holding her at arm's length. There was turmoil in his eyes as he stared at her.

He was as shocked by that kiss as she was. What might have been interpreted as simple attraction had now manifested itself as something else entirely. And he wasn't at all pleased.

Great. Trust her to finally find the right man and then have him turn out to be someone who wasn't interested in finding the right woman.

To relieve him of any sense of responsibility when he'd done too much for her already, she tossed her hair and said with a superior lift of her eyebrow, "Told you so."

Then she turned on her heel and went back to work.

CHAPTER SIX

BEAZIE HAD NEVER SEEN ANYTHING like the Christmas party at the Whitcombs' home. Even when her father was alive, their family had been small and holidays had involved quiet celebrations with a few close friends.

This reminded her of Mardis Gras with turkey. The energy level was high, the noise level very loud, and she couldn't turn around without being offered a plate of hors d'oeuvres. The living room and dining room were strung with fat, ornament-encrusted garland, and a tall Christmas tree was wound with gauzy gold ribbon and decorated with bird ornaments.

Adults numbered fourteen or fifteen; it was difficult to count, as people moved in and out of several connected rooms. Cam and Mariah were there, as well as Mariah's sister, Parker, who was also married to a Wonder. Bart and Haley Megrath were arranging a relish tray while their foster son paced the kitchen with their squalling baby. All the single men who worked for Hank had been invited, and Beazie spotted Randy in the crowd, talking with several other young men she didn't recognize.

Children were everywhere—infants, toddlers,

older, bright-looking children with the happy confidence of the lovingly indulged.

She met Glory Anselmo, who was engaged to a Wonder, and found out that she, too, had been born in Buffalo. They compared memories of familiar high school haunts and went through a list of people they both knew and what had become of them. When Glory was called away to replenish the punch she'd brought, she called over Parker, to keep Beazie company.

Parker introduced Beazie to her stepchildren— Jeff, a college freshman home for the holidays, and Stacey, a junior at Maple Hill High. Stacey held one of Hank and Jackie's twin boys, who were about eight months old.

"Jeff and Stacey have brilliant voices, both of them," Parker bragged. The teenagers closed their eyes in simultaneous mortification. "They're part of the high school's Madrigals."

"I'm impressed," Beazie said frankly. "I love music, but I can't sing and I can't play an instrument."

"They're going to sing when Jackie lights the tree on the common," Parker went on. "And the Madrigals have been offering their services in small groups to take your musical greetings anywhere in the county for a very small fee. So, if you want to serenade anyone with carols, just call the high school."

Jeff put an arm around Parker. "I don't think you can serenade with carols. I think you just...carol.

Nice to meet you, Beazie. Excuse me, I have to go watch the game.''

"Have to?'' Parker repeated.

"Yeah," he replied, and was off.

Someone appeared with a cordless phone and put it in Stacey's hand. She passed the baby to Parker and went in search of a quiet corner to take her call.

But Parker immediately passed the baby to Beazie. "I'm sorry, but would you, please? I'm supposed to be mashing potatoes, but I wanted you to meet my kids. Well, they're Gary's kids, but aren't they great?''

"Yes, they are." Beazie took the warm little bundle into her arms. The baby was wearing a bright red one-piece romper with a smiling snowman on the pocket. He gave her a wide, gummy grin, and she grinned back. "You're one of those sweethearts, too, aren't you.''

She looked around for Evan but couldn't spot him. Then, noticing a simple wooden rocker in a quiet corner of the room, she headed for it.

EVAN SAT WITH THE GUYS in Hank's downstairs den off the kitchen and watched one of the many football playoffs. Mike McGee, Bart and Haley's foster child, was stretched out on the floor with Brian, Cam's foster son, and Jeff, Parker's stepson.

Evan, Cam, Hank with one of his twin sons, Bart, Gary, Randy and Jimmy Elliott were sardined on two full-size sofas and several chairs pulled up within view of the screen.

While they alternately cheered and booed, Evan

found himself wondering what Beazie was doing. Last time he'd spotted her, she was in conversation with Glory Anselmo, who dated Jimmy. Glory was studying accounting and was a part-time nanny for Hank and Jackie. Glory and Jimmy's wedding was scheduled for Valentine's Day.

Beazie had looked comfortable enough, and he couldn't imagine why he was worried about her, except that he always seemed to be now—ever since he'd spotted the red SUV and felt an overwhelming need to protect her.

Everyone seemed to accept that Beazie was a girl-friend from his past, and the role was easy to assume. The room was filled with cozy couples, so melding in one more was a simple thing. It required only a smile exchanged across the room, a touch when they reconnected in the crowd.

He'd tried all night not to give too much weight to yesterday's kiss, but it had kept him awake, anyway. He'd been stunned by the impact of it, surprised by the light it seemed to flash inside him.

The truth was, he didn't really want that kind of light. There were still a lot of unanswered questions concerning Blaine's death, and he'd come to believe that was probably best. His parents and his sister-in-law had been spared any additional trauma, and his move to Maple Hill had spared him from having to try to reconnect with them when the accident stood between them like an open grave.

But there was some cosmic plan afoot that seemed to ignore whatever it was he wanted. He'd come to Maple Hill in search of a quiet life, and found himself surrounded by friends determined to make him a part of their lives. He'd wanted to forget, but the love of his family had been too strong. It nagged at him all the time.

And he hadn't wanted to get involved with a woman. Yet here he was, hip-deep in Beazie Deadham's problems.

Not to mention her smile, her charm, and her drop-dead beautiful little body in borrowed clothes.

Restless, he wandered out of the den unnoticed and through the kitchen, which was alive with tantalizing aromas, female laughter, and children at waist and knee level like beautiful undergrowth in a domestic forest.

Jackie held a fork up to his mouth. She wore a cobbler's apron in a floral fabric over jeans and a yellow sweater. Her cheeks were pink from the heat of the kitchen, and her smiling eyes said she was a woman who had everything. "Turnip and carrot mixture. Need more salt?"

He tasted the hot combination of vegetables and shook his head. It was perfectly seasoned.

Addie, stirring gravy in a pan, held a spoon up to his mouth, her other hand under it to catch drips. "How's this?"

He knew what she wanted in reply, and fortunately he could give that honestly. "Perfect."

"About that Evans you're looking for..." Addie said.

"Yeah?"

"I can't find anybody who knows one in Maple Hill. There was a Susan Evans in the county clerk's office a few years ago, but she married a pilot and moved to Alaska. Rita's not doing much better than I.''

Evan hugged her. "I appreciate your trying." He was almost glad she hadn't come up with anyone. To his surprise, he realized he wasn't anxious for Beazie to move on.

Haley took a roll from a towel-lined basket and grinned at him. "I know they're good. Mom made them. Just wanted you to have one."

He kissed her forehead. "Bless you. Have you seen Beazie?"

She pointed toward the living room. "She's on nursery duty. And doing very well, I might add. Good choice in the mother of your children, Braga."

He smiled in response to her praise, just what the role he'd assumed called for. Then he went in search of Beazie.

He found her in a corner of the living room. Now that the men were in the den, the women in the kitchen and the older children playing upstairs, the living room was relatively quiet. She sat in a rocker, a baby in each arm, her eyes closed as she pushed herself gently back and forth, one leg crossed over the other.

Alex Whitcomb, in a red jumpsuit, had the general dimensions of a snowball. And Henrietta Megrath, wrapped in a quilt that Addie had made, slept serenely, tiny little hands protruding and working the air.

Sensing his presence, Beazie opened her eyes lazily to look in his direction. She smiled slowly. "Hi," she said very quietly.

He went to squat beside her. "Hi. You look as though someone should be rocking you."

Her smile widened at that, and she gazed from one little face to the other. "I don't think I've sat quietly for this long since—well, maybe never. It's wonderful, you know? Even your breathing seems to slow down in sync with theirs, and you find yourself wondering what the rush was ever about. And every breath brings you something new—the smell of baby powder, of turkey and hot rolls." She drew a long breath. "Your cologne..."

As he gazed into her languid expression, he felt himself drawn into her time decelerator. All the noise and activity in the other rooms seemed to recede, and all that existed for him was this moment, with Beazie smiling into his eyes, her arms filled with babies.

He wanted to be distressed by the happiness he felt, but it was too strong. The contented-baby/serene-woman vibe cancelled out everything negative. And his system had slowed too much to fight it, so he let himself be happy.

"Is this what you want?" he asked, raising an index finger to the little hand that opened and closed on thin air. The tiny fingers latched around his first knuckle and held with a strength that surprised him. It was one life reaching out to another, innocence searching for something secure. "A baby in each arm?"

"It feels wonderful," she replied. "I suppose it isn't in the middle of the night, whcn the babies can't sleep and you don't know why, but right now, it seems like a worthy goal. What about you?''

He shook his head. ''Humans that tiny make me nervous. I like kids, but I'd be more comfortable if they came in Rachel's size.'' Rachel was Jackie and Hank's seven-year-old.

''I wonder if Caleb and Elizabeth had children?''

''You should ask Jackie.''

As though on cue, Jackie appeared in the neighboring dining room, bearing a platter in each hand and followed by a small army of women, also carrying platters or bowls.

''Evan, could you go get the guys?'' she asked, placing her platters on the table as someone else moved plates and water glasses aside to make room. ''And tell Hank I need him to carve the turkey, please. Beazie, do your salads need anything, or are they ready to put on the table?''

''They're ready.''

Jackie did a double take as she caught sight of Beazie in the chair. ''Are you still holding those babies? My goodness, Haley, do something.''

Her plates arranged, Haley came quickly to take her baby. ''I'm sorry,'' she said. ''You should have had Evan put her in the carrier when she fell asleep.''

Haley took the baby to the carrier resting in a chair and did just that.

Evan had gone to do Jackie's bidding, so he missed Beazie's small performance. ''He's terrified of little babies,'' she said with the amused tolerance of a lover. ''He says when we have one, he won't touch it until it's Rachel's size.''

Haley came back and carried Alex to one of two carriers in a playpen set up in a warm corner of the big kitchen.

"Well, we'll have to give him a few lessons," Haley said when she returned, "or you won't have any help with changing diapers or midnight feedings." She pursed her lips in suspicion. "Of course, it's entirely possible he isn't afraid at all, just setting you up to have to do everything. He's so capable when it comes to most things, it's hard to imagine he really is afraid."

"Who's afraid?" Hank asked, walking into the room with the second twin sound asleep on his shoulder. The other men and boys followed him to the table and began to pull out chairs.

"Evan," Jackie replied.

Hank frowned. "Afraid of what?"

"Babies."

Evan, deep in conversation with Mike, looked up at the sound of his name and the public airing of the fact that he was afraid of babies. He knew precisely where to look for the source of his betrayal.

"Well, Beazie had to share that with someone," Haley chided him. "We're your friends. We're here to help you when you feel inadequate."

"Right." Hank turned to hand him the twin, expertly balanced on the palms of his hands.

Evan took a step backward. "I don't think…"

Ignoring him, Hank placed the baby in his arms. "Put him down in the carrier in the playpen. It's good practice for you. But don't drop him. Jackie gets really upset when you do that."

Glory blinked. "Have *you* done that?"

"Only once," Hank replied with a wince. "And I didn't drop him very far. Just from the changing table to the floor."

A room full of horrified women shouted, "Hank!"

He shrank away from the sound. "I know. Well, I didn't do it on purpose. He had a diaper rash, and I had ointment on my hands and..."

Haley stared at him in theatrical disbelief. "And to think I let you baby-sit my daughter."

Hank made a face at his sister. "I baby-sat you enough times when you were little, and you survived."

Addie pulled out a chair and sat down. "There *was* that time you locked her in the utility closet."

"She wouldn't listen to me."

"You wanted her to go to bed so you could smoke," his mother recounted. "It was seven o'clock."

"Rest would have been good for her. She was always hyper."

Evan listened to the affectionate ragging go on as he walked like a robot into the kitchen, the weight of the small bundle in his arms scaring him spitless. He'd been afraid even to hold his own nephews until they were rough-and-ready toddlers.

The transfer of the baby's head from his elbow to his other hand was terrifying, but he did it without mishap. Supporting the thickly diapered bottom in his left hand, he lowered the baby next to his twin.

He felt a moment's panic when a pair of blue eyes opened and studied him with seriousness.

"It's okay," he said quickly, softly. "I'm your uncle Evan. Your mom and dad are right there through that doorway. We're having a Christmas party and you might find a drumstick a little difficult to handle. But I'm sure somebody'll bring you milk or something later."

The baby's brow furrowed. Instinctively Evan stroked the bald head and shushed the infant gently, certain his reputation would be ruined forever if the baby started to scream and woke his brother.

"I'll see that you get mince pie, or something," he bargained with the baby, who kicked, gave him a toothless smile and dropped his heavy lids again in sleep.

"Everything okay?" Beazie asked, appearing behind him with a salad bowl in each hand.

"Yeah, I think so." He straightened, and she put a bowl in his hand.

"Great. Would you carry this, please?"

Remembering what had started this whole threat to his peace of mind, he took the bowl with a teasing yank and accused, "Nice going, telling them I was terrified of babies. I bared my soul to you in confidence."

She smiled tentatively, as though not sure if he was really upset or not. Then, after a moment of staring into his eyes, she smiled with affection. It occurred to him that he could watch that happen all day.

"I was just sharing with the girls, you know. They like to dish on their husbands and boyfriends. It's a bonding kind of thing. And it makes them believe we're lovers.''

"Really. Well, wait until I get something on you."

She shrugged, wide-eyed. "But I'm fearless."

He remembered the nightmare she'd had, but was too much of a gentleman to mention it.

She must have read that memory in his eyes, because she rested a hand on his shoulder for balance and stretched up to kiss him on the cheek. "Thank you for not throwing that back at me," she said. "See? A sweetheart."

"Oh, get a room!" Cam grumbled as he walked past them, a hand held up against his face like a blinder. "But before you do, would you take those salads to the table? Everybody's waiting and you're in here having dessert."

THERE WAS ENOUGH FOOD to feed all of Maple Hill. Every time Beazie thought she had some of everything on her plate and could actually begin eating, another bowl was passed to her.

She liked the fact there was no separate children's table. Card tables had been placed at each end of the big table, and the children, each distributed between the adults, tried all the exotic dishes and joined in the conversation. Only the sleeping babies were missing but within sight.

Everyone raved over Beazie's salads, and she delighted in the compliments while Evan took a good-natured ribbing over his choice of a woman who could cook. Beazie played her role and smiled at him, wondering if this group would be as welcoming if they knew she hadn't so much been chosen as thrust upon him.

She let that thought go, the warm and wonderful moment too precious to dismiss with the truth of why she was here. She considered it a miracle that Gordon's horrifying murder and her pursuit by his killers had culminated in the sanctuary she'd found in Evan's home and her welcome into the lives of his friends.

With the other women, she helped clear the table and set out dessert, an array of six pies served plain or à la mode with regular or spiked coffee.

She tried a sliver of Addie's pumpkin custard pie, and another of her pecan. Then Evan dipped his fork into the pie on his plate and offered the bite to her.

"You have to try this," he said.

She'd been eating for what seemed like hours, and it was such an easy thing to open her mouth and nip off the little cube of pie. It was apple with a caramel-and-pecan filling, and she melted into a puddle of hedonistic delight.

"Glory made it," Addie said from her place between Hank and Erica, the Whitcombs' other daughter. "She once made a meat loaf Jackie used as a doorstop, but I'm teaching her everything I know."

While everyone laughed and praised Glory's success, Beazie helped herself to another bite of Evan's pie.

"Okay, that's enough," he teased quietly. "I'm not a sweetheart when it comes to sharing my dessert."

She couldn't imagine that was true—that a situation could exist where he wasn't the epitome of kindness he'd been so far.

Clearing away was a lengthy process that involved several cycles of the dishwasher, and storing leftovers in the extra refrigerator in the basement because the one in the kitchen was already full to bursting.

Beazie helped Haley, Mariah, Parker and Glory, while Jackie conducted a sort of informal meeting in the living room about the opening of the homeless shelter. Addie, who'd done so much of the meal preparation, had been banned from the kitchen.

Haley was eventually called to the meeting to discuss publicity for the event, which would solicit clothes and canned goods for the food bank. Then Mariah was asked to join the discussion on collecting and repairing toys.

Jimmy Elliott came into the kitchen with Glory's coat. "Gotta go, love," he said, "if we're going to be at my sister's by six."

Glory pulled off her apron and turned to let him help her into her coat.

"I was going to leave you whatever was left of the pie," Glory said when she had her coat on, giving Beazie a hug. "But there was nothing left." Then she grinned. "Although I'm not sure if that hungry look in your eye when you sampled it was because of my pie, or because Evan was feeding it to you."

Jimmy, too, gave Beazie a hug. "You take good care of him," he said.

The kitchen door closed behind them, and Parker, standing on a stool and putting plates away in a tall cupboard, pointed to a stack of plates Beazie had just removed from the dishwasher. Beazie carried them to her.

"Funny that Jimmy wants *you* to take care of Evan, when it seems as if it should be the other way around." Parker reached down for the plates. "But I know what he means. Evan's all muscle and determination since he recovered from that accident. He's calm and funny and has answers for every problem, but I've given him massages a couple of times when the old injuries were giving him trouble, and there's something in him that's…festering."

Beazie stared up at Parker, wondering what accident she was talking about.

"What do you mean?" she asked carefully.

Parker rearranged the plates in the cupboard. "Muscle knots have a number of health-related causes," she explained, "but many of them are simple tension. Evan has one right between his shoulders that defies all my efforts. I can make it go away, but almost before the session's over, it's back again."

"It's probably the painting," Beazie guessed. "He does a lot of work that involves reaching over his head, holding both arms up and…"

Parker was shaking her head before Beazie had finished. "I can make that kind of knot go away. This is something else. Sometimes, in an unguarded moment, it's in his eyes."

Beazie knew what she meant. She'd seen it, too. Somewhere behind the soft brown serenity was a dark turbulence that never quite surfaced, but never went away.

"I'm sure it would help him to talk about it," Parker said, turning slowly on the step to look around the kitchen. She pointed to two messy turkey roasters and abruptly changed the subject. "Let's just fill the double sink with detergent, and you do one and I'll do the other."

Parker was half finished when Stacey appeared, the cordless phone she'd been handed hours earlier still in her fingers. She held it to her chest. "Polly Bishop's mom is coming to pick me up and she'd like to meet you. Is that okay? Dad's involved in the meeting in the living room, and she's going to be here any minute. We have a gig tonight at the Breakfast Barn."

"A gig?" Beazie looked up from the sink.

"Somebody hired the Madrigals to sing for a group of seniors who are having dinner tonight at the Barn." She rolled her eyes. "They want a lot of old songs, but at least the harmony's fun."

Parker turned apologetically to Beazie while drying her hands on a towel. "The show must go on. I'll just run out to meet this lady, and I'll be right back."

Beazie shooed her away with soapy fingers. "Don't worry about it. I'm almost finished. Good luck, Stacey."

"Thanks. Your layered salad was killer." Stacey put an arm around her stepmother's shoulders, and Beazie saw Parker's delight in the small expression of affection.

"You'll have to give Parker the recipe," said Stacey. "She's determined not to pollute us with preservatives and carcinogens, but I do miss mayonnaise and bacon.''

Parker hugged her, then pushed her gently toward the door. ''You'll thank me when you live to be ninety-seven.''

Stacey pulled the door open, then said with the brutality of youth, ''But you'll be long gone. Oh, there she is!''

They were laughing as the door closed behind them.

Beazie smiled and went back to scrubbing. She finished the pans, wiped off the counters, took a last look around to make sure everything had been put away, then left the kitchen to join the others just as Parker returned.

It seemed that everyone had gathered in the living and dining rooms, even those not involved in the informal meeting. Children were sprawled in front of the television in one corner, and dining room chairs had been pulled closer to the living room for more seating.

Haley and Bart and the baby occupied a love seat, Jackie and Hank shared a large sectional with Cam and Mariah, and Gary beckoned Parker to join him on a padded bench. Addie sat in a rocker, and the single men occupied the dining room chairs.

There was not an empty seat anywhere.

Randy got up to offer her his chair, but Evan, seated behind him in a tapestried wing-chair, said quietly, ''Stay there, Randy. There's room here.'' He held out his hand to Beazie.

Jackie stopped talking, waiting for Beazie and Parker to settle in.

Beazie hesitated, because the seat Evan offered her was in his lap. It was a role he played for his friends, who believed her to be his old girlfriend, but she was such a puddle of vulnerability, she was afraid to let herself slip into that scenario again.

She wanted this. She wanted it a lot! And how was she going to deal with it a few days down the road when she found the Evans she was looking for, handed him the tape and had to say goodbye?

Evan raised an eyebrow, his hand closed over hers but not applying pressure. He'd let her walk away if that was what she wanted, though he clearly didn't understand what caused her hesitation now, when she'd been the perfect actress all afternoon.

As she studied the confusion in his eyes, she saw beyond it to the undefined problem Parker talked about. The one that caused the knots in his shoulders. She saw darkness and pain there, and…need. He'd never expressed it, would probably never admit to it, but it was there. He needed her.

Suddenly everything ceased to be about her and became about him. She wanted to know all those things he never talked about to anyone. She wanted to get to the bottom of that look in his eyes and somehow make it better.

She sat in his lap and wrapped an arm around his neck, as he put one hand to her back and rested the other familiarly across her thighs.

Jackie smiled indulgently at them, then continued the meeting.

"OKAY, THAT'S THE COMPLETION SCHEDULE taken care of, an update on the clothes, the day-to-day supplies, the toys." She looked up at the group and smiled. "I need someone to be in charge of baked goods for the holiday table. Addie's cooking a ham dinner and all that goes with it, but we need someone who can be in charge of baking or collecting cakes and cookies for the opening on the twenty-third, then for the families' dinners on Christmas Eve."

Evan heard the words and understood instantly how they could assist his cause. He hadn't even realized he actually had one until Beazie sat in his lap and wrapped her arm around his neck. Suddenly, all the half-formed, unexplored feelings he'd experienced since she'd fainted in his arms a few days ago took on shape and purpose. The easy weight of her, the sturdy softness of her legs and backside, the scent of her—it all seemed to make complete sense.

He wanted this. And he couldn't think beyond that. He didn't want to call it love, because it felt like lust mixed with some element heretofore unfamiliar to him. It wasn't the simple desire created by having a woman's body close to his. It was...

He gave up trying to analyze it. He just knew that his tenuous hold on sanity was being challenged by a woman who'd wormed her way into his life by threatening to kill him.

God. He needed help.

So, on the chance that she found this Evans guy tomorrow, he wanted to make sure Beazie would be around long enough for him to analyze what in the hell was happening to him.

He pinched her thigh between his thumb and fore-finger.

Beazie's indeterminate little yelp made Jackie sit up and ask, "Beazie? Are you volunteering?"

Beazie turned to Jackie with a smile, but not before giving Evan a punitive glare that only he saw. "Sure," she said.

"All right!" Jackie crossed something off in her notes, then smiled at the assembly. "Great. We've covered everything. Randy, if you and your committee can check our drop-off locations for toys once a day this week, that'd be great. The opening's getting close." She looked up and smiled at the assembly. "I guess that's it, until our next meeting—same time, same place next Thursday night?"

There were nods and a chorus of affirmatives.

"Okay." She put her notes aside and got to her feet. "More coffee and pie for anyone?"

There were several groans, but a few hands went up, and the children, their attention never diverted from the television, shouted, "Pie, please!"

"Ready to go?" Evan asked.

She closed her eyes and grinned. "I hate the thought of moving, but if you're ready, I'm ready. I wouldn't want to find out in a room filled with your friends that I snore."

"You don't snore," he said, pushing her to a sitting position, then standing with her. "You're too busy screaming. But we'd better keep that to ourselves, too. I'll find our coats."

Their departure started an exodus of families, though the single men stayed behind for that last piece of pie and cup of coffee. Thank-yous and good-byes were shouted as everyone wandered off toward the long line of vehicles parked outside.

Horns honked, and Jackie waved from the door-step as car after car headed home.

Once she was settled in the passenger seat, Beazie leaned her head back and closed her eyes sleepily. "That was the best Christmas party I ever attended. Thank you for—" she sighed languorously "—for sharing your friends."

He smiled to himself as he turned right at the high-way and headed home. He had a lot more he wanted to share with her, but he wasn't sure she was ready for that. Or that he was. So he let her sleep.

CHAPTER SEVEN

THE AIR IN THE SMALL HOUSE crackled with tension as Beazie gave Lucinda leftover giblet pieces that Jackie had saved for the cat, and Evan made a pot of decaffeinated coffee.

Beazie understood the problem perfectly. It was as though their day-long pretense had changed something between them. The sudden acceptability of touch after she'd sat in his lap brought to life the attraction that had been simmering between them for some time and now made the whole living-together drama unbearable.

But she was being pursued by murderers, and he had dark secrets in his eyes. They couldn't simply pretend those problems didn't exist.

Still, for a woman who'd never found lovemaking all that exciting, Beazie was now desperate to know what it would be like with Evan. She could remember in crisp detail every time he'd ever touched her, and now that he'd looked at her lovingly and held her in his lap—even if it had been for the sake of a harmless little drama—her heart was selfishly demanding that those moments become real.

She was behaving like her mother, she reasoned with herself, falling in love with a man she considered her rescuer. An indignant voice inside her said, *No, this is nothing like that!*

But she couldn't be sure.

While the coffee brewed, Evan leaned a hip against the counter and watched her as she made a production of putting away the few things she'd left out this morning when they'd set off for the Whitcombs'. She pretended not to notice.

"No one's coming to inspect the kitchen," he teased as she scrubbed the tiled backsplash.

"I'm just trying to hold up my end of the bargain," she replied, scrubbing harder.

"I don't remember a bargain."

"There was one," she said. Her voice was weak and clearly distracted. She hated that. "You gave me shelter, and in return I was supposed to help you—"

"Paint," he interrupted, "not regrout the tile. And if you scrub any harder, we're going to have to."

She dropped the cloth in the sink with a splat and turned to face him. "I don't want to talk about today."

He shrugged. "Neither do I."

"You don't?" She was so surprised by his response that when he crossed the small space to reach her, she wasn't sharp enough to see what he intended.

He took her in his arms and kissed her until she lost all sense of reality. All that existed for that space of time was his arms, his lips, his hands—wandering over her and creating a fiery path from her scalp to the juncture of her thighs.

She surrendered to it, responded to it, was almost lost to it...until she remembered that today had been fiction, and she was acting like a vulnerable ninny. She pushed against his chest to force a space between them.

"Today wasn't real!" she insisted, her breath coming in gasps. "We were acting."

"At first," he allowed, "but then it wasn't acting anymore. That's what's wrong right now. You don't know what to do about it."

She challenged him with a look, pushing hard against his arms to prevent him from drawing her back into them. "Are you claiming you do?"

"It's not that complicated." He pinched her chin between his thumb and forefinger and studied her face with unsettling concentration. "I'm falling in love with you, you're falling in love with me...."

Her eyes widened in disbelief. "I'm being pursued by killers!" Then she narrowed her focus on him and said with a shake of her head, "And you're being pursued by something else entirely, but it looks as though it could be just as lethal."

Her words had the desired effect; he dropped his hands. But the moment she lost physical contact with him, she regretted the move. She saw a war go on in his eyes over whether or not to withdraw emotionally, as well.

He backed away from her, turned to the coffeepot and poured a cup. When he faced her again, she still couldn't tell by the set of his jaw what he'd decided. "Coffee?"

"No, thank you," she replied.

"What's wrong with a man and a woman taking comfort in each other during a difficult time for both of them?" he asked coolly.

The answer came easily to her. She knew this stuff well. "The fact that I saw my mother look for comfort," she said, "and it never worked out. She wasn't looking for someone to love, she just wanted someone to comfort her after what she'd lost, to understand her grief and lift the darkness." She sighed and admitted with a rasp in her throat, "And I think that might be what I'm finding in you. You make me feel safe, and you make me feel...so much less lonely. But I can't make love with you out of gratitude."

His eyes met hers and the smallest smile played at his lips. "You're sure?"

She wanted to smile in return, but she was so sure of this that she had to make him understand. "I'm sure. Love offered just to put a warm body beside you always ends badly."

He nodded, though the gesture didn't seem to express agreement so much as simple acceptance. "So, you consider temporary comfort a bad thing?"

"No," she admitted. "Any kind of comfort is a good thing, but if you're looking for love, that isn't going to do it."

"And you are."

"Absolutely. I had family life for ten years, life with the tennis player for five months, life with the alcoholic for a little less than a year, and life with Hal. Then my sorry choice of boyfriends. So far, the only thing lasting in my life has been the loneliness. I don't want anything temporary anymore, even comfort." She met his eyes frankly. "Is that all you want in a woman? Temporary satisfaction?"

"Not deliberately, no," he replied, "but that seems to be the pattern. It's probably me. Cops are notoriously self-contained, just a little out of reach."

"But you're a housepainter," she reminded him.

He conceded that point with an arch of his eyebrow, then pointed toward the living room. "Can we sit by the fire? This is exhausting."

Lucinda, having finished her treat, occupied the middle of the hearth rug, so they sat on either side of her. Evan leaned back on an elbow, his cup at hand, and Beazie sat cross-legged, closer to the flames.

Evan resumed their conversation without losing a beat. "Being a cop is like being a priest," he said. "You never really shed the responsibility. Or the habits. You see a lot of awful things you never forget. You know a lot of truths that are hard to reconcile with life as most people know it. And sometimes you struggle to hold on to hope. It's hard to invite a woman into that, except temporarily."

HE'D DUG DOWN DEEP for that explanation, and thought it accurately expressed what he felt. She seemed to understand, but didn't appear impressed by his honesty.

"Then, you've seriously underestimated the women who've crossed your path. I'll bet a lot of them would have been happy to be invited in."

"You aren't."

"You didn't invite me in," she argued. "You

stopped me at the door with an offer to make love to me for the purpose of comfort. Haven't you been paying attention to this conversation?''

"I have," he replied, struggling to hold his own. What had happened to the frightened and weary young woman he'd found in his office? This new side to Beazie was both annoying and confounding him. "But I don't see how you can determine what's going to last forever, if you aren't willing to try it temporarily. Unless maybe you're afraid to trust your judgment."

"That's it exactly," she admitted with an ingenuously frank expression on her face. "Being wrong hurts."

"But the only way to guarantee you'll never be wrong," he pointed out quietly, "is to never make a decision."

She stared at him, obviously absorbing that and finding it unpalatable. Finally she sighed and pushed herself to her feet.

"This is getting much too heavy after a wonderful but very long day. Where are we working tomorrow?"

"The shelter." He sat up, put his cup on the coffee table, then got to his feet. "Carpet layers are coming to the mill tomorrow, and Cam's going to meet them."

"Okay," she said. "I'll set my alarm for six."

"Why don't you just come down when you wake up?"

"Because I promised to hold up my end of the bargain. And there *is* a bargain, remember?"

He remembered. He just wished there were different components involved. Shelter in exchange for lovemaking. Protection in exchange for lovemaking. Cooking in exchange for lovemaking.

He waved good-night as she headed for the stairs. He was hopeless. She'd just presented a well-reasoned case for holding out to build a permanent relationship, and he still wanted to make love to her, whatever tomorrow brought.

He couldn't quite believe himself.

And she said she saw things in his eyes. He'd prided himself on being able to conceal the tangled web of confusion he'd felt caught in since Blaine died. He'd moved to Maple Hill, but he hadn't really escaped it. And Beazie knew it.

BEAZIE PREPARED FOR BED, longing for the relative sanity that had been her life before Gordon was murdered. She longed for a good dose of zany Horie and an afternoon at the mall.

Horie! Tomorrow was Horie's birthday and she'd promised weeks ago to take her friend to dinner and a movie. She had to tell Horie she wouldn't be there; otherwise her friend would worry. Horie might be worried already. They usually spoke on the phone several times a week.

She picked up the phone, anticipating a chatty conversation. But Horie's answering machine came on, so Beazie left a brief apology and a promise to explain as soon as she returned.

Then she hung up the phone and climbed into bed,

troubled but sufficiently exhausted to fall asleep immediately.

EVAN STEPPED OUT OF THE SHOWER the following morning to a high-pitched sound coming from Beazie's room. Lucinda sat up in the middle of his bed, eyes wide, whiskers bristling.

Afraid Beazie was having another nightmare, he pulled on his robe and raced for her room—to find her sound asleep on her stomach, arms wrapped around her pillow. The high-pitched cry was the sound of the alarm clock, screeching unnoticed. It probably had been on for several minutes.

Evan turned it off, then pulled the covers up over Beazie's shoulders, clad in his striped pajamas. She looked so relaxed in sleep, a far cry from the sharp, quick woman who'd argued with him last night. But it occurred to him that she must be really exhausted to sleep through that alarm.

When he was dressed and ready to leave, he replenished the cat's food, then started to write a note, telling Beazie that if she called the shelter when she got up, he'd come back for her. But he stopped at the sound of footsteps racing down the stairs and her sudden appearance in the kitchen on a skid, hair wild, pajamas billowing around her. She clutched the waistband in one hand. Apparently the safety pin had failed.

She looked disheveled and anxious, and his heart melted.

"Are you ready to go?" she asked.

"Yes, but take your—"

"You didn't wake me."

He took several steps toward her. "It's all right. When the alarm didn't rouse you, I figured you needed to sleep."

"Can you give me five minutes? I know you jog with the guys first, but you could leave me at the shelter and start me off."

"You don't have to—"

"Four minutes?"

"Okay."

She ran upstairs as fast as she'd come down. He was going to have to take abuse from the guys for being late. Wonders were always on time, for work or play. They'd start the run without him and he'd catch them on the third or fourth lap, but they'd harrass him, anyway.

In four minutes she reappeared in the old sweats and jacket she wore to work. Her hands were turning and twisting in her hair, and when she lowered them, her hair was caught in a slightly lopsided but interesting topknot, curly ends sticking out.

She headed for the door and opened it, turning back to him with a teasingly superior look. "Let's move it, Braga. I'm not waiting for you any longer."

He went to the door and gave her a gentle shove through it. "You're buying lunch today."

"You just want to see me get my money out," she teased, running around to her side of the van. "Whoa!"

She stopped short in the middle of the drive. Overnight, fresh snow had covered Maple Hill, turning the world into a winter wonderland postcard. Snow frosted all the trees, the cottage, the mailbox—even the van.

He unlocked the doors, then walked around to the back in search of the scraper.

"It's wonderful!" Beazie cried in what sounded like genuine wonder, as Evan finally climbed in behind the wheel. "I've never seen snow in the country, just in the city. It's still pretty, but it never looks untouched like it does here. It's beautiful."

She exclaimed continually as he drove into town past classic New England saltboxes, their sloping roofs uniformly outlined in the pristine snow, the Berkshires rising up in white-covered mounds behind them.

An old station wagon approached from the opposite direction, Berskshire Cab emblazoned on the side.

"I didn't know Maple Hill had a cab company," Beazie said, turning to watch it drive past.

"It's run by two sisters," he told her. "They were born here, so the story goes—one went away to law school, and the other married a senator, or something. Anyway, they're both back and they run this little cab business in two nine-hour shifts. They're friends of Parker and Mariah, I think."

The statue of Elizabeth and Caleb Drake had collected snow on every flat surface—his hat, shoulders and blunderbuss, her hair, shoulders and the curve of her bosom. The evergreens that stood behind them had been strung with lights and somehow changed the scene from one of heroism in the face of danger to— He wasn't sure what.

Then Beazie said it. "With Christmas all around them," she remarked, "it looks just as though they're on their way to Grandma's house for dinner." She wrapped her arms around herself. "I wish I could put a scarf and mittens on them."

He pulled up in front of the bakery. "Have something to eat," he directed, and handed her a ring of keys, holding it by the square-headed key to the shelter. "You can let yourself in if you want to, or just stay here and keep warm. I'll be back in an hour."

"I can't believe you guys jog in this," she said, shaking her head at him.

He shrugged casually. "We're tough dudes."

She smiled. "You're sweethearts. I watched them in action yesterday, and they're the same breed you are. I'll get a doughnut and coffee and look around the shelter. I won't do anything until you get there." She pushed her door open and began to climb out, then turned back to him. "What was that last doughnut I had the day I found you?"

The day she found *him?* Technically, he'd found her. But he liked the implication of her version better.

"Ah...maple bar?"

"No, that was the first one."

"Well, I'm not sure. As I recall, you ate everything I had."

Unoffended by that reminder, she went on. "It had nuts and a buttery, brown-sugary..."

"Caramel nut-roll," he said. "My personal favorite."

"Okay." She leaped down and waved at him before closing the door.

He watched her walk distractedly in front of the van, her hands and face held up to the falling snow. She moved carefully over the slippery sidewalk, then pulled open the bakery door. Even through closed windows, he caught the aromas of sugar and yeast.

To his surprise, he found himself reluctant to leave. He'd have happily forgone the morning jog to be able to sit across from Beazie in the bakery and listen to her observations on snow, and Caleb and Elizabeth, and whatever else she wanted to talk about.

Determinedly, he pulled away and headed for the high school track. God. Was he turning into the lovesick male his friends had warned him he'd become when the right woman came along? Scary to contemplate for someone who'd always been his own person, whose sense of self had never been dictated by anyone else—at least, until Blaine died, and he hadn't been sure what the hell had happened.

He had to keep some distance here, he told himself as he drove. Beazie didn't want a relationship that was only physical and he didn't want one that would require they share feelings and dreams. He had too much of the former and none of the latter.

Just as he pulled in to the school's parking lot, Hank, Bart and Cam jogged around the end of the track. Hurrying out of his van, he fell in beside them and was treated to the jibes he'd fully expected.

"Did you put in a long night and just couldn't get up?"

"Nooners are for later in the day."

"Sex before breakfast depletes your energy."

They picked up the pace in an attempt to leave him in their wake and prove their point.

He ignored them and kept up, eventually passing them to loud hoots and hollers. Sexual frustration, he discovered, was a powerful energizer.

BEAZIE WALKED through the new building, caramel-nut roll and coffee cup in hand. The two-story, gray-blue structure was large and sprawling, but in keeping with the colonial architecture of its neighbors. The kitchen counter boasted a covered recess for small appliances, and in the bottom cupboards was a corner shelf that turned and came forward in the deep cabinet. Beazie coveted it. In her Boston apartment, she had a corner cabinet built long before such amenities existed, and she had to practically crawl into it to find the seldom-used items she stored there.

A microwave and a coffeepot with Whitcomb's Wonders labels stood on the edge of the counter for the use of the long line of workmen involved in the project. Beside them was a wall with heavy-duty outlets probably waiting for the stove and refrigerator.

Beazie knew from the tour Evan had given her last week when they'd painted the common room that the shelter had beautifully appointed bathrooms and rooms that would be used to house families. Though small by some standards, the rooms would contain four or six bunk beds and allow families to live with relative privacy.

There was a large, dormitory-like room upstairs,

already painted and filled with bunks constructed of bolted two-by-fours. Mattresses still covered in plastic lay atop them. Addie's quilting circle, Beazie had learned yesterday, was making the curtains and coverlets for all the shelter's beds with fabric and batting donated by The Maple Hill Store. The shelter's budget provided for sheets and pillowcases.

The large common room was where clients could socialize. Tall, small-paned windows and a brick fireplace dominated the outside wall. Painted a warm color, and with comfy furniture and a fire in the fireplace, the room would be a cozy place to gather.

Beazie wondered where she would find coffee for the coffeepot. One cup simply wasn't going to get her started today. She'd lain awake half the night, going over and over her argument with Evan. Sometimes she wished she'd been able to take a less grave approach to his invitation, then at other times remembered what her mother had been through and was grateful she'd resisted.

Just after four she'd finally fallen asleep and slept through her alarm. At the moment, she felt very much like a woman who'd had only two hours' sleep.

As she went from cupboard to cupboard looking for coffee, she wondered what color of paint Jackie's committee had chosen for the kitchen. If it were up to her, she'd paint it yellow, just like Evan's.

At last she found the coffee and several mugs in a drawer under the microwave, and knew Evan must have chosen the blend. It was the same one he used at home.

The pot was brewing and she was perched on the

counter when he arrived at seven-thirty. She was surprised to see him so soon.

"Cut the run short," he said, putting a bag of doughnuts on the counter.

There was snow in his hair and on the shoulders of his jacket, and she found herself wondering what he'd look like in Caleb's hat. Gorgeous, she was sure. Just as he always looked.

"The wind's picked up and it got too nasty," he added.

She checked her watch. "But the girls said you guys always have coffee for half an hour before you go to work."

"Not this morning," he said, shrugging out of his jacket. "Bart's got court, Hank's meeting a client, and Cam has to be at the mill for the carpet guys." He grinned. "And I thought I'd better get over here before you decided to start painting the kitchen Horie Metcalf–purple." He sniffed the coffee aroma appreciatively. "But I see you were constructively engaged, after all."

She leaped off the counter and poured two cups. "What color's the kitchen going to be?" she asked, handing him one.

He put down the cup and consulted a work order in his pocket. "Daisy Eye?" he read, clearly confused about what that meant.

"Yellow!" she said, pleased. "All right!"

He gave her a dry look over the sheet of paper and read with disgust, "The wallpaper border is called Shelf of Teapots." He rolled his eyes. "Those poor homeless guys are going to love that."

"They'll like the yellow."

"As long as we don't tell them it's called Daisy Eye."

It was a beautiful, sunny color that deserved its name, Beazie thought a little later as she knelt on newspapers on the counter and applied the first coat to the wall above the cupboards.

EVAN APPLIED PAINT with a roller to the wall at the entrance of the kitchen.

Beazie had the radio cranked up and was singing at the top of her lungs to a country-and-western tune about love and family and pulling together. Then she shouted over the music, "Have you thought any more about going home for Christmas?"

"No!" he shouted back.

He hoped that was the end of it. She was quiet for a moment while the tune played on, promising happily-ever-after to those willing to give love. Then she reached down and lowered the volume on the radio.

"Is the china in your cupboard your mom's?" she asked.

That seemed like a non sequitur, but probably wasn't. She was going to connect the china with holidays and family dinners or something.

"No," he was happy to reply. "It was Millie Evans's. She gave it to me when she moved into the nursing home."

"No children or grandchildren?"

"She was a single lady and has outlived most of her friends. She took a liking to me, for some reason."

"Because you're a sweetheart."

"Please."

"You're spoiled because you have friends who feel like family, but that doesn't mean you can ignore them. Your family, I mean," she clarified, as though that was necessary.

Her remark didn't seem to require comment, so he kept on painting.

"Does it have something to do with the accident?" she asked intrepidly.

He turned, wondering where she'd heard about that. She'd stopped painting, too, to look at him. Kneeling on the counter, a paper cap pulled down over her wild hair, her curves hidden by the old coveralls, she looked like one of the guys, albeit a young and skinny one.

"Parker told me. She also said you have knots."

"Knots?"

"In your shoulders. From tension or some problem you haven't dealt with."

He dropped the roller in the pan and leaned it against the molding. He needed a break. Suddenly he found himself *wanting* to explain a few things to her, and he knew that meant he was tired.

"I thought I had doctor-patient privilege with her, or something," he said, going to the coffeepot and finding it empty. He pulled the basket out, tossed away the old filter.

"I don't think you're guaranteed that with a massage therapist. And she wasn't gossiping. She told me that because Gary had told me to take good care of you."

He looked up from rinsing out the pot, indignation rising in him.

"Don't get upset," she said, resting her roller in the tray. "It wasn't as though we were dissecting your life. No one knows enough about you to do that. Gary thinks I'm your significant other, as we wanted him to think, so he told me to take care of you."

"Well, please don't take the advice to heart." He measured coffee into a fresh filter, avoiding her probing gaze, then set the pot on brew. "I'm fine. I'm going for lunch. What do you want?"

"Yeah," she said wryly, moving her tray and roller down to the counter. "You're fine. I'm supposed to get lunch today, remember? The bakery had stew and a roll, as I recall."

He knew every to-go menu in town by heart. "Perk Avenue has a wedge of lasagna and garlic bread."

"Okay. Soon as I wash my hands, I'm on my way."

"I'll just sit on the floor and relax," he said, doing just that. "I have knots, you know."

On her way out into the hallway, her jacket over her arm, she doubled back to rap her knuckles lightly on his head. "And the biggest one's right here."

When he aimed a swat at her, she dodged him with a squeal of laughter. He heard the rush of water through the pipes as she washed her hands, then the sound of the front door closing behind her.

The room was enveloped in silence. It pulsed around him, rang in his ears, bringing with it a certain loneliness he'd never experienced before. It had never bothered him to be alone. He'd played for hours by himself when he was a child, before Blaine was born. Then he'd spent a lot of time alone as a teen. Blaine had all the friends, since he'd inherited Barney's gregarious personality, whereas Evan was edgy and angry, very much aware he was the son of a man who'd abandoned his mother and made her cry. He'd thought, then, that he deserved to be left alone.

Eventually, he'd gotten over that feeling, but even when he became a cop, he found dating difficult. Either women didn't want to date a police officer because of the potential for danger, or else they were somehow turned on by it.

After several casual relationships, he came to the conclusion they weren't really that much different from being alone. The company was sometimes nice, but very superficial, and whenever he had something difficult to deal with, he did it on his own.

But now, he was very much aware of his solitude, and it wasn't so much that he didn't like it, it just felt…empty.

Heaven help him, he thought as he groaned and stretched out his legs. He wasn't *falling* in love, he'd already landed with bone-jarring impact.

BEAZIE HAD A LARGE PAPER BAG in her arms, the insulated packages inside warming her nicely as she waited in the gently falling snow for the light to change. At the flash of green, she hurried across the street, head held down as she watched her step on the slippery road.

She was almost beside the red SUV before she saw it. She had stepped up on the sidewalk on the opposite side of the street when she felt it like a malevolent presence. The feeling was strange, ridiculous even, except to someone who understood the ominous rising of suppressed fear.

When she turned her head, she saw the New York license plate, 357 HAR. With dread, she raised her eyes to the windshield and discovered that the vehicle was empty. Her relief was a palpable thing. A little cry escaped her and the urge to run as far and as fast as she could overtook her. And then she thought of Evan.

Where were the occupants of the SUV? Had they found out she was staying with Evan? Were they inside with him right now, demanding to know where she was? She'd seen what they were capable of. She just couldn't leave him.

It wasn't heroics; she was terrified. But she couldn't abandon Evan to their ruthlessness, after all he'd done for her.

Forcing herself not to hurry, she started up the path. *Be calm,* she told herself. *Act natural.*

And then she heard a voice. She hadn't even known she remembered it, but she now recalled hearing it as she escaped out the back of her apartment building. The person had been shouting instructions. Holding the paper bag high against her shoulder, she glanced over it and spotted four men walking out of St. Anthony's rectory, next door to the shelter.

Terror had a sharp memory, she discovered. There was a slender gray-haired man, medium height, in a

MURIEL JENSEN   141

dark overcoat that looked like cashmere; a tall, burly man with a broken nose and a thick head of dark hair; a wiry young man in jeans and a fleece-lined jacket; and a stout, balding man in glasses who looked more like an accountant than someone who would help kill a man and pursue a witness.

Her heart punched against her ribs, and all her breath escaped as though her heart had made a hole in her lungs.

She was just going to miss them. She kept walking, fighting hard to control the urge to run. They went by her so closely that she smelled cologne and…an orange.

"Murray, for God's sake, put it away. We're going to stop for lunch."

One of the men sneezed. "That's what you said an hour ago, but I need the *C*. I thought you said the Deadham girl was working with the guy who's painting the shelter. But the basement of that church hasn't seen paint in years. And what kind of a church is this? No priest, no housekeeper, no homeless!"

"There was a note on the front door that said the priest was on sick call and would be back in an hour."

"Or maybe Brick here just didn't get the address right. I'll call the boss and straighten it out. One way or the other, this girl's—"

She didn't hear the rest because she'd kept walking and so had they, but she could only imagine it was something like *days are numbered,* or *going down!*

Frantic now, she pushed her way inside the front

door of the shelter, her breath coming in noisy gasps. Her hands shook as she tried to lock the door behind her, but it was new and stiff and resisted her cold fingers.

Her need to see Evan had become desperation. She walked into the kitchen, sure something had called him away and she'd be stuck here alone with the four men banging on the door.

But he was there, using a brush to touch up a spot against the decorative picture rail. He grinned at her as she walked in.

"'Bout time," he teased. "I was beginning to think you'd wandered—"

Fear must have been visible on her face, because he dropped the brush instantly and reached for her. "What?" he asked.

She could hardly find air enough to speak. "They're out there," she whispered finally. "They found me! How did they *find* me?"

"Where out there?" he began, heading for the door.

"Right out front!" she said. Air seemed to be rushing out of her now, and she had to struggle to speak. "You have to lock the door!"

Men's voices sounded nearby, and she knew with a sickening dread that they'd corrected their misconception about the shelter and were on their way there.

CHAPTER EIGHT

EVAN YANKED HER BACK at a run toward the kitchen. He put the billed paper hat on her hair and boosted her up to the counter with a hand to her backside. "Work on that wall and keep your face turned away. Let me handle them."

He took the bag that contained their lunches and stuffed it into a bottom cupboard, then picked up his brush again and went back to work.

His heart was thumping—adrenaline, he knew, not fear. Well, maybe not fear for himself. But fear for Beazie was a new and unsettling reality to deal with. It took the edge off his focus, he noticed. He resolved to correct that.

He swept the brush up and down in easy swipes, pretending to be completely absorbed in the task, when the doorway was suddenly filled with three men.

With an inquiring smile, Evan glanced over at them. A gray-haired man in an expensive coat looked him up and down. Somehow the guy seemed familiar, though Evan couldn't imagine why.

Maybe it was just that he knew the look. Men who lived by grasping power assessed everyone who crossed their path. Evan forced himself to squelch his own "touch me and die" response, acquired after so many years as a cop. Instead, he portrayed affability, simple interest.

"You Braga?" the man asked.

Evan nodded, placing the brush across the top of the open paint can. "Yeah."

The man took something out of his pocket and flashed it at him. It was a badge. Withholding surprise took a little effort. Then Evan realized he shouldn't withhold it entirely. A badge would likely unnerve a simple housepainter in western Massachusetts.

"Ben Carstairs," the man said. "Boston PD. Homicide."

Evan offered his hand. "What can I do for you?"

The man took it. *Good grip,* Evan thought, instinctively reading it: *Determination. Something to lose.*

"We're looking for a woman," Carstairs said, replacing the badge and pulling a photo out of his pocket.

Evan grinned genially. "Aren't we all?"

Carstairs humored him with a nod, then showed him the picture. It was a portrait of Beazie—maybe a college graduation photo. She looked a little younger, and her hair was smoothed back tidily with a headband. What a criminal thing to do to her hair, Evan thought absently.

"Have you seen her?" Carstairs asked.

Evan was aware of a big man walking into the kitchen, noticing Beazie for the first time. Carstairs turned to watch him, glancing briefly at the shapeless form in coveralls on the counter, then focused his attention back on Evan.

"Well?" Carstairs prompted.

Frowning, Evan pretended to study the photo. "I think I may have."

Beazie didn't say a word or betray herself with a sound, but Evan felt the tension emanating from her. She kept working while the big guy looked up at her.

"Where?" Carstairs asked urgently.

In a bid for credibility that would either save or swamp him and Beazie, he carried the photo to her, getting between her and the big guy to hand it up.

"Mel," he said. "This is the babe from Cromwell's Bar, isn't it? You remember. The one that seemed so scared and said she was on her way to Buffalo? Her hair was wilder than this, and she kept looking around. Isn't this her?"

Beazie studied the photo of herself, her hand remarkably steady, then she handed it back and said, her voice an octave lower than usual, "Think so."

"You're sure?" Carstairs demanded.

Evan headed toward the two men at the door, and the big man followed him. "Hard to be sure," Evan said.

"She made a call from your place."

What? Evan thought in frustrated disbelief. Aloud, he said, "Yeah. So? She came home with me."

Carstairs tried to look inside him. "You just had to have your buddy confirm that this is her, and yet you took her home?"

Evan smirked. "I wasn't that interested in her face."

"When did she leave?"

It was a trick question. Evan could see it in his eyes. The safest guess was "This morning."

"Did she say why she was going to Buffalo?"

"Had a brother there, I think."

Carstairs studied him a moment, unsure whether to believe him or not. Then he nodded, probably deciding a shaky lead was better than no lead at all.

"She's wanted for murder in Boston," Carstairs said, handing him a business card.

It was the card of the captain of detectives in the South Boston Division and looked genuine. Suddenly Evan remembered why the face and the name were familiar. There'd been an incident when he was a rookie where he and half a dozen other officers were pinned down by automatic weapon fire while responding to a bank robbery. Carstairs and his men had come to their rescue with a Swat Team. Evan held his breath, wondering if Carstairs would recognize him. But that had been a long time ago; they hadn't met face-to-face, and their paths had never crossed since.

"She stole incriminating evidence from the scene," Carstairs added. "Call me if she shows up again."

"I sure will," Evan promised gravely. He walked Carstairs and his men to the door, trying to analyze the big guy and the bald one. Cops, too? He didn't think so, though he couldn't be sure. It was sometimes hard to tell cops from perps. They often had the same skills but were dedicated to opposite sides of the law.

He noticed the kid outside in the fleece-lined jacket, probably posted as lookout. That one looked particularly dangerous, hard-core. But then, a cop on the brink of a bust sometimes had that same look in his eye.

Carstairs gave Evan a last once-over that contained the threat of retribution if he was lying. Then he followed his men.

Evan smiled as though he hadn't noticed, and closed the door behind them. The moment they were out of earshot, he locked it and stood just out of sight until he saw the red SUV pull away.

For a full minute he stood where he was, trying to regain his emotional equilibrium.

He didn't believe for a second that Beazie Deadham was capable of murder, but Ben Carstairs had been a good cop. A great cop. Was he truly investigating a murder in which Beazie was a suspect, or was he somehow involved and tracking her down for reasons of his own? Evan remembered her saying that Hathaway had told her not to trust the police.

But she'd taken something from the murder scene. He guessed that was what she was trying to get to Evans—not just a message.

And she'd made a phone call!

He went back into the kitchen. Beazie stood doubled over in the middle of the room, hands on her knees as she drew in deep breaths. She'd torn off her hat and pulled her hair free. When she heard him approach, she straightened, her face pale, her eyes wary.

"Are they gone?" she asked softly.

He nodded. "I watched them drive away." Then he accused, "You made a *phone* call?"

She looked hurt by the sound of his voice. "I was supposed to take Horie to dinner today. I had to tell her I wouldn't be there."

"And it never occurred to you that if someone really wanted to find you, they'd tap the phones of your friends, your workplace, waiting for you to call?"

"But I was careful what I said! I didn't tell her where I was, just that I wouldn't be there!"

He spread his arms in exasperation. "Well, that didn't work, did it? You've never heard of caller ID?"

By the look of surprise on her face, he could only conclude that the thought hadn't occurred to her. He could also accept that after all she'd been through, it was probably understandable.

"Was one of them the man who hit Gordon?" he asked, lowering his voice.

"No." She put fingertips to her temples and massaged. "He wasn't here. But they're the ones who came to my apartment and chased me."

"Carstairs really is a cop," he said.

BEAZIE DIDN'T LIKE THE WAY Evan was looking at her. Of course. If Carstairs was a cop, Evan would believe him above her. She'd broken into Evan's office, threatened him with a bat, lied about why she was here and made him lie to his friends.

Sensing his suspicion made her feel cold to the very center of her being. That cozy sense of belonging she'd experienced in his house and among his friends was wiped away, and loneliness was now an even darker thing.

She fought a paralyzing depression to find a way to explain. "Carstairs must be the reason Gordon told me not to go to the police," she said, straightening, squaring her shoulders. "I did not murder anybody. The guys in the SUV did it."

"Was one of them wearing a fleece-lined jacket?"

"Yes. But he wasn't here."

Evan nodded. "He was waiting outside as a lookout."

"I did not kill Gordon." She felt compelled to repeat herself. "They did."

He folded his arms. "I believe you," he said. "But what did you take from the crime scene?"

Certain he was humoring her, she suddenly felt exhausted, and emotionally and physically off balance. She closed her eyes and braced herself. She should have cleared this up earlier. Drawing another breath for strength, she said, "I don't know what I have. I haven't been able to listen to it. But it has to be important if it was Gordon's only thought while dying."

His jaw firmed. "What? A tape?"

She reached into her shirt to pull it out of her bra, where she always kept it. She handed it to him. "I have no idea what's on it, but Gordon wanted me to take it to Evans. I'm beginning to wonder if that *is* you. Even if you *didn't* know Gordon."

"Why didn't you tell me?"

"Because I wasn't sure who *you* were at first,

and…'' She rubbed her eyes. ''I know it's weird, but time seems to have flown.''

He studied her a minute, then looked at the tape. ''I can't imagine this is for me. I haven't been a cop in a year and a half.'' He tucked it in his shirt pocket. ''Stay here. I've got a small tape recorder in the truck that I use for bids and estimates.''

As he hurried outside, she laid her jacket on the floor and sank onto it, feeling the little fortress she'd built around her since coming here crumble to dust. She was alone again, exposed, completely vulnerable. She blinked back tears and swallowed the painful lump in her throat.

Evan was back in an instant with the small machine.

''I didn't kill Gordon,'' she said again, as he sat on the floor opposite her.

He glanced up at her as he inserted the tape. ''I said I believe you.''

''How can you?''

''Seems I have more faith in you than you have in me.'' He hit the play button.

There was the sound of crackling paper, a subtle clink of crockery, then a quiet voice said, *''We have to do something. I know we talked this over once before and decided against it because it could mean we don't get paid, but the kid's trouble, I'm telling you. Trouble.''*

''You recognize the voice?'' Evan asked quietly.

Beazie nodded, a chill running along her spine at the sound of the disembodied voice. Evan stopped the tape.

"He was here today," she said. "He didn't come in with the other two, but somebody called him Murray. He has a cold."

"Good. Okay." He pushed play again.

They sat quietly as another voice chimed in. *"I think Murray's right."* This one was anxious, agitated, definitely a New Yorker. *"We gotta do it now. Home run, just like we talked about. It'll be easy. Fenway Park will be full of people, everyone watching the game. We wait till he hits the men's room."*

Evan raised an eyebrow in silent question. Beazie shook her head.

"Park full of people." Still another voice. Gentle, affable. *"It's not a good idea, gentlemen."*

"That's Gordon!" Beazie whispered urgently.

Evan nodded and raised a hand for silence as Gordon's voice went on. *"We don't have to kill anybody. It just isn't necessary."*

"I disagree." A fourth voice. Beazie recognized it, too.

"That's somebody called Brick," she said. "I heard him when they were going up to my apartment. I think he might be the big guy."

Murray's voice chimed in. *"He's dangerous to us because his primary concern is himself, not us, not the payback, not the woman. That kinda guy'll get you in trouble every time. I say it's time to waste him. The park's a good idea."*

The details became a free-for-all discussion.

"But not the men's room. He won't be the only one who has to go. We don't want witnesses."

"Something in his coffee or his beer."

"That's too uncertain. It has to be a bullet."

"The parking lot?"

"Nah. People come and go all the time."

"In his car, then. Ricky'll wait for him. What do you think, Ricky?"

Ricky's voice was an addition to the mix. *"I think it'll be easy. But what are you paying me?"*

"The usual."

"If he's such a danger, he should be worth more than the usual."

"Give him double the usual," the first voice recommended. *"It's worth it to get rid of him. He makes me nervous. I don't like to be nervous."*

"Okay, double. Home run's a deal, Ricky?"

"Deal," Ricky agreed coolly.

The rest of the tape was blank.

Beazie looked into Evan's eyes. "You'll notice," she said, "that my voice is absent from the tape."

He shook his head at her. "I said I believe you. Besides, that wasn't a plot to kill Hathaway. You recognized his voice. He was there. What business was he in, anyway, that he got involved with what sounds like big-time criminals?"

She shrugged. "Just insurance."

INSURANCE.

That information registered with Evan like a punch. And left him with a bad feeling. A really big one.

Cops learned to trust bad feelings, because they were often intuition's way of explaining what wasn't clear to the brain, and often turned out to be more reliable than hard information. Still, evidence was critical.

The word *insurance* brought Blaine instantly to mind. But Blaine had only borrowed from his holding account, not from loan sharks. And judging by the talk of payback and the possibility of not getting paid, he guessed that the men on the tape were part of a loan shark's organization.

And then the obvious occurred to him. Maybe Blaine had borrowed the money from his holding account to pay back a loan shark.

Evan dismissed the thought. It was foolish to speculate until he had more information.

"Tell me what you know about your boss." He pushed the tape recorder aside and faced Beazie across the small space between them.

"He was married, no children, always *seemed* honest. Most of our clients really liked dealing with him." She looked tired and upset, but he couldn't stop yet. "What else do you want to know?"

"When'd you go to work for him?"

"About two years ago. He'd just opened the Boston agency, and a man I was dating recommended me for the job of office manager."

He asked the next logical question. "Who was that?"

"His name was Blaine Turner," she replied. "He sold insurance, too. They'd been friends since they worked together for another company."

Evan heard Blaine's name, but not the rest of it. If the word *insurance* had struck him like a punch, his brother's name hit him like a tree trunk to the gut. Gordon Hathaway and Blaine had been in-volved.

That *had* to mean Hathaway had intended that the tape get to Evan, and not *Evans,* as Beazie had mis-understood. It provided proof that there'd been a plot afoot to kill his brother—even though it hadn't been carried out. The automobile accident had probably occurred before they could put the plan into action.

And then something else occurred to him. Some-thing that felt even worse than the tree trunk to his stomach. Beazie said she'd been "dating" Blaine. He remembered that Blaine had tried to explain away his "borrowing" funds from the holding account by saying that his girlfriend was expensive.

It was hard to equate that kind of woman with Beazie, but the evidence was clear. The fact that Evan didn't want to deal with it wouldn't change it.

His brain was chaotic with this new information, and his heart in turmoil. He got to his feet, needing to move, to put some distance between him and Bea-zie.

He made it as far as the doorway, then turned to face her, leaning a shoulder against the new molding. "You dated Blaine Turner?" he asked. He believed she hadn't committed murder, but now to learn she'd endangered his nephews' family life…

"Yes," she replied, watching him warily. "Why?"

"He was married."

"No, he wasn't," she denied calmly. "We dated for a couple of months. He wasn't married."

"He was married," he insisted. Her disbelief

seemed genuine, but then, it would. She'd lied to him about the message. "He had two little boys."

She frowned and got to her feet, breathing deeply in agitation. "He was single!" Her voice rose, her fists balled at her sides. "He had a studio apartment on Summer Street."

"How many times did you sleep there?"

"I never slept there!" she shrieked at him, her eyes filled with hurt and uncertainty. "Why are you doing this? How would you know if he was married or not?"

"Blaine Turner," he said, his voice quiet, "was my brother."

Now she looked as though she'd been struck.

He took his wallet out of his pocket and flipped through the plastic sleeves of family photos to show her the picture he'd taken at Mark's second birthday party. Blaine, Sheila and Mark in front of a birthday cake decorated with Scooby-Doo, in Blaine and Sheila's kitchen.

"Matthew wasn't born yet," he said.

She looked at it, made a small sound of distress, then stared at him, the hurt in her eyes deepening as the uncertainty disappeared. She finally believed him.

He put the wallet away. "What was it you wanted that he couldn't provide?" he asked. There was a perverse pleasure in hurting her, in having someone else to blame for the tangled mess of Blaine's theft and his premature death. "What did you want?"

Her eyes had lost focus for a moment, but finally settled again on him. "What do you mean?"

"He stole money for you," he revealed brutally.

"He told me he had an expensive girlfriend. What did you ask him for?"

"Nothing!" she shouted at him. "I didn't ask him for anything! We dated for a month, but I never slept with him. I soon discovered that I'd mistaken for charm what was just a slick sort of performance to get what he wanted. We broke up, and I read later that he died in an automobile accident. I was *not* the expensive girlfriend."

THIS WAS A NIGHTMARE from which Beazie could not awaken. Seeing suspicion and condemnation in Evan's eyes after the comfortable relationship that had developed between them was difficult to bear. She didn't know what to say or do to convince him that she hadn't known Blaine was married, and that she was not responsible for the fact that he'd stolen money.

"When did he tell you this?" she asked.

"In June," he replied. "The day of the accident."

She spread both arms in a that-proves-it sort of gesture. "I dated him at the end of February and the beginning of March, and we never went anywhere. I usually cooked or ordered pizza. He was a brief attempt to find that soul mate again, and it failed completely. He was very self-absorbed. If he had an expensive girlfriend that he had to support by stealing, it wasn't *me!*"

She remembered the details in the newspaper about his death. She'd been at work when she read the article, and remembered breaking it gently to Gordon, knowing he and Blaine had been friends.

When he'd asked her how it had happened, she'd read him the article. It had said Blaine had been riding with his brother.

So that explained the pain in Evan's eyes, the family he didn't want to visit. "You were driving when he died," she said, suddenly understanding, "and you blame yourself."

That observation seemed to hurt and surprise him.

"That wasn't an accusation," she put in quickly. "I remember the news story said it was a sunny day with no hazards on the road, and that alcohol wasn't involved. Even though I've only known you a short time, I can't believe you were reckless or in any way directly responsible. I'd just like the same consideration from you. Things may look as though everything is my fault, but it isn't."

Now he looked stunned and off balance. Perhaps because he'd been making accusations, he'd expected her to do the same to him. But she was in such distress over the fact that Blaine had been married and had children, and she knew turning the blame on someone else wouldn't help. Besides, how could she see Evan in anguish without wanting to help?

"We were arguing over the money," he said finally, still rooted to that spot in the doorway. It felt as though he was miles away. "I'd found the money in his gym bag while we were at the gym, and I was determined he would put it back in the account that very afternoon. I made him get in the car with me. But as we argued, he started to fight me for the wheel, and we were hit by a truck at an intersection."

If he'd told her that this morning, she could have touched him in sympathy, maybe wrapped her arms around him. But now she didn't think he'd want that.

"I'm sorry," she said softly. "But doesn't that absolve you of responsibility for his death?"

"I made him get in the car."

"You wanted to help him return the money. That was a good thing. The truck was just one of those awful turns of fate we can't explain. Couldn't the other driver...?"

Evan shook his head. "There was nothing about him in the police report. It was hit and run. The car was incinerated, and all I can figure is that the money burned up, too. I woke up a few days later in the hospital."

She nodded and said again, "I'm sorry." She reached to the floor for her jacket, feeling as though a large hole had been drilled into her world and precious things were falling out. "Do you think, under the circumstances, that I could go home?" she asked.

In answer, he grabbed his car keys off the counter and picked up his jacket. "I'm pretty sure they're gone," he said, "but on the chance they decided they didn't believe my story and came back, put your hat on to cover your hair."

That sounded almost like concern, she thought as she did what he asked. Except, it wasn't visible in his face. He still looked as though she'd betrayed him.

Snow was falling heavily. Small cars struggled on the road, and a few had already been abandoned at the side, but Evan's all-wheel drive made it home easily.

He pulled up in front of the house and turned off the motor.

"Aren't you going back to work?" she asked.

"No," he replied.

She scolded him with a look. "You're afraid to leave me alone."

"I have things to do at home," he insisted, climbing out of the van and coming around to help her down. But she was already on the snowy pavement, closing her door.

"This morning you said we were going to put in a few hours after dinner."

"I changed my mind. Road conditions are getting worse—I'll make it up when it stops snowing."

Great, she thought, following him as he unlocked the door and went into the house. So much for the quickly made plans she'd thrown together on the drive home. She would have to carry them out, anyway.

"I'll be doing paperwork at the table in the kitchen," he said, pulling off his jacket. "And I'll get the coffee going. Our lunches are still in the cupboard at the shelter. Why don't you get some rest?"

She smiled agreeably. "Good idea." She glanced at the clock. It was shortly after three. "I'll be down at six to fix dinner."

He nodded.

All right, she thought. *Three hours.* She ought to be able to work the plan in that amount of time.

"Bea!" he called as she began to walk away.

She turned, wondering if her eyes had betrayed her.

"I'm going to call a friend in Boston," he said. "See if he can nose out some details of Hathaway's case for us."

"A cop friend?"

"Yes," he replied. "But this one's trustworthy. Clay Markham used to be my partner."

"Okay," she said.

It didn't really matter now, but she nodded so that he would think it did. Then she ran upstairs.

CHAPTER NINE

MARKHAM SOUNDED GENUINELY HAPPY to hear his voice. "It's been forever!" he said. "How the hell are you? What's keeping you in the boondocks, anyway?"

"It's a great place," Evan said. "You should come visit."

"*You* should come home once in a while. I'm keeping an eye on Sheila and the kids like you asked me, but the boys are missing you. You coming home for Christmas?"

"I'm thinking about it," he said noncommittally. "Look, Clay, I need a favor."

"Sure."

"Can you fax me the reports from my wreck?"

"Sure. But why?"

"Just a little detective work I'm doing. And while you're at it, an insurance agent named Gordon Hathaway was shot in the parking area in the Bentley Building. I'm sure there has to be a case on it."

"There is. Our division's working with South Boston on it."

"Can you read over that stuff so I can ask some questions?"

There was a moment's silence. "Do I want to know what's going on?"

"Nothing yet, but if it does get interesting, I'll call you. Okay?"

"Okay."

"Thanks, Clay. I owe you one."

"You owe me three or four, as I recall." His voice turned serious. "Evan?"

"Yeah."

"What do you think Sheila would say if I asked her out?"

He smiled to himself. He'd suspected Clay had been interested in Sheila for a long time. "There's only one way to find that out, you know."

"Yeah." A deep sigh came down the line. "But I've loved her since long before Blaine died. I'm afraid she'll see that in my face."

"She won't. She knows I asked you to keep an eye on her and the boys, and she'll just think your feelings developed from proximity. Do it, Clay."

"I'm scared."

"You carry a gun. You're the district's top contender in boxing."

"You know it's not about muscle or power."

Yes, he did. "Yeah, well, you're also a good man. I'll bet she's ready to date one about now."

"If this blows up in my face, I'm coming after you."

"Get in line."

Clay laughed. He probably thought Evan was kidding about the line.

When he hung up, Evan called the Suffolk County

Courthouse and asked for the records of sale for Blaine's business.

"Service is iffy today, probably because of the snow," the clerk said. "But I'll take care of it as soon as I can get through."

"Fair enough. Thank you."

He spent a brief amount of time telling himself that his efforts could result in nothing at all, and if that happened, he had to accept that he might never know the truth.

Or it could result in all kinds of things he didn't really want to hear but would have to live with, anyway. He reminded himself that the truth was the truth, and hiding from it didn't change it.

He spread his paperwork for the mill on the kitchen table and drank an entire pot of coffee while going over the supply list for the next office to be renovated. Cam had left a message, telling him the carpet had been laid at the mill and looked wonderful, and that he should call Baldwin Engineering because he'd run into Ben Baldwin at a party and Baldwin was interested in renting two adjoining suites. "Call him and set up a meeting," Cam had told him. "And we'd better get busy on the upstairs apartments, because someone asked me about them today."

Trent and Braga Development seemed to be heading toward success. Evan found that exciting. At first it had been primarily Cam's baby, and all Evan had done was help him fund the purchase. But now he found it a thrill turning the ancient relic of Chandler Mill into a safe, updated replica of its former self. It gave him great satisfaction and helped him feel even more a part of Maple Hill.

Now, if he could just be as successful in his private life. He sipped at the last cup of coffee and listened to the silence upstairs. When Beazie had first gone up, he'd heard the shower, then nothing.

In the silence, he thought about Blaine. Now that he was calmer, less shocked that his fate and Beazie's were linked, after all, he could imagine how Blaine had charmed her into believing he was single, then tried to keep a low profile with her so that no one would see them together and report to Sheila that he was fooling around.

He wondered if his brother had some ulterior motive in setting Beazie up in the job with Hathaway, or if all that had simply been coincidence. Beazie had said something about Blaine using his charm to get what he wanted. She denied that they'd ever made love, but he could believe Blaine had wanted to.

That brought back thoughts of Beazie and an even deeper, rougher frustration. He imagined her curled up in bed, her wild hair spilling over the pillow. Longing, desire, every kind of lustful emotion ignited inside him, and he had to stop thinking about her, or explode.

Finally he put the paperwork aside and went to the back porch for more firewood. He built up the small fire in the living room to a cheerful blaze, then returned to the kitchen to clear the table in preparation for dinner.

He was bent over the table in the nook when he

noticed the headlights through the darkness beyond the kitchen window. It looked as though someone had parked halfway up the drive.

His first thought was that the red SUV had returned, but he remembered from his glimpse of it, that afternoon when he'd walked Carstairs and his men to the door, that the lights had been higher off the ground. These were lower, like those on a small car.

He wondered if someone had pulled into the snowy driveway to turn around and gotten stuck.

Evan was about to investigate when he saw Beazie's figure come from the back of the house in the old jacket and watch cap, a plastic bag dangling at her side. The moment she reached the driveway, she made a run in the direction of the headlights.

Ignoring his sudden and complete confusion, he raced out the door after her. "Beazie!" he shouted.

She stopped and spun around at the top of the drive, surprise and distress visible on her face in the light from the kitchen. Then she turned back toward the driveway and began to run. But the troughs made by the van's tires had iced over, and she went down on her backside halfway down the drive.

As he ran toward her, sticking to the snow at the side of the drive for steady footing, he watched her try to scramble to her feet in the glare of the headlights. But he reached her before she could gain purchase.

"What are you doing?" he demanded as he grabbed under her arms and tried to haul her up.

She struggled against him and they both went

down. This time, her head collided with his arm as she fell, dislodging her watch cap. What he saw in the glare of the headlights made him stare in shock and anger.

Beazie's luxurious red hair had been cut off so that it was barely longer than his, and it was...purple.

"I'm leaving!" she said, swinging at him with her plastic bag. "Let me go."

"Bea!" Her name escaped him in a kind of gasp. He couldn't believe she'd done that, even though he realized it was probably her most recognizable feature.

He forced his attention away from the atrocity perpetrated against her hair, handed her the hat so she could put it back on, and made himself focus on the more important issue at hand.

"To go *where?*" he demanded.

"Anywhere the cab will take me!" she replied. "I got the tape to you, so my job is done."

"Beazie, your life is in danger."

"Not anymore. Now *you* have the tape."

"Carstairs and his men don't know that."

"Well, they're not here, and if you'd let me go—" she yanked against him again, her voice rising "—I could get out of here!"

He held on. "That's thoughtless and irresponsible. Have you forgotten that you have no money? Have you failed to notice the blizzard?" He suddenly realized what might move her. "Did you forget that you promised to oversee the baked goods for the opening of the shelter?"

Before she could reply, a new voice injected itself into the argument.

"Hello?"

Evan looked up. It took him a moment to recognize the young woman wrapped in a blue parka, a striped scarf around her head. It was Paris O'Hara, one of the sisters who owned the cab company. Paris and Prudence attended St. Anthony's, and he'd worked with them on a couple of parish projects.

She leaned over them solicitously. "Evan," she said. "Are you two all right? What's going on?"

"Hi, Paris." He was growing uncomfortably aware of the frigid night air and the ridged ice on which they sat. "This is Beazie Deadham, my…"

"Oh, your girl!" she said with a bright smile. "I drove Rita Robidoux to work this morning because she didn't trust her little car on the snow. She told me all about her." Paris turned the smile on Beazie. "Welcome to Maple Hill," she said, helping Evan get Beazie to her feet. "I was gone for a few years and I'm so glad to be back. Now…" She looked from one to the other. "Where did you want me to take you?"

"We've changed our mind about the cab," he said, reaching into his pocket and handing her a bill. "I'm sorry to have called you out."

Paris turned to Beazie with a woman-to-woman look.

"Is that true? Or is he making decisions for you?"

Evan waited. Beazie stared at him with complete exasperation coupled with a curious desperation that seemed to require something from him he couldn't quite define.

"I'm here," he said, hoping that assured her that he'd cover the need, whatever it was.

She smiled thinly at Paris. "Thanks. But I think I'll stay, after all."

"You're sure?"

"Yes."

"Okay." Paris smiled from Beazie to Evan, then turned carefully on the icy ground and headed back toward her cab. "From now on," she called over her shoulder, "try to conduct your arguments in the warmth of the house!"

Evan took the plastic bag from Beazie, wrapped an arm around her waist and led her cautiously up the now dark path and back to the house. In the kitchen, she pulled off her jacket but left the hat on. Her eyes were wide and distressed, and made him feel helpless.

Helpless and angry, he decided. Not a good combination. One tried to prevent you from dealing with the other.

"What were you *thinking?*" he asked, the anger easier to cope with. He didn't want to mention her hair, but his eyes kept going to the woollen watch cap. "I can't believe you would have run off in the darkness in a snowstorm."

She leaned against the counter, the jacket folded in her arms and held to her like a shield. "If I stay," she replied calmly, "I put you, or anyone else who might be with me, at risk." She met his eyes, real misery in hers. "And I don't blame you for doubting me about Gordon's death, or about luring Blaine away from his wife.'' She heaved a ragged sigh. ''But it makes me...uncomfortable and—'' She swallowed audibly. ''And really unhappy...so I thought the best thing to do was leave.''

His anger subsided in response to a rising sense of guilt. ''I told you I believed you about Gordon,'' he insisted. ''And I did jump to conclusions about Blaine, and I'm sorry. But that was a tough time for me, and it was handy to have someone else to blame for it—if only for a couple of minutes. I believe you didn't kill Gordon, and I believe you didn't know Blaine was married.''

From across the room, she assessed his expression, the cap pulled down to her eyebrows. Her blue eyes were enormous and uncertain.

''I'm not one of your stepfathers, Bea,'' he said gravely. ''I'm here. I will be here tomorrow and the next day.''

She finally nodded, deciding to trust that.

''I'll fix dinner,'' she said, turning her back on him and opening cupboards. ''You should get out of your wet clothes.''

He studied her back suspiciously. ''You promise me you won't run off?''

''I promise,'' she said, pulling down a jar of spaghetti sauce.

With a minimum of fuss, he changed into old cords and a turtleneck sweater and hurried downstairs again, not entirely trusting her to do as she'd promised.

But when he walked into the kitchen, he was relieved to find her scrambling hamburger and onions in a frying pan. He reached around her and into a drawer for utensils to set the table, and when he looked down at her purple hair, tapered in a mannish style, he felt a pang.

"How'd you do your hair?" he asked.

"Diluted bleach and your grape Kool-Aid," she replied.

"Kool-Aid?"

"All the kids are doing it."

He winced privately at the cartoon-colored spikes and thought that he'd never understand women in general, and this one in particular.

Once he'd distributed knives, forks and spoons on the place mats, he reached into an overhead cupboard for the Parmesan. He was carrying it back to the table when she stopped him.

"I bought fresh Parmesan," she said. "It's on the bottom shelf of the fridge."

He replaced the shaker-Parmesan and dug out the fresh. "Fancy," he said with a teasing note of snobbery in his voice.

"Just tastier."

Evan found the simple brass candlestick his mother had insisted he take with him when he left Boston. "For refinement at the dinner table," she'd said. "Or to light the room if the power goes out."

Now he put it in the middle of the table and lit the half-burned red candle that remained in it from one such power outage.

"Vegetable sticks or salad?" she asked.

"You have a preference?"

"No." She added a jar of spaghetti sauce to the mixture in the pan.

"Then, vegetable sticks. I can handle cutting those up."

He retrieved carrots, cauliflower and a cucumber from the vegetable bin and set to work, keeping up a running patter of conversation, which she responded to politely, if in monosyllables.

"I'm getting the police report about Hathaway's death, Blaine's death and the sale of his agency," he said, longing for the ease with which they used to talk. "There's got to be something we can use to build a case."

"We have the tape," she said, stirring the sauce.

"The tape proves that they hatched a plan, but that's all. Blaine died in the crash. And, anyway, the tape isn't admissible in court because the men were taped without their knowledge."

She frowned over that. "I don't understand. If it doesn't prove they killed him, why did they kill Gordon for it? Why are they chasing me to get it if it can't be used in court?"

"I think they killed Gordon for some other reason. But when you happened along and saw the red SUV, they came after you because you can identify the vehicle, not necessarily because of the tape. And Carstairs would know we can't use the tape."

In her frustration, she rested the spoon on the side of the pan and turned to him, apparently forgetting she was angry. "Why did Gordon give me the tape to take to you, if it doesn't prove anything?"

"I'm not sure. Revenge, maybe. Or..." He'd been

thinking about this since he'd first heard the tape, but was afraid to actually form the thought into words. "Maybe the truck that hit Blaine and me…did so on purpose."

Her mouth opened and she put a hand to it. "They were *trying* to kill you?"

"Well, they were trying to kill Blaine, and the fact that I was in the car wouldn't stop them. You heard the tape. They're ruthless, and he'd apparently done something to tick them off."

She nodded her understanding. "So, if we could prove that, you could stop blaming yourself for his death."

"I'd like that a lot."

"Okay." She checked the saucepan and found the water boiling, then dropped in a handful of angel hair pasta and set the timer. "I'll stay around to help you prove it as a thank-you for your initial kindness."

"My *initial* kindness," he repeated with an arched eyebrow. "Before I doubted you, you mean."

"Yes."

"And you're completely discounting the fact that you lied to me?"

There was injury in her eyes when she turned to him. "I was being pursued by killers and doing the best I could to survive. You just believed another cop over me."

"No, I didn't," he said calmly. "If I looked doubtful, it was just that I needed a little time to figure out the truth."

Her eyes filled with tears. "You said you were falling in love with me. If that was true, you'd have believed me. But you're just like every other man who crosses my path, you and Gordon. I thought he was my friend and an honest man, and he was involved in God-knows-what with those men on the tape. And you thought I was a murderer.''

''If I'd thought you were a murderer,'' he pointed out slowly, deliberately, ''you'd be in the red SUV with Carstairs right now, on your way back to Boston. But you're not, are you? You're here with me. I just needed to hear the truth from you and figure out how it all fit together.''

Tears spilled over, and she stirred the sauce with one hand while swiping them away with the other. ''Ow!'' she complained, and rubbed the back of her wrist across her forehead.

''What's the matter?'' He got up off the stool, intending to investigate.

She raised the tomatoey spoon. ''Nothing's the matter. I'm fine.''

''You said 'Ow.'''

''Yeah, well, my whole life's one big 'Ow!' at the moment. Do we want wine with this, or coffee?''

He poured wine, she prepared two plates, and they sat down across the table from each other to eat their meal in relative silence. Evan insisted on cleaning up afterward, and Beazie helped put things away.

''I'm sorry,'' she said when the kitchen was spotless once again. Her eyes still held him at bay, but at least she was talking. ''I'm more mad at myself than I am at you. I hate knowing that I dated a married man with two little boys.''

"Blaine knew how to use his charm," Evan admitted. "It wasn't your fault."

"I thought I was going to be smarter than my mother."

"You were. You broke it off."

"If I'm smarter," she said, her voice raspy, her lips quivering, "why am I stuck in a cottage in the woods in a blizzard with killers after me?"

"Because you tried to help your dying boss. Your friend."

"Yeah," she said doubtfully. "Well, if things don't start working out better for me, I'm going to begin acting really foolish."

"Relax," he said with a grin. "You covered that when you tried to run away."

She almost smiled, but not quite. "I'm going to bed early," she said. "Good night."

He stayed where he was. "Why don't you have a hot bath? Might help you relax."

"I showered this afternoon when I..." She ran a hand over her short crop and winced. "When I did my hair."

"I'm sorry about your hair," he said sincerely.

She hunched her shoulders, her eyes filled with misery. "I'm sorry about a lot of things. Good night."

CHAPTER TEN

BEAZIE TIDIED UP THE ROOM she'd left in a mess when the cab had arrived ten minutes earlier than planned. She hung up her small wardrobe in the closet, used a paper towel from the bathroom to dust her dresser top and bedside table, and did her best not to think about the events of the day.

In her heart, she didn't blame Evan. She didn't know why she felt called upon to blame him to his face. Of course he'd want to shout at the woman he'd thought had made his brother steal money and cheat on his wife and children.

At eight o'clock she went to bed, but tossed and turned until ten, then got up to take a couple of aspirin. Her scalp burned and her hairline itched and stung. The diluted bleach, she concluded, had not been a good idea.

At midnight she got up again, since even the soft pillow against her head was making her uncomfortable. She didn't know what to do. Her short, abused hair felt woolly and looked ridiculous against her pale face. Her scalp stung abominably, preventing her from sleeping even though she was so exhausted she wanted to scream.

Evan, still dressed, took one step through the open

bathroom door. His face appeared over her shoulder in the mirror.

Though she was a woman who seldom cried, she burst into tears for the third time that day. Her misery was too overwhelming to fight anymore. She put both hands over her eyes and succumbed.

"I'm fine," she sobbed as she heard his footsteps behind her. "You can go to bed. I'll be fine."

She felt his hands fall on her shoulders and turn her, then he slipped his arms around her and pulled her to him. She didn't want to lean into him, but her arms seemed to have a will of their own and wrapped themselves around his waist.

How something as solid as the wall of his chest could be so comforting, she had no idea, but it was. She'd been alone for so long, *lonely* since the day her father died and her mother forgot that she was there. Since the men she'd thought she loved turned out to be cheats of one kind or another.

And then when Evan had looked at her with accusation in his eyes because she'd dated Blaine, she'd felt friendless and bereft. Somehow all the grief she'd known in her life burst out of her in the misery of the moment, and she could hear her own noisy sobs without being able to stop them.

As he rubbed her back and rocked her gently from side to side, round after round of sobs flowed from her. She cried out her three miserable stepfathers, her years of loneliness in the big city, Gordon's death and the long, cold night she'd spent fleeing his killers. Then the truth about Blaine, and Evan's resultant anger.

At last she was free of it all, if only temporarily. Her tears quieted, and she felt less distraught.

Still, she kept her grip on Evan, hating to let go, afraid it all might come rushing back if she did.

"Better?" he asked gently, his hand still rubbing up and down her spine. She decided she could stand like this forever.

But that would be cowardly behavior, and she had to straighten up, toughen up. Taking a step backward out of his arms, she smiled at him ruefully. "Yes. Thank you. I'm sorry you got dragged into that, when you should have been sleeping."

"I dragged you into my arms, as I recall," he said, then frowned at her head. "You burned your scalp, Bea. And you've got this purple wire-scrubber thing going with your hair."

She put her hands to her eyes again, this time in embarrassment. "I know, I know. But it'll work if Carstairs shows up, don't you think? He'll take one look at me and figure 'Martian!' and keep looking."

"Mmm. Unless he decides making big bucks on an extraterrestrial would be easier than loan-sharking or insurance fraud, or whatever he's up to."

She lowered her hands and made a face. "You certainly dropped your comforting efforts in a hurry."

"Sorry." He opened the medicine cabinet and removed a tube of hydrocortisone cream. "This should help, hmm?"

"I guess. It's worth a try."

With a gentle touch, he worked the cream into her scalp, tracing it along her hairline. That made her look like a Martian with one of its fingers stuck in an electrical socket.

But Evan didn't seem to notice. He left briefly and returned with a large bandana, which he tried to fold for her. She finally took it from him and placed it over her head turban-style. The sting began to subside.

She heaved a sigh of relief. "That's feeling better," she said. Then she yawned mightily. "I think I might be able to sleep now."

"Good. Lay your head down on the pillow and see how it feels."

Evan stood over her and drew the blankets up as she eased her head down on to the pillow. Contact with a surface, even the soft pillow, hurt considerably. She tried lying on her face, but she couldn't breathe.

"All right, I can fix this," he said, toeing off his shoes.

"What...?" she started to ask, but he'd already pulled her up to a sitting position, propped the pillows around the headboard, then climbed into the bed with a leg on either side of her. He drew her into his arms so that she could lean against his chest and rest her cheek on him.

She tried to object. "You can't sit up all night."

"Just be quiet and cooperate so we can get *some* sleep."

"You promise you'll move when you get uncomfortable?"

"I promise."

"Really?"

"Really."

"You wouldn't lie to me?"

He put a hand over her mouth and reached out to turn off the light.

Beazie awoke to gray daylight, alone in her bed. Her head felt considerably better, but the rest of her body seemed to be experiencing a weird discomfort she couldn't quite identify. Until she remembered that the same sensation had awakened her during the night and she'd stirred, confused about just where she was.

She'd found herself lying awkwardly, half sitting, yet sprawled across a hard surface. When she'd put a hand out, it had connected with flannel, then stubbly chin and jaw.

"What are you doing?" a groggy voice had asked.

Evan! Joy had swelled in her when she'd remembered where she was. She also remembered his suspicion of her and her heartache over it, but somehow she was able to take it all philosophically. Who wouldn't have suspected her in the drama of the moment?

But she was happy that they were no longer angry at each other, and that he'd tried to make her comfortable after the fiasco with the bleach.

"Are you uncomfortable?" he'd asked, trying to sit up.

She'd pushed him back and settled in against him. "No, I'm fine. Sorry I woke you."

"How's the head?"

"Better."

"Want to try lying on the pillow?"

"No." She'd burrowed her nose into his neck and heaved a sigh, aware of her body relaxing again.

And then she'd become aware of a pulse deep inside her, at the heart of her, that was quickening, wanting something. Needing something. *Evan.*

The instant she identified it, her physical comfort fled and she felt edgy and anxious.

"Beazie..." his voice said on a warning note.

"I know," she whispered. She wasn't surprised that he seemed to understand what she was feeling. They were, after all, body-to-body in a darkness that seemed to press them even closer together. "I'm sorry."

"Don't be sorry," he replied quietly. "Just stop moving."

She tried, but acknowledging the tension seemed to somehow aggravate it. Her skin tingled, there were tremors in her stomach and the need to move screamed from muscle-to-muscle.

With a growl of annoyance, he'd tipped her face up, and his bristly chin came down to pin her with a kiss that clearly understood all she yearned for. Well, most of it.

He'd held her to him with a hand in the middle of her back and explored her mouth with debilitating thoroughness. It felt as though he drew out of her every negative thought she'd ever had and dispelled it. Then he replaced it with a score of tender and positive thoughts. Hopes, dreams, longings she wanted to explore.

When she reached up to let a hand wander into his hair, he drew back and caught it. He shifted to lift her off him and laid her down beside him. Her heart began to beat frantically, until she felt him move away.

She caught the front of his shirt in a fist and held on. "Where are you going?" she demanded in a disappointed whisper.

"Now is not the time," he said, his voice a little ragged. "We can't afford to be distracted."

She was sure that was true to a point, but Carstairs was supposed to be on his way to Buffalo, and even if he was here, she couldn't imagine that he and his men would be prowling around on a frigid, snowy night.

What held him away from her? They'd resolved the Blaine issue. It was something else.

He put a strong, warm hand over the fist she'd dug into his shirt and pried her fingers open.

"You're afraid of me," she said with sudden certainty. She could feel his thundering heartbeat under her knuckles, hear his efforts to control his breathing, taste the urgency in the kiss she still wore.

"Yeah," he said, and pulled her hand from his shirt. Then he reached around her waist to hitch her up to the pillows once again, folding one lengthwise so she could rest the back of her neck on it without hurting her scalp.

"Go back to sleep," he encouraged.

"It'd be easier if you were here," she said, reaching for him blindly.

He caught her probing hand, kissed her knuckles, then tucked the hand back under the covers. "If I were here," he corrected, "it wouldn't happen." And he walked away.

She'd closed her eyes then, feeling precisely the same frustration she was feeling now. It was coupled with a curious excitement, because after that incident in the night she was certain he cared as much as she did. Odd, she thought, that the man who seemed to know what to do about everything else didn't know what to do about that.

The sounds of him puttering in the kitchen and the smell of coffee floated up to her as she swung her legs out of bed. Carefully removing the scarf, she felt her hair gingerly. Haley and Mariah had brought her baby shampoo and a small bottle of conditioner, she remembered, and decided to try it.

The conditioner worked reasonably well, and subdued the purple somewhat. Combing or brushing her hair was still uncomfortable, so she simply arranged what there was of it with her fingertips and left it to dry. She dressed in the black jeans and poinsettia sweatshirt and went downstairs.

To her surprise, Jesus, Mary, and Joseph stood in a corner of the kitchen. She wondered if news was out about her lascivious, middle-of-the-night attempts to get Evan to stay with her and heaven had sent the A-team to straighten her out.

Closer examination revealed that though they were life-size, they were constructed of some sort of durable outdoor material and not flesh and blood, though they had a real-live cat. The figures were grouped on newspaper spread out on the kitchen floor, and Evan was touching up Mary's garment with light blue paint. Lucinda sat under the manger, purring.

"This is the old Nativity set Father Chabot found stored in the basement of the rectory," Evan explained. He seemed like his usual self this morning, unaffected by what had passed between them last night. Beazie felt great relief. She didn't want to have to deal with it, either, until she had some idea how to do so.

"He thought if they were painted," Evan went on, "they'd look better than the plastic ones in use now. He dropped them off this morning."

Beazie glanced out at the snow. "He's getting around all right?"

"Yes. Seems our weather's improved a little, though New York's still a mess and should be for several days. Somebody's looking out for us."

That seemed to be true. She pointed to the Holy Family. "Were there just the three pieces?"

"The Wise Men, shepherds and angels are in the living room, along with a couple of camels and a few sheep."

"You're not going to work today?"

"Yeah. I was just waiting for you to get up. Everybody's meeting at the shelter this afternoon to work on various projects before the weather gets bad again. Jackie's had some offers of furniture and she wants to chart the place, make sure she gets the right things. Mariah's bringing the clothes they've collected so far, and Randy claims to have received a great toy contribution from the firemen. He's on duty, but he's dropping the toys off. New stuff we don't have to repair or buff up.''

''Sounds like a busy day.''

He lowered his brush into a coffee can of turpentine and stood. ''How long until you're ready to go?''

''Depends on whether you want breakfast before or after I'm dressed.''

''We'll go to the Breakfast Barn.''

''Then, fifteen minutes.''

''Okay. Meet you in the van.''

After a hearty breakfast, they applied a second coat of Daisy Eye to the shelter's kitchen.

At lunchtime they were invaded by Evan's friends. Cam and Mariah arrived with Ashley and Brian, trash bags filled with donated clothing, an ironing board and a slow cooker of chili.

Court had been canceled because of the weather, so Bart came in right behind them with the baby and a square, foil-wrapped package. ''Corn bread, I think,'' he said, handing it to Beazie. ''Haley called from the office and told me not to forget to bring it. She'll be along later. She's doing a story on the snow and following Jackie around as she makes sure all our winter emergency systems are in place. Hank's sticking with her in case there's a problem…with the…power. Beazie!'' he exclaimed with a wince. ''Your hair's purple. And…'' He was obviously searching for the right word as he studied the short spikes. ''What did you *do* to it?''

Beazie grimaced and searched her mind for some explanation they'd accept. ''I…it…was an attempt to just…I don't know. Be adventurous, I guess. I cut it and colored it with Kool-Aid.''

Ashley came to study it. "I think it's cool!"

"It's…um…" Mariah struggled to be diplomatic. "Very trendy. Lots of kids are doing it."

"Molly Baker's big sister's hair is blue!" Ashley added. "But the purple's cooler."

Bart turned to Evan with such sympathy in his eyes that it was almost comical. "Are you okay?" he asked, as though what Beazie had done to her hair had affected him physically.

Evan hooked an arm around Beazie's neck and pulled her closer, his expression indulgent. "I haven't been okay since she walked back into my life. Purple hair is the least of my problems."

Beazie thought that was a little overstated, but it turned everyone's attention subtly in a different direction, and she was grateful for that. And being held close to Evan was always good.

"Randy's bringing salad," Mariah said, taking the baby from Bart. "And the toys the firemen donated. All we have to do is wrap them. Do we have paper?"

"Sutton Stationery donated some," Evan said. "We just have to pick it up."

"I'll go do that," Bart offered, "if you'll keep an eye on Henri, Mariah. Do we have something to eat the chili out of?"

"I brought bowls and silverware." Mariah bounced the baby, who giggled uproariously. "And of course I'll watch Henri. Ashley, honey, please go into the kitchen and plug in the slow cooker. Aunt Beazie can show you where it is."

Beazie liked the title of "aunt," particularly the way Mariah meant it—as a friend dear enough to be considered a relative. It was really Evan who was dear to Mariah, and Beazie acquired the title only by association. But that was fine.

"Are you and Uncle Evan going to get married?" Ashley asked Beazie as they pushed aside the coffeepot to make room for the slow cooker.

That was a nice thought. Beazie could see herself in a lacy white dress and veil, walking up the aisle toward Evan. But there was too much unresolved in both their lives. And he'd admitted to being afraid of his feelings for her.

"I've never been a flower girl," Ashley prodded, obviously hoping Beazie would agree to a wedding so she could gain that experience.

"Well, if and when we do get married," Beazie said, "you can be our flower girl."

Ashley's eyes widened and she gasped. "You *mean* it?"

There was no harm in humoring her. "Yes, I do."

The little girl held both hands to her bony chest and said eagerly, her voice high with unconcealed delight, "Do you think you'll get married before Christmas?"

Uh-oh. Unfamiliar with children, Beazie was a bit surprised by the speed with which a casual idea could be rushed toward the desired conclusion.

"Well…" She tried to backpedal.

"'Cause I just got this beauuutiful dress for Christmas that's red and flouncy! It'd be perfect!"

"Ashley, I—I…"

Ashley did a pirouette, her slender hands floating out to her sides, indicating the movement of the dress. Then she stopped short, her eyes reigniting. "Do I get to wear a veil? Or a crown sort of thing with flowers? I'd *love* to wear a veil."

Beazie stammered too long, and Ashley took off for the common room, shouting, "Mom! Mom! I'm going to be in Uncle Evan and Aunt Beazie's wedding! And it's gonna be at Christmas!"

Oh God. Beazie remained in the kitchen, wondering if she could fit into the corner cabinet and disappear into its dark recesses.

She heard Mariah's squeal and practiced an explanation. *Actually, Ashley misunderstood, Mariah. I was just speaking speculatively, and she—*

Mariah ran into the kitchen, Henri clutching the shoulders of her sweater. She wrapped Beazie in a one-armed hug, Ashley jumping up and down beside her.

"Oh, Beazie, I'm so happy! *Everyone* will be so happy. And you won't have to worry about a thing. Evan said you have no family, so just count on us to help you plan and organize."

"I get to wear a veil!" Ashley exclaimed.

Beazie opened her mouth to set them straight, but it soon became apparent why Ashley had leaped to conclusions. She'd obviously learned it from Mariah.

"Frankly," Mariah went on, "I've never understood people who get married at Christmas when there's so much else to do—particularly for us with this shelter—but, hey, we're nothing if not resourceful, and committed to each other's happiness."

"Mariah…" Beazie began, when her friend drew a breath. "I didn't…"

"I know you didn't ask for our help." Mariah hugged her again. The baby squealed and pulled Beazie's nose. Ashley wormed her way in between them. "But we're offering it, anyway. Who'll we get to give you away? What do you think about Hank?"

Beazie's head was beginning to spin. Over Mariah's shoulder, she saw Evan standing in the kitchen doorway. He raised an eyebrow in amused surprise, but when Mariah sensed his presence and drew out of Beazie's arms to turn to him, he smiled convincingly, assuming the air of a prospective bridegroom.

"Evan, I'm so happy for you!" Mariah gave Beazie the baby and went to hug Evan. "Cam will be ecstatic." She grinned. "He couldn't wait for you to be as married as he is. I can't believe you didn't tell him. I mean, I know you're a private man, but such happy news should be shared with everyone." She slapped his chest. "And you get more presents that way. Have you set a date? If we're going to get this done before Christmas—"

"We…were just talking about that," he said with a quick glance at Beazie. "There are still a few details to iron out."

"Well, speed it up," she encouraged. "Christmas, as they say, is coming. I'd better call Jackie and Haley. And Addie! She'll want to know so she can organize her ladies for the reception."

"Mariah!" Beazie tried to stop her, but she was already running out of the room, Ashley in pursuit, asking how long her veil could be.

As Evan came toward her, Beazie patted the back of the baby Mariah had forgotten in her excitement.

"Married?" Evan asked, leaning against the counter beside her. The baby smiled at him, two bottom teeth just pushing through pink gums. He leaned toward her and nuzzled her cheek. She smacked his forehead. "I don't remember accepting a proposal," he said, straightening.

"I'm sorry," Beazie said in a half whisper. "It's all a misunderstanding! Ashley asked if you and I were getting married, and if we were, if she could be in the wedding. I just said if we *did* get married, we'd let her be the flower girl, and I'm not even really sure what happened after that. She said she had a dress and got ecstatic over the possibility of wearing a veil. Then she told Mariah, and Mariah came running in here and never really gave me a chance to say anything!"

The baby studied her seriously, a small pleat forming between wide blue eyes, probably distressed at the urgent sound of her voice.

"Oh, please don't cry." Beazie began to rock her from side to side, making a point of lightening her voice. "Why didn't you say something to Mariah?" she asked in a cheerful tone intended to relax the baby.

Henri pushed away from her, anyway, and reached for Evan.

Evan took the baby and perched her on his hip. "Because I thought you might have told her we were getting married for purposes of your own."

"Why would I do that?"

"Why would you cut your hair and dye it purple? I haven't a clue. I was just trying to be supportive."

"Well, you might have supported us right into a wedding!"

"You have a remarkable talent for shifting the blame onto someone else," he observed, tipping his head sideways as Henri grabbed his earlobe and pulled. "Ouch. You do all these outrageous things, and then when it drags me into trouble along with you, you blame me. Ow. *Ow.*"

Beazie reached out to pry the tiny fingers from Evan's ear. "At least I'm not afraid to get married," she said.

He shifted the baby in his arms so that she could face Beazie. "I'm not afraid to marry you. I'm just afraid of being unable to figure out whether you're telling me the truth."

She rolled her eyes impatiently. "I lied to you once. *Once.*" At his narrowed gaze, she reconsidered, then insisted again, "Only once!"

"You're forgetting the announcement that we're getting married."

She closed her eyes and heaved a long-suffering sigh. "That was a misunderstanding for which I'm not responsible."

"Right."

Beazie gave him a disgruntled look for his skepticism. Henri, taking offense, reached a hand up to Beazie's chin and tried to insert a dimple.

Evan pulled the little fingers away. "Jeez!" He laughed. "What I am afraid of is having one of *these.*'' He indicated Henri. ''You could wake up and find yourself dismembered.''

''Oh, I'm sorry.'' Mariah hurried into the kitchen. ''Was she trying to rearrange your features?'' She reclaimed the baby, who squealed her delight, then tried to rip the top button off Mariah's sweater. ''Haley thinks she's studying to be a sculptor. She and Jackie and Hank are meeting us for lunch. And Bart's back with the wrapping paper.''

Mariah ironed, while Ashley and Brian played with Henri and Beazie wrapped toys. Cam and Evan repaired a bicycle one of Hank and Jackie's girls had outgrown and donated to the cause. It had a broken chain and a basket dangling by one screw.

When Randy arrived with salad, he ran into Beazie coming out of the kitchen, took one look at her hair and screamed, hiding behind Evan. Evan rescued the large stainless steel bowl of salad before it fell to the floor.

Beazie laughed, finding his reaction a relief compared to the agonizingly polite attempts by everyone else to pretend she looked fine.

''I knew living with Evan would be hard on a body,'' Randy said, moving cautiously out from behind his friend, ''but I thought it would be more of an emotional thing, you know? I didn't realize it could take magnificent red hair and…and—'' he pointed to her spikes ''—and turn it into an eggplant crossed with an artichoke! An eggchoke? An artiplant? How did it happen?''

Before Beazie could answer, Evan handed Randy

back his bowl of salad. "She wanted a change. She was feeling adventurous. Let it go."

He didn't seem to be able to. "You mean, you did it *on purpose?*"

Beazie admitted with a nod that she had.

"With brass cleaner?"

"With Kool-Aid."

"Pardon me?"

"Kool-Aid," she repeated. "All the kids are doing it and I was feeling frisky."

"Kool-Aid." Randy considered that, then handed Evan the bowl and put a hand to his forehead. "I have to go sit down."

Mariah came through with an empty coffee cup. "Did you hear that they're getting married?" she asked Randy.

He looked from one to the other in surprise. "What?"

"You're not invited," Evan said.

Randy grinned broadly, his expression changing from confused to congratulatory. "Well, that's great." He hugged Beazie. "He's really a nice guy, even though he makes your hair turn purple and stand up like that." Then he shook hands with Evan. "Happy for you, Evan. I knew the right woman would come along for you."

Beazie cast Evan an apologetic look, sorry that the deception seemed to be compounding itself. He looked away from her as though it didn't matter, and clapped his friend's shoulder.

"You're going to fall in love again, too. Addie will see to it."

Randy put both hands to his eyes. "I was at the *Mirror* this morning with a news story about the new ambulance, and she tried to fix me up with the cab driver who'd dropped her off. I guess her car's in the shop again."

"One of the O'Hara sisters?" Evan asked. "They're nice girls. Which one?"

"Was hard to tell, she was so bundled up. Green eyes, though. I noticed that."

"That's Paris. Let her fix you up. You know you can't get a date unless Addie sets it up for you. Or they've had a head injury."

"Ha, ha." Randy hugged Beazie again. "I can help you escape him," he said in a theatrical whisper. "I have lights and a siren. Call me."

"I will," she said with mock gravity.

When he'd left the kitchen, Beazie put a hand up to her hair and sighed at Evan. "I guess some impulses shouldn't be indulged, no matter how dire the situation."

In a move that completely surprised her, he pinched her chin between his thumb and forefinger and studied her feature by feature, his eyes finally moving to her hair. He looked it over, then smiled affectionately. "Maybe not all of them, but some should." And he kissed her lingeringly. "I don't know how you manage to still look beautiful despite the hair, but you do." Then he handed her the salad bowl. "Here you go. You're in charge of lunch."

CHAPTER ELEVEN

JACKIE WAS JUST GETTING READY to go back to City Hall after lunch, when Ashley rubbed her arms and asked, "How come it's so cold in here?"

Hank checked the thermostat and whistled. "Furnace is off. I hope it's just a matter of hitting the reset button." He headed down to the basement with his friends right behind him.

The reset button did nothing. Hank called Jimmy on his cell phone and asked him to come by.

"He won't be free for another hour and a half," Hank said, leading the way back upstairs. "You'd all better go home. I don't want you getting pneumonia just in time for Christmas. We'll divvy up the packages and wrap at home."

"We got a lot done," Mariah said, when Hank explained the problem. "We can still be ready by the twenty-third. Ashley, Brian, gather up your stuff so we can go."

While the children complied, Mariah handed Beazie a large plastic bag. "Can you sew?" she asked.

Beazie nodded. "When I have a machine."

"That bag's full of odds and ends of fabric and trim donated by a friend who makes wearable art, but I don't know what to do with it. Maybe it'll inspire you. I thought we might use it for Christmas trim in here, or something, but if you can find a use for it, go ahead. I have no needlework skills.''

''Okay. I'll see what I can do.''

They parted on the front porch and went their separate ways.

Evan was almost out of town, when Beazie shouted, ''Christmas trees!''

He slammed on the brakes, certain there was one in his path, threatening his life. They rocked to a stop, the brakes rumbling and the van pulling slightly sideways. He glanced in the rearview mirror and noticed, mercifully, that there was no one behind them.

''Sorry,'' she said, wincing. ''I got a little excited. We should get a tree, and one for the shelter.'' She pointed to a roped-off stand strung with lights. The bundled-up proprietor turned off the lights just as they pulled up.

''I can see you're closing,'' Evan said, ''but can you give us just a minute to pick out a couple?''

''Sure.'' The older man smiled genially. ''Business has been slow today, so I was going to quit early. Guess everyone who's getting a tree has already got one.''

Evan nodded. ''Right. Except for us. We'll do this quickly.''

Beazie went straight to the ten-foot trees, leaning against the fence at the back of the lot. He dragged her to the shorter trees.

''We have nine-foot ceilings,'' he said. He stood one up. ''This one?''

''Flat on one side,'' she said, moving on.

196 MAN WITH A MIRACLE

The proprietor picked out another and turned it around for her. "Even all around," he said.

She shook her head. "A little skimpy on the bottom." She spotted a tree and pulled it up with both hands. Evan reached out to steady it for her.

"What do you think?" she asked.

"Perfect," he said.

He hauled it to the van, leaped in to lower the seats, then placed it carefully in the back. By then, the proprietor had a second one for him, and when Evan tried to pay him, he said, "The lady's already paid, sir. Thank you. Drive safely."

With the van smelling like the heart of a forest, Evan headed home. "He said you paid him."

"Yes. We were in a hurry to let him go home."

"You didn't dig the cash out of your bra, did you?" he teased.

"As a matter of fact, I did," she replied, her nose in the air. It was her pseudo-haughty look, which had worked when she'd had long, luxurious hair to toss around, but was less effective with her eggplant-artichoke spikes. "He was very impressed. Wanted to give us the trees for free, but that hardly seemed in keeping with the Christmas spirit."

He had to touch her. He put the back of his hand to her cheek, and to his surprise and near destruction of the van, she turned her face and kissed his knuckles.

Tension sparked between them and exploded. He saw it in her eyes, and felt it in the swift, demanding reaction of his body.

He focused deliberately on the road, afraid if he

didn't, he'd kill them both. But the instant he stopped the car at the foot of his porch steps, he turned to her.

She flew into his arms across the small space, landing in his lap and kissing him like a madwoman. The horn honked as her elbow hit it.

After reaching behind him to open the door, he climbed out, pulling her with him. They walked up the steps arm in arm, and he unlocked the door with unsteady fingers. Together they blundered into the kitchen, lips still connected, feet entangled.

Absently, he heard Lucinda meow a greeting and noticed the chill in the house, but he didn't stop to reach for cat food or turn up the heat. Beazie's lips were so avid that he was warmed by an inner fire—and Lucinda would have to wait.

He lifted Beazie into his arms and carried her upstairs. His room was dark and cold. He set her down on her feet beside the bed and could see nothing but the gleam in her eye from the hallway light.

She framed his face in her hands, and the intense concentration in her expression froze the moment. He felt the pulse in her thumb, his own heartbeat.

"I love you, Evan," she whispered. "I know it's not the time, I know it isn't wise, I know you don't want—"

He covered her mouth with his to stop her. He couldn't think about what he didn't want. His mind and his emotions were too filled with what he *did* want—her. All of her, everything about her—and *now*. Right *now*.

"I love you, too," he said with complete honesty,

ignoring all the issues that should have made them cautious. This was a gift from destiny.

She wrapped her arms around him and leaned into him with a little sigh—her surrender to destiny.

"There's no one but us," she said, drawing back to look into his eyes. "Okay? For tonight? Just you and me. No fear, no second-guessing, no past. Just all this love between us."

"Yes," he agreed. He kissed her gently to give himself time to let it all slough away. He was conditioned to hold on to all the details, to constantly remember and review his position—as a cop and a man.

But he realized this wasn't about him, but about her and him together. So he shrugged it all off—Blaine, Hathaway, all the emotional stuff that was hard to trust because he couldn't fit it into place.

"You and me," he said, feeling the burden fall away, "and Christmas."

She nuzzled his throat. "You smell like the trees we brought home." She pushed his jacket off his shoulders. "I always wanted to spend Christmas in a cabin in the woods, with a fire in the fireplace and snow everywhere."

"We can still stop to build a fire," he said, unzipping her jacket, letting it fall to the floor.

She reached for the buttons of his shirt. "I'll settle for flannel sheets."

"Then, let's get into them."

They shed the rest of their clothes in a hurry, the only hesitation coming when she caught the clasp of her watchband in a loose thread as she pulled her sweater over her head.

She struggled with it, then Evan turned on the bedside lamp. ''I love this sweater,'' she complained as she fought with the tangled thread.

Evan leaned over to help her, his larger fingers having trouble with the tiny clasp. He finally flicked it open with his thumbnail, and she freed the thread, looking up at him with a wide smile.

''There! No damage done,'' she said.

And that was when he was reminded of how exquisite her body was. He'd seen it before, the night she'd kicked off all the covers and dreamed she was freezing. But she'd been frightened and cold after her ordeal in the back of the truck, and he'd covered her as quickly as he could.

But now she was restored to good health, the slenderness of arm and thigh dramatizing the subtle roundness of her curves.

He watched gooseflesh form on her pale skin, and realized that while he was taking in her beauty, she was probably chilled. Quickly he tossed the blankets back and turned off the light.

Her arms wound around his neck the moment he climbed in after her, and they settled into the middle of the bed. He felt the tips of her breasts bead against his chest as he enfolded her, the soft sole of her foot running along the side of his leg.

It occurred to him that he had everything. In the fullness of this magical capsule of her and him and Christmas, he could think of nothing missing.

BEAZIE SNUGGLED CLOSER as his lips explored the curve of her shoulder and his hand wandered the length of her. His shoulders were warm and solid as she skimmed them with her fingertips, then trailed down his long and supple spine.

All thought was suspended as his palm opened over the curve of her buttocks, shaped it and stroked gently, then moved down the back of her thigh. He hitched her leg over him so he could chart the hollow at the back of her knee.

She could not remember ever experiencing such complete rightness. This was her place, she thought. The niche she had searched for all her life and had never been able to find. Here in his arms, wrapped so tightly that it was difficult to move. It might have felt confining if it wasn't so freeing to finally know where she belonged.

She strained closer and planted a kiss in his ear.

He nipped at her lobe, then traced kisses along the side of her neck to her shoulder, and lower. When his lips closed over the tip of her breast, every nerve ending inside her fluttered.

"Evan," she whispered.

"Yes?" He raised his head to look into her eyes.

"Nothing," she replied, so sorry she'd stopped him. "I just felt…" There wasn't a word for what she felt. "It was the only right thing to say."

He kissed her mouth, then the other breast, then strung a line of kisses down the middle of her body to her navel. When his lips found the inside of her thigh, her brain seemed to shut down—obvious system failure because her brain was overloaded with sensation. It was disorienting to feel as though she couldn't control her body, and for an instant she forgot the Christmas capsule. She gave a murmur of distress.

He lay down beside her again, propped up on an elbow, his hand resting lightly on her stomach. "It's all right," he said, leaning down to kiss her lips. "You're safe."

She fidgeted under his hand. "I know I'm safe, I just don't have…"

"What?"

It was hard to admit. "Control," she finally blurted, her voice sounding anxious in the darkness. "I don't have control."

"Take it. It's yours."

"No, I don't mean control of the lovemaking. I mean control over…me!"

"You don't need control," he said, his hand rubbing her tenderly. "You need the courage to let it go."

On one level she didn't know what was happening to her. She'd never panicked during lovemaking before. But on another level, she knew exactly what was wrong, and it didn't make sense. She was remembering her mother, abdicating control to the men in her life, men who hadn't come through for her or her daughter. Beazie had promised herself she'd never let someone else take control of her life.

But this was her body, she told herself, not her life.

She hated herself when tears started to fall.

"Do you want to stop?" Evan asked, clearly concerned.

She thought about that for a moment and knew she didn't. She wanted to go forward, not back. But this was a significant moment, and she couldn't help but wonder if it had already lost its importance for him.

"Do you?" she asked.

He ran a hand through her spiky hair. "Silly question. Of course I don't. But that doesn't mean we've reached some point of no return. There's no such thing. If you've changed your mind, or suddenly don't feel comfortable for whatever reason—"

She stopped him by kissing him quickly and hard.

"That's it right there!" she said. "You're everything I ever wanted."

"And you're afraid that while I might look good now," he guessed, "I could still fail you eventually."

"No," she said. "I know you wouldn't. I've trusted you with my life, so there's no reason..."

"Your life and your feelings are very different things."

"In my heart," she said firmly, "I trust you with everything." She added a little lamely, "My body just doesn't seem to understand that."

"Then, why don't you just *take* control and go as far as your body's willing to go."

Curiously, she felt hesitant. She'd always found lovemaking more interesting for the potential it presented than for the pleasure it actually provided.

He lay back against the pillows. "No pressure,"

he said with a small smile. "No standard to measure up to. Just do what pleases you."

"It would please me a lot," she said, leaning over him to plant a kiss between his pecs, "if I could somehow erase what brought me here and pretend I'm just a...a designer or somebody looking for office space in the old mill, and that's how I met you. Then, I wouldn't have lied to you and you wouldn't have doubted me."

He rested a hand on her naked back. "You're forgetting we put that all aside when we walked in here—we decided that it's just you and me and Christmas."

She kissed him again. "Snowbound in the woods."

"That's it. The wind and the cold outside, the fire and the passion inside."

"We didn't build a fire," she reminded him.

His hand ran gently down her back. "We still have personal fire."

She smiled and pushed the control issue aside. "I still have spiky purple hair. We can't pretend that away."

"I don't have to," he said. "It doesn't diminish your appeal to me at all."

His sincerity humbled her, and she was suddenly fueled with a new determination to show him just how much appeal he held for her.

IT WAS TORTURE; he'd known it would be. But abdicating control seemed to be the only way to help her, once she'd decided to go on.

He hadn't suspected that she'd have a diabolically tactile interest in every muscle in his body, but he remained dutifully still while she explored every plane, every ripple. Inside, he was a bubbling cauldron, but outside he lay patiently docile, letting her do what she needed to do to come to terms with the control issue.

He was amazed his brain didn't explode.

Her hands were everywhere except where he longed for them to be. Her mouth followed them down his body, then back up, again evading that part of him now desperate for her touch.

"You're still okay with this?" she whispered, throwing a leg over his waist, the soft inside of her thigh silken agony as she slid astride him.

"Yes," he replied, his voice strangled.

But he was going to have to be committed to an asylum, he thought feverishly, if she didn't touch him *now!*

BEAZIE CLOSED BOTH HANDS over him, fascinated by his warm strength. It wasn't about control, she realized suddenly, but trust.

She heard his hoarse gasp. "Evan!" she said.

"Yeah?" His whisper was ragged.

"Are you all right?"

"Are we stopping?"

"No. I just…discovered something remarkable!"

"Uh…"

"Yes, I know. This really isn't the time to talk about it. Except that it's what we're all about here. Right now."

"Okay." He gasped again. "What?"

"Control," she replied. "I don't have to have it."

"Why not?"

"Because I love you completely, I trust you entirely. So I can…be free in the knowledge that I'm… Oh!"

Her newfound sense of self was tested as he wrapped an arm around her and brought her swiftly down beside him.

"You're sure?" he demanded.

She was delighted to discover that she was. "I'm sure."

He rose over her and she moved to accommodate him. Her epiphany and his charming patience as she worked through it had melted her, and he entered her in one swift, sure stroke that brought them heart-to-heart in a blazing instant.

She clung to him, their bodies spasming in unison, everything of which she'd ever been afraid disappearing in the wonder of the moment. She felt as though new life had been breathed into her, and the loneliness that had always been part of her life vanished.

Evan sank atop her, bracing his weight on his forearms.

She giggled, wrapping her arms tightly around him.

"Tell me that's delight and not amusement."

She giggled again. "It's bigger than delight. It's…I don't know. Bigger than anything I've ever felt. And all with the abandonment of control."

He grinned and kissed her chin. "The world can't

give you its surprises if you don't loosen up enough to take them in.''

"Yes.'' She squeezed him tighter. "I thought of it as a miracle, rather than a surprise.'' She smiled into his eyes. "I'm sorry there was so much talking.''

He laughed. "Sometimes you just have to share what's on your mind.''

"It seemed important.''

"It proved itself to be important.'' He slipped an arm under her and rolled onto his back, taking her with him. "You know what's on my mind now?''

She was sure she was going to like it. "What?''

"I think we should try that again and play it out the way it began. So you have one experience to compare with the other.''

Leaning her forearms on his chest, she studied the love and passion in his eyes. The wonder of it made her feel whole, essential, complete.

"Well, in the interest of research…''

CHAPTER TWELVE

IT WAS AFTER EIGHT O'CLOCK when they got up to have dinner. Beazie fed a loudly complaining Lucinda, then made soup and sandwiches while Evan continued to work on the St. Anthony's Nativity figures. After dinner, Beazie decided to help Evan. A lazy voice on the radio said that though the weather had improved in New England, the Great Lakes area was now under several feet of snow, and Buffalo had been particularly hard hit.

Beazie smiled at the report as she spread newspaper on the floor beside Evan. "Do you have Christmas ornaments for the tree?" she asked.

With a very fine brush dipped in a paper cup of white paint, he made a light dot in St. Joseph's eye. "Uh...I have a box somewhere that my mother gave me when I first moved out. "I think it has some ornaments I made in school, and a few extras she had. Nothing fancy."

"Oh, good!" she said with relief. "I had visions of having to make enough ornaments to cover the entire tree."

"Well, don't relax yet. What I have might cover a two-foot tree, but not an eight-footer. We may have to pass the word among our friends and see what we can mooch.''

Once the Holy Family was finished and drying in a corner, Beazie worked on one of the Wise Men while Evan painted a shepherd.

''Who do you suppose this is?'' she asked Evan as she painted a flowing cloak bright red.

He was confused by the question. ''What do you mean? He's one of the Magi.''

''I know, but which one?''

''Not sure. Why?''

She shrugged. ''Just wondered. I know one of them was Melchior.''

''Right. Gaspar and Balthazar were the other two. I remember that from grade school.''

''Do you know who brought what? You know, who brought the gold, who brought the frankincense…''

''No. Just that they were from the East and followed the Star.'' He smiled, amused by her interest.

She studied the king she painted, her brush poised in the air. ''Painting them is like doing someone's hair or makeup. You have to get close enough to invade their personal space, and something about that makes you want to understand them, and hope they understand you.''

He smiled as she went back to work, thinking she was a puzzle, but a wonderful one.

They went to bed again after midnight, all the members of the Nativity lined up on newspaper in two rows reaching from one side of the kitchen to the other.

Evan liked the way Beazie lay in his arms, her back to his chest, their legs entwined.

"I know this is odd," she said quietly as he was drifting off, his nose in her hair, "but I have never been this happy."

He replied in all honesty, "Neither have I."

HE WOKE UP to another gray day. The sky was leaden, but there was no snow. He stretched, feeling mellow and languorous, and noticed that Beazie's side of the bed was empty.

Just as it occurred to him that he'd never felt mellow and languorous in the morning since he'd become a cop, he turned to the clock to see what time it was.

9:32! He never slept that late! And where was Beazie?

There was no call to panic, he told himself as he jumped into jeans and a sweatshirt and pulled on his shoes. She was probably just making breakfast.

It wasn't normal for him to sleep that soundly, either. He usually woke up when Lucinda jumped off the bed.

A curious uneasiness settled in his stomach as he ran to the kitchen. He was losing his edge. Great timing, with Beazie being pursued by killers. Of course, he knew it was happening because he was in love with her and had lost all sense of reason and proportion. Thoughts of her were always crowding his mind. And the fact that he'd awakened around three a.m. to find her watching him, and had been so entranced by the love in her eyes that he'd had to prove his love to her again, didn't exactly make him fresh now.

He had to sharpen up, he told himself. At least until the danger was over.

He found the Nativity entourage in the kitchen, but no sign of Beazie. Lucinda was playing soccer with an empty thread spool. Her food bowl had been filled, but Beazie was absent.

Evan's attention was snagged by the glittering jewels that had been added to the Magi's cloaks. He noticed that the bag of fabric trims Mariah had given Beazie was open on the kitchen table, spilling out a few of the colorful glass beads that now bedecked the hem of one of the Wise Men's robes. Elegant gold braid trimmed another hem, and wide, textured ribbon decorated the third. Jewels and gold piping jazzed up the camel's saddle, and gold tassel dripped from his harness.

Father Chabot would be thrilled. But where was Beazie?

"Bea!" he shouted from the middle of the kitchen.

The front door opened suddenly, and a tree standing in the doorway spoke to him. "Good morning," it said. "You bellowed?"

He went to the door, reached a hand into the prickly needles to grasp the slender trunk and held the tree aside. Beazie stood there in her trusty sweats, her purple hair parted and combed into a sort of funky order. Her cheeks were pink, her eyes bright, her smile wide.

"You slept well," she observed. Then she seemed to notice his displeasure and frowned. "What?"

"Don't go running off without telling me where you're going," he barked, then pulled her inside and closed the door.

At his tone she raised an eyebrow. "I didn't go running off. I couldn't sleep, so I came downstairs."

"You could have told me."

"You were asleep."

She studied him, as though trying to assess his bad mood. "I was tossing and turning," she explained patiently, "so rather than wake you, I came down to work on the Magi. But I've finished that, so I went out to get the tree." She grinned tauntingly, apparently deciding against barking back at him. "I'm glad you're finally up. It weighs a ton."

It wasn't fair to be angry at her because he'd slept well, he decided. In most circles that was considered a good thing. But among those being pursued by killers and needing to be vigilant every moment, it wasn't desirable.

"This has to stay on the porch," he said, "until we get a Christmas tree stand. We'll do that on the way back from delivering the Nativity to Father Chabot."

She started for the door. "I'll get the other tree out of the back so there's room for..."

He caught the back of her sweatshirt and pulled her to a stop. "I'll do it. Why don't you make breakfast?"

"Because I'm in an artistic mood," she said, arms spread theatrically, indicating the Magi. "I've just accessorized the Wise Men and have great plans for decorating the tree. Cooking is kind of limited in scope for the mood I'm in.''

She was teasing him, her eyes dancing and her smile barely kept in check. Their lovemaking had left him moody, unsettled to discover he could be subject to his emotions, but it had obviously had a more positive effect on Beazie.

She finally sighed and went to the refrigerator. ''Fine. Bacon and eggs in ten minutes.''

He laid the tree down on the porch, then went to the van to get the second tree and placed it beside the first. He took a moment to stop and look around.

Snow was falling, and the morning was quiet except for a barking dog somewhere down the road. He wondered if Carstairs was on his way back yet, or if, like a good cop, he was tracking the Buffalo lead to earth. There was no way to be sure.

When Evan went back into the house, he found Beazie working away at the stove, bacon already sizzling, a carton of eggs on the counter, the toaster plugged in and ready. She moved efficiently from stove to table to refrigerator, and he felt evil for having grumped at her. He was sure she'd revised her ''sweetheart'' opinion by now.

''I'm sorry,'' he said abruptly.

She spun in his direction, a turner in hand. She looked puzzled. ''Why?''

''For yelling at you.''

Her eyes widened and she was about to smile, then seemed to think better of it, maybe afraid he'd misinterpret the gesture.

''I understand,'' she said. ''You think you compromised my safety by sleeping well. But that's silly, isn't it? I mean, they're probably still in Buffalo somewhere, and how are you going to protect me when they come back, if you're not rested?''

Her assessment of the situation delivered, she swiped the air with the turner and said, "It's all right. I'm not that sensitive."

He stood there, watching her back as she turned the bacon and put bread in the toaster. If he'd been worried about his edge before, he was now certain it was a major problem.

Beazie had seen right inside him. She'd smiled in the face of his bad mood and read him like text on a high-resolution monitor. Making love with her had robbed him of his self-imposed isolation. He felt vulnerable, exposed.

The fax machine rang and he walked into the office to see what was coming, hoping it was information from Clay Markham. He was disappointed when he saw that the fax wasn't from Clay, but cheered up instantly when he realized it was about the sale of Blaine's insurance franchise.

"Breakfast!" Beazie called from the kitchen.

Evan carried the paperwork in with him and set it down at his place. He poured coffee while she served breakfast.

"Is that the fax you've been waiting for from your cop friend?" she asked as they sat across the table from each other.

"No, it's a copy of the sale of Blaine's insurance franchise." He skimmed it and was disappointed to find nothing in it to confirm his suspicions.

"So, a sale transpired and no one suspected that the capital was two-hundred thousand dollars short?"

"Apparently."

"I wonder how that could be? Certainly there would have been an audit."

"You'd think so."

"Who bought it?"

"Uh…" He checked the sheet. "Claudia Boughton."

Beazie's eyes widened. "The sale went through without a hitch," she said breathlessly, "because Claudia Boughton was Gordon's ex-wife!"

"What?" He looked over the sheet again.

"Yes. His ex. But I don't understand. It sounds like she was in collusion with him, but they hated each other. Just before I went to work for him, they'd had a very hostile divorce."

"Maybe he offered to make it worth her while," Evan said.

BEAZIE HAD BEEN FEELING like a stranger in her own life for a long time. Now it seemed as if she were watching someone else's life. Gordon Hathaway had been such a considerate boss; she couldn't imagine him involved in fraudulent deals or criminal activities.

Why hadn't she been suspicious of what he and Blaine were up to when they went into his office and closed the door? And how could she not have picked up on the fact that Blaine was married? It was obvious now that he hadn't taken her anywhere because he didn't want to risk being seen with her.

She took a sip of her coffee and asked morosely, "Was I particularly stupid, or would anyone have suspected Gordon and Blaine were up to something?"

Evan spread jam on his toast, then passed her the jar. "If they weren't good at deception, they wouldn't have gotten away with whatever they did in the first place. So, it's not surprising you didn't suspect anything."

She pushed the jam away, still working on the puzzle. "What *did* they do?" she asked. "And did they do it together, or separately? I mean, it hardly seems possible that whatever Blaine had going a year and a half ago is the same thing that Gordon was killed for, does it? I mean, if it is organized crime they're mixed up in, they just don't let something float that long, do they?"

Evan speared a bite of egg. "I'm not sure. Before we even speculate, I'm going to see if the investigating officer in Gordon's murder has subpoenaed his bank records."

"Is that legal?"

"Clay was going to read the report over for me so I could ask questions. Eat up. We've got to get the Nativity back to Father Chabot. I promised I'd return it in time for the music program tomorrow night."

"Do you think they'll still have it?"

"The weather's supposed to break tonight."

Beazie wondered if the roads were clear enough to drive in New York state. Carstairs could already be on his way back from Buffalo if they were.

That possibility was too unsettling, so she

switched her thoughts to Evan. She'd been worried, when he'd awakened in such a bad mood, that last night hadn't meant as much to him as it had to her. But she'd have sworn his tenderness had been the result of real feelings. Then she'd seen something in his eyes when he looked at her that suggested the bad mood was caused more by fear than displeasure, and she'd put it all together.

He was afraid for her, not for himself.

Now he seemed to be relaxing again. She didn't want to do anything to discourage that.

They arrived at the rectory to find Father Chabot on a hospital call. When they explained their mission to Mrs. Corrigan, the housekeeper, she suggested they simply go ahead and replace the plastic Nativity with the restored figures.

The snow had stopped, though the day was over-cast and cold, so they worked quickly. As Beazie removed a plastic figure, Evan put the restored one in its place. When they were finished, Evan put an arm around her shoulders to admire their work.

"The Magi are beautiful. Your touches with the phony stones are perfect."

"They do look good, don't they? But I wish I knew who was who."

"I'm sure you made a friend of each one of them."

"You don't think Father will think they're gaudy?"

"Father does not!" came a voice from behind. The priest pushed his way between them, slipping an arm around each of them. "I can't believe you got these done so quickly! They're stunning. Are you the fiancée I've heard about, young lady?''

Father Chabot was a short, rotund man with bright eyes and a wide smile. In a dark suit and an overcoat, he could have been an affable businessman—except for the clerical collar.

Beazie opened her mouth to reply, but glanced at Evan for direction. Did one lie to a priest?

''Father Chabot,'' Evan said, ''Beatrice Deadham. We call her Beazie.''

The priest shook her hand. ''A sibling's nickname for you?'' he asked.

''No, Father. I'm Beatrice Zoe. B.Z. I think my father started it, believing Beatrice or Bea was just too adult a name for a baby.''

''And what do you do, Beazie?''

''I'm a secretary, Father. But…between jobs at the moment.''

He smiled from her to Evan. ''I understand the two of you quarreled when Evan left Boston, but you finally decided you couldn't live without him, so you followed.''

Unwilling to admit that was true when it wasn't, she simply smiled, hoping he would take that as assent.

''Even winter fails to slow down Maple Hill's communication system,'' Evan said. ''Who told you all this?''

''Oh, there are all kinds of people in town happy to know you're in love,'' the priest replied. ''Rita told me when the ecumenical council met at the Breakfast Barn this week. Addie Whitcomb mentioned it when her Sunday School dropped by to see what a Catholic church looks like, and Glory Anselmo is coming to me for pre-marriage classes. Her fiancé, Jimmy Elliott, is one of ours, you know.''

Evan winced at Beazie. ''Keeping things to yourself isn't encouraged in Maple Hill.''

She smiled. She loved everyone he'd mentioned, and the priest himself was so warm and kind, it was hard to be upset that she and Evan had been talked about. Except, it wasn't the truth.

''I see that,'' she said.

''I understand you're planning a pre-Christmas wedding,'' Father Chabot said to Evan. ''So, why haven't I seen you to schedule it?''

''I always put things off,'' Evan replied easily.

She admired his aplomb, but couldn't help the feeling they were both going to hell. Lying to a priest had to be punishable by fire. Lying to a priest at Christmas while standing in front of the Nativity scene had to guarantee a place in the hottest flames.

''The last week before Christmas is open,'' the priest said with a grin. ''Most people are reluctant to get married at such a busy holiday, but some of you apparently realize the blessings attached to a love contract entered into at such a miraculous time. Call me and I'll put it on my calendar.''

''Thank you, Father.'' Evan shook his hand. ''Well, if you'll excuse us, we'll carry the plastic Nativity down to the basement and be on our way.''

''No, no,'' the priest said. ''A couple of boys who live nearby are coming over this afternoon to shovel my walk. I'll have them take the old statues down and pay them off in cocoa and cookies.''

Father Chabot took another look at the brightly painted Nativity with its bejeweled Wise Men and spread his arms in an all-encompassing gesture. ''Thank you again. I can't tell you how grateful I am.''

''Father,'' Beazie said, pointing to the Magi. ''You wouldn't happen to know which Wise Man is which, would you? Or who brought what to Baby Jesus?''

The priest frowned. ''I'm not sure anyone knows, Beazie. If I was to speculate, it's known that Balthazar was the king of Babylon. I suppose it's possible he brought the gold. But that's just a guess.''

She liked knowing even that much. ''Thank you, Father. I'm happy to have met you.''

''I'm happy to know you, Beazie. Call me to set the date.''

''We lied to Father Chabot,'' Beazie said a few minutes later as Evan drove slowly toward the highway.

''No, we didn't,'' he said. ''I was careful not to lie. I just answered him with things that were…appropriate. But true.''

''I doubt that St. Peter will split hairs like that when you try to get into heaven.''

He made a scornful sound. ''I'm not even going to try. I'll just take the down elevator when the time comes.''

She backhanded him on the arm. ''That's ridiculous. Where are we going to find a Christmas tree stand?''

''We'll try The Maple Hill Store. They have everything.''

He was right about that, Beazie thought as she wandered up and down aisles. Evan had headed toward a display of lights and ornaments, assuming he would find a stand there.

She found clothing, books, small appliances, cologne and makeup, plumbing and electrical supplies, linens, and two aisles devoted to groceries. She bought a box of brownie mix, remembering that Evan had eaten several brownies at the Christmas party.

Beazie found him at the checkout, just as Randy ran into the store, spotted them and hurried to hide behind them. He pulled them close together as he ducked down.

''Hide me!'' he whispered urgently.

''Jealous husband?'' Evan asked.

''It's Addie!'' Randy whispered. ''She wants me to come to dinner tonight to *get acquainted* with Paris O'Hara, and I told her I was going to Springfield and couldn't make it.''

''You'd like Paris,'' Evan said over his shoulder.

Beazie elbowed him as Addie came through the front door. She waved at them and headed in their direction.

''Here she comes!'' Evan said under his breath. ''Stay down.''

''Don't worry!''

Addie approached them with a warm smile.

"Well, hi, you two! Are you out in this weather making wedding plans?"

Evan gestured with the tree stand he held. "Putting up the tree tonight. What are you doing in town?"

"Hank brought me in," she said. "I forgot the sauerkraut for a country-ribs dish I'm fixing tonight."

"Having company?"

She nodded. "The O'Hara girls. I invited Randy, thinking he and Paris might hit it off, but he's going to some class in Springfield. More training."

"I think he'd like Paris—" Evan said, his voice just a shade louder than required to communicate with Addie.

Fortunately, she didn't seem to notice, but Beazie felt Randy shift behind them. "You should try again to get them together."

"I'm going to. He just doesn't realize I'm not easily discouraged."

Addie sidled by them in the narrow checkout aisle, and Evan and Beazie, remaining shoulder-to-shoulder to conceal Randy, rotated like a turntable. She eyed them oddly.

"You two really have become joined at the hip, haven't you." With a wave, she turned and walked on.

Randy, still bent down, peered over Evan's shoulder until she was out of sight. Then he straightened with a groan. "That woman has the persistence of a terrier."

"And the jaws," Evan said. "What's it worth to

you for me not to tell her you were hiding behind us like a lily-livered coward?''

''I'd be careful about threatening to reveal *secrets,* if I were you,'' Randy reminded, raising a judicious eyebrow. ''You'll recall I'm keeping a few of yours.''

''And we appreciate it.'' Beazie wrapped her arms around him and hugged him gratefully. ''But a little romance would be good for you,'' she prodded gently. ''It's a long, cold winter.''

Randy sighed at her. ''I'm happy with my own company,'' he said. ''But thank you for your concern. If I hide in my car, will you go back to the freezer section and buy me a carton of Cherry Garcia and bring it out to me, so Addie doesn't find me?'' He handed Beazie a bill.

''No, she won't go...'' Evan began, then called, ''Bea, come back here!'' Beazie had already headed off toward the freezer section at a quick pace to do as asked.

By the time she returned, Evan had checked out and was waiting for her by the door. She paid for the ice cream, then followed him out to the parking lot. Randy was hunkered down in a red pickup.

''You're an angel,'' he said, opening the window and taking the bag from her. ''He doesn't deserve you. But I might reconsider marriage if you'd have me.'' He seemed suddenly to notice her hair. ''And if you let your hair go back to red. What happened to it, anyway?''

''It's a long story,'' Evan said, glancing back toward the market. "And Addie's in the checkout line. You'd better get out of here."

Beazie laughed as Evan drove home. "You think he can hold out against Addie?" she asked.

"I seriously doubt it. It's just a matter of time. And I have a feeling about him and Paris."

"But Addie was trying to fix you up, I understand, and you resisted."

He gave her a quick grin. "Are you suggesting I have her put me back on her list?"

"Of course not," she replied. "Your friends think we're planning a pre-Christmas wedding. It would look as though you were fickle and a bounder."

"A bounder?"

"You know. A cheating rat."

"Ah. So it's not because you feel undying love for me?"

"Yes, I do, but that's beside the point."

CHAPTER THIRTEEN

EVAN FROWNED AT HER as the traffic slowed down for a pickup making a left turn. "How could that ever *not* be the point?"

"Because we can't trust the circumstances," she replied without turning to him. "I mean, making love was fantastic, but you woke up grumpy, and I woke up..."

"Yes?"

She hitched up her shoulders close to her body, as though using them to shelter herself. "I woke up a bundle of nerves."

She turned to him then, misery in her eyes. He felt panic. She was going to tell him she didn't love him, after all.

"What if...what if Carstairs and his men come back, and...and something happens to you?" she asked.

Relief flooded him. It wasn't that she didn't love him, but that she *did*. "Nothing will happen to me. I'm experienced at this sort of thing."

"There are four of them."

"I have friends, too."

She did not seem impressed. "A lawyer, an electrician and a plumber?"

"I wouldn't underestimate the Wonders."

"I should have run away the day I dyed my hair."

"I'd have tracked you down and brought you back."

"You might not have found me."

He felt such a connection to her that the possibility she might be somewhere he couldn't home in on seemed ridiculous. "I'd have found you. I have ESP where you're concerned."

She tried to hold back a smile and failed. "ESP?"

"Evan's Special…" He thought over the third word. "Possession?"

She frowned over his choice.

"Not that I own you," he said quickly, "but that your love owns mine and mine yours. We're as committed as if a deed changed hands."

This time she looked startled. He couldn't tell if it was because she was stunned by that admission, or because she didn't like the analogy.

"Evan's Special Passion?" he suggested. "Princess? Prize?"

She considered the possibilities, then swallowed. "I think I like Princess best. Particularly if it comes with ball gowns and a crown."

He accepted her need to lighten the moment and nodded. "I'll see what I can do."

At home, he sawed the bottom inch off the tree for the house, and they set it up in front of the living room window.

"You bought lights!" she exclaimed, as he pulled out three sets of twinkle lights. "I forgot to mention it and wasn't sure you'd remember."

"Of course I thought of it. Do you think I'm completely out of step with Christmas?"

"You do have a lot on your mind."

"Yes," he said with a wink, "but a lot of that is you, and you suddenly seem to be the personification of Christmas." His eyes roved her hair as he handed her one end of the light string. "An elf come to life, all mischief and good cheer."

It was clear she didn't know whether to be offended or flattered. "But being an elf doesn't come with ball gowns and a crown."

"Elves can do magic," he placated.

She shrugged. "It's Christmas. Miracles abound. Who needs magic?" She plugged the string in near the baseboard under the window, then straightened. "See? A string of lights that actually works!"

"We're in the zone now," he said, walking around the tree and placing a string of lights on the branches.

As they connected the second, then third string, they had to reposition the bottom loops closer together until they spiraled upward evenly. Then they stood back to admire their work.

Beazie joined her hands at her breasts. "This is going to be the most beautiful tree I've ever had," she predicted.

Then she leaned into him, and wrapped an arm around his waist, the first time he could recall that she'd initiated touch rather than responded to his.

"I suppose with a family," she said a little wistfully, "you've always had wonderful Christmases."

"Yes, I have." That was true. His mother loved Christmas and made a great fuss. She decorated every inch of the house, baked for days, and when Blaine's boys were born, even Barney, who encouraged frugality, stood out of her way and let her shop. "But I agree that this is going to be a spectacular tree."

She turned to him, suddenly serious, and wrapped her other arm around him. "You know, you should really go home for Christmas," she said. "I'd be fine here, and I'll bet it would make your mother's holiday if you walked in the door."

It probably would, but his mother had always read him like a book. He couldn't go home until he had the answers to Blaine's death. And he wouldn't consider leaving Beazie under any circumstances. She was now the single most important thing in his life.

Beazie was reading his eyes. "I'm serious," she said with sudden firmness. "You should do this. You can't bring me because this is such a significant holiday for your family. Last year their grief over your brother was too fresh for them to enjoy it, but this year they're probably trying to move on, and I'm sure it would help them…"

He put a hand over her mouth, then replaced it with his lips. "I'm not going home," he said when he raised his head. "I called my mother and explained, and she understood."

"When?"

"The other day."

Her lips firmed. "I don't believe you. When?"

"When we were at the shelter and you went to pick up our lunch. Carstairs showed up, and I forgot to mention it to you." He pointed toward the garage.

"I'm going to see if I can find those ornaments. You keep decorating."

It took Evan half an hour to dig them out. It wasn't that he had too many possessions, it was just that none of the storage boxes was labeled. After a laborious search through knickknacks his mother had insisted he take, kitchen gadgets she'd given him, school memorabilia, and all his cop gear, he finally found the corrugated box that had once held manila envelopes.

He carried it into the living room and was astonished by how much progress Beazie had made. Somewhere she'd found red-and-black-check ribbon, made bows and arranged them on the tree. She was now attaching ornament hangers—something else he remembered—onto gold braid tassels from the same strand she'd used for the camel's harness.

"Found it!" he exclaimed triumphantly. "Looking good, Beazie. Where'd you find the ribbon?"

"It was in the bag of trim Mariah gave me." She put her project down on a chair and stood to reach for his box. "What have you got in there?"

He removed the lid, tossed it aside and rummaged through the box. Inside was a very rustic ornament made of tree bark, moss and pine cones.

"Oh! A red ribbon on that, and it'll look beautiful." She did just that and hung it near the bottom of the tree. Lucinda, watching them with great interest, took a swing at it. When the pinecone swung back and struck her in the nose, she yelped with healthy respect.

Evan held up something made with elbow macaroni that was unidentifiable, except for the small plastic Santa glued to the middle.

"Let's just throw that one away."

She tsked at him. "Give me that! It's an example of your artistic skill at a particular stage. It's a milestone."

He rolled his eyes. "Whoever came up with the idea that children should make artwork out of pasta should be shot. Now, this one's not too bad." He handed her a small plastic circle painted like stained glass to depict Bethlehem.

She ran gold thread through a loop at the top and hung it on the tree along with the macaroni ornament.

There were a few cutout snowmen and snowflakes, and a round paper ornament with his family's photo glued to the center.

Beazie sat down to study the picture. "Wow," she breathed. "So that's your mom."

He leaned over her shoulder. It was a photo of his mother a good twenty-five years ago, slender and dark-haired, and looking very contented. Sitting beside her with an arm wrapped around her was Barney, young and robust with an open and friendly face. Blaine sat between them, curly blond hair rioting over an angel face, and Evan sat beside his mother, leaning a little backward, not smiling. He and Blaine wore matching ski sweaters in a blue-and-white snowflake pattern.

Beazie looked up at him worriedly. "You weren't a happy child," she said.

"I wasn't *un*happy." He found that period of his life hard to understand, much less explain. "My father had left and my mother cried a lot. Then Barney came into our lives and…you know how children are. I thought he was mine. Then Blaine came along, looked just like him, and though Barney never slighted me, I began to wonder just where my place was in the world. Blaine grew up to be smart and charming and good at everything. I didn't resent him for that, but I had to work hard for everything I accomplished, and I was shy and more serious."

"Were you jealous of him?"

"Sometimes," he admitted honestly, "but when he was first born, I thought he was so amazing, and that thrill of having a sibling never really left me. Even when I began to notice there was a selfish, self-serving streak in him, he was still my little brother, and I was always trying to save him from himself."

"Did he appreciate you?"

He smiled. "Occasionally, when I got him out of trouble. But usually I think he just considered me an impediment to fun."

"I'm sorry," she said with a sigh.

He took the ornament from her and put it on the tree. "Don't be. Your life is your life. You just deal."

"Did your parents see the truth about him?"

He'd never been sure about that, and he'd certainly done his part to conceal what he could of the truth. "I don't think so. At least, I'm not sure. He married a wonderful girl and gave them two of the smartest, cutest grandsons, so that made him pretty marvelous in their eyes."

"His wife must have known."

"I'm not sure about that, either. He loved her and was good to her, until whatever was happening at the end there, and the money he owed made him reckless and ruthless. But I'm not sure Sheila knew any of that."

He dug into the box, needing to change the subject. He came up with a crocheted snowflake. "My grandmother—my mom's mom—made this." It hung on a simple piece of fishing line, and Beazie reached for her spool of gold-colored string.

"It's still a little bare," she said half an hour later, when every ornament they had was on the tree. "We need garland."

That was something he *hadn't* thought of.

She disappeared into the kitchen and returned with a bag of cranberries. She threaded a needle and handed it to him.

He studied her doubtfully. "What are you expecting me to do with this?"

"Thread cranberries onto the string while I make popcorn and do the same."

"But..." He tried to protest. He sanded and painted and wallpapered. He didn't have the hands for small projects.

"It's easy," she encouraged. "And when you've finished that bag, the shepherd's pie will be ready."

"You made shepherd's pie?"

"This morning while you were still sleeping. I'll go put it in the oven."

"I should be above bribery, but I'm not."

Stringing was a long, tedious process, and they worked for two more hours after dinner. It was late when they finished and stood arm in arm in the darkened house, with only the lights from the Christmas tree shining.

"Wow," Beazie said, her voice unsteady. "It sure beats a three-foot tabletop tree."

Evan kissed her forehead and admired the tree with her, thinking that perhaps because he had an investment in this one, it did seem more beautiful than any tree from his childhood.

"Look at that stunning cranberry garland." He made no pretense at modesty. "I slaved long and hard over that."

She leaned into the hollow of his shoulder, wrapping both arms around him. "I'm sure Santa will reward you."

"I was thinking of a more immediate reward."

"Leftover shepherd's pie?"

"No."

"Another brownie?"

"No."

She finally caught on, but she was grinning. "Have you no shame?"

"I don't think so."

The grin turned to laughter. "Then, come on," she said, and led the way upstairs.

EVAN LOOKED OUT THE WINDOW at the clear skies the following morning and wondered where Carstairs and his men were. He hadn't heard the news yet, but he hoped snow was still falling over Buffalo.

He had to get to the shelter today. Everything was pretty much under control, but he still had to put the wallpaper border up in the kitchen. The furniture that had been donated for the common room was now being stored in Cam's garage and had to be transported. The stove and refrigerator were due to arrive the day after tomorrow.

And they had to set up the tree.

Christmas was only—he counted—a little more than a week away. Could that be? He counted again. Yes. Still, that was plenty of time, he told himself bracingly.

Even if Carstairs showed up again between now and then, he could handle it. He had a plan. He just had to alert his friends.

Beazie emerged from the bathroom in black jeans and the flowered sweater. The shade of her hair was somewhat subdued, and she'd managed to get the spikes to curl a little this morning. But it was definitely still purple.

His heart reacted to her presence as though it would never matter what she looked like. She'd somehow taken possession of him and he'd never belong to himself again. It amazed him that he felt at peace with that.

It had been a wild night. There'd been something almost frantic about her response to him, something desperate in the lovemaking she'd initiated at three this morning. He'd wondered about it for an instant, but was too quickly entrapped in her arms and her spell to really think about it.

He looked for a clue in her eyes this morning, but they were clear and happy. Perhaps he'd imagined the whole thing because he was so frantic himself to be with her.

He held out a hand to her. "How are you this morning?"

She came to him eagerly. "Wonderful. How are you?"

"Great," he said, drawing her to him and wrapping his arms around her. She slid right into his embrace, but he felt a little stiffness in her that was at odds with her insistence that all was well.

"What are you worried about?" he asked directly. "Carstairs is too far away to hurt you. We're still in our Christmas capsule." He wanted to make her smile. "Or are you afraid that Christmas is closing in and we're going to have to explain to my friends why we're not getting married? Because if you are, I have a solution."

He could tell that wasn't it. She was just humoring him when she asked, "What is it?"

"I thought we'd get married," he said, dipping her backward in his arms, "and save having to explain."

She didn't struggle, apparently trusting him not to drop her. He sensed something significant in that.

"Okay," she said.

As he swung her upward again, he caught a whiff of her soap and shampoo. *"Okay?"* He feigned hurt feelings. "A man you purport to love proposes, and your answer is '*Okay?*'"

He'd caught her close to him, her hands resting lightly on his shoulders. He could feel the charge of their middle-of-the-night madness in her as she looked at him under her lashes.

"When the man who purports to love me proposes in lieu of having to come clean to his friends, I think that's all the proposal deserves." Then she wrapped her arms tightly around him, negating the claim she'd made. "Evan, I just love you so much. I was thinking in the shower that we're going to have to deal with Carstairs eventually. And I'm worried about you and all we have here."

He framed her face in his hands. "Do not worry," he enunciated. "I'll keep you safe, and I'll have an airtight case to present to the DA."

She opened her mouth to speak, but was fore-stalled by the peal of the doorbell. "I'll get it," she said, heading for the stairs, "while you get dressed."

Catching her arm, he yanked her back, his old instincts kicking in. "No. You stay up here. I'll get it."

"Why?" she asked, still poised to go.

He pulled her back firmly. "Just in case."

"In case of…?" And then it seemed to dawn on her. "You said Carstairs would still be snowbound outside Buffalo."

He nodded. "I'm sure he is. But it always pays to hedge your bets."

He ran down the stairs, wondering who'd be calling at this hour on a Thursday morning. Trouble. It had to be trouble.

He pulled the door open—and congratulated himself on being right. It was trouble, all right. Two of the people whose faces had haunted him for some time now stood on the porch.

His mother flew into his arms, and Barney reached out to shake his hand.

"Hi, Mom," he said, surprised by how good her hug felt, how great it was to see Barney's face. "Hey, Dad."

But he didn't want them here. They could be in danger, despite the assurances he'd given Beazie. Carstairs could return tomorrow, and Evan couldn't risk their safety.

"Evan." His mother said his name with a sigh, as though she felt great relief at seeing him safe and sound. "I'm so happy." She hugged him fiercely. "So happy!" she said again. "I thought you'd never be able to do it."

"Do what?"

Her black leather purse banged his elbow as she dropped her arms from him. She crossed one gloved hand over the other and just stared at him. "Do what?" She repeated his question as though he teased her with it. "You know what. That must be the reason you look so wonderful. You've finally let it all go. Barney said you just needed time on your own to sort everything out, but I didn't believe him. You know, once a mother, always a mother, no matter how old your child gets. You still think the safest place for him is under your roof, at your table. But you're really going to do it!"

Evan turned to Barney for help, but Barney simply shook his head at his wife and took a step forward to wrap an arm around her shoulders. "You'll have to forgive her for running on. She's a little excited."

And that was when Evan noticed Jackie, who'd

been standing behind Barney. She came forward with a chagrined and apologetic expression on her face.

"I ran into the Barn to pick up a quick cup of coffee, and Rita told me that your parents were there, having breakfast and asking directions to your place. So, since I was going to the inn for a staff meeting, I told them to follow me. But I didn't realize you hadn't told them, and I congratulated them."

He was beginning to wonder if it was lack of sleep or if everyone was talking in riddles. "Told them what?" he asked.

"That you were getting married," she replied. She gave him a quick hug, then did the same to his mother and Barney. "I just wanted to apologize for ruining your surprise!" she called over her shoulder as she beat a hasty retreat. "Enjoy your visit!"

God. He should explain right now, but there were tears in his mother's eyes and she drew him to her arms again and began to weep.

"For God's sake, Alice," Barney said. "The boy has to breathe. And I have to get warm. Could we please go inside?"

"Where is she?" his mother demanded as she slipped off her boots and he took her coat. "Jackie says she lives here. That she's someone you knew in Boston but broke up with when you came here." She was frowning, perplexed. "I didn't realize you'd been seeing anyone." Then she grinned broadly and walked through the living room into the empty kitchen. "But I'm thrilled! We're thrilled—aren't we, Barney?"

"Yes, we are, Alice," Barney replied. He fell into

a convenient chair. "Aah, that feels good. Don't mind me, son. And the best thing to do is just let your mother wander around. She'll probably check your fridge, your closets. She'll just keep looking until she finds her."

"Well, where is she?" Alice Turner came back to the living room and stood in the middle, arms akimbo. "I'm finally about to acquire a second daughter-in-law and she's nowhere to be found." She glanced at the stairway. "She isn't still asleep, is she?"

According to his mother, anyone in bed after seven a.m. was sluggardly and destined to social and financial failure.

Evan was preparing to shout for Beazie, wondering how to explain to her without words what his parents thought, when she came running lightly down the stairs.

"Here I am!" she said cheerfully, heading right into his mother's arms. "Hello! Welcome to Maple Hill!"

He saw his mother's smile at the sound of Beazie's voice, then watched it grow wider as Beazie's slender form in jeans and flowered sweater became visible on the stairs. She maintained the smile at the sight of Beazie's pretty face, but it froze when her short purple hair came into view.

Evan wasn't sure if he wanted to groan or laugh. He wisely kept silent.

But Beazie hugged his mother with affection, then stepped back to look into her face. Everything about her was utterly genuine.

"I'm so happy to meet you at last," she said. He could only guess by her behavior that she'd overheard at least some of their conversation. "Evan's told me all about you."

Beazie moved on to Barney, who was about to struggle out of the chair.

"No, no," she said, pushing him back. She leaned over to hug him. "You must be Barney. We just put your photo on the tree last night."

Alice turned to the tree with sudden interest. "You did?"

Beazie took her arm and drew her closer to it, to point out the ornament. "Here. And here's your mother's ornament." She touched a fingertip to the crocheted snowflake.

Except for the purple hair, Alice was clearly charmed by Beazie. She politely said nothing about the oddly colored spikes, but couldn't help looking perplexed.

Noticing his mother's reaction, Beazie laughed and ran a hand over her hair. "You're probably wondering why my hair's purple," she said.

Alice nodded. "I'm afraid I was."

Beazie shrugged. "Overprocessing. My own color's kind of drab, and I wanted to look perfect for the wedding, so I was trying different shades of red. Unfortunately I picked one that didn't go with a perm I also tried…"

"But your hair is straight," his mother pointed out.

"Yes," Beazie replied quickly. "The perm didn't work, either, so I cut it off. I'm Beazie, by the way.

B. Z. for Beatrice Zoe. Strange, I know, but I'm named after my grandmothers."

Alice seemed to experience a moment of indecision, then wrapped Beazie in a hug and tried to squeeze the life out of her.

"I'll bet you could use some coffee," Beazie said, drawing away at last and catching Alice's hand. "Or maybe some breakfast?"

"We had breakfast," Alice replied, "but an English muffin or something would be nice."

"We can do that. Come and help me, and tell me how you got here in this awful weather."

As Beazie drew her away, Alice turned to Evan with a shushing finger to her lips. "I have a surprise," she said softly.

Evan sank into a chair opposite Barney, relieved and terrified at the same time.

"I know how you feel," Barney said wearily. "Your mother's like a tornado passing through. Some things are left standing, but a lot of things are beaten to the ground."

Evan was afraid of the answer to the next question, but had to ask it. "So, how long are you…" He rephrased his query diplomatically. "How long can you stay?"

Barney pointed toward the kitchen. "Oh, your mother has every intention of staying through Christmas."

CHAPTER FOURTEEN

"THEY CANNOT STAY HERE!" Evan whispered urgently to Beazie as he stood over the toaster, waiting for the English muffin to pop. He'd sent his mother out to sit with Barney while he helped Beazie. "I don't care what you told her."

She arranged cups and cream and sugar on a tray and gave him a stern look. "Evan, they're your parents!" she whispered back. "And it's Christmas!"

"I know that! But this isn't the safest place to be. I'll put them up at the Yankee Inn. Jackie will see that they're well taken care of."

"They want to be here with you!"

"Well, they can't! They don't know anything about Blaine's criminal connections, or his connections to you. I'm just afraid one of us will say or do something that'll *really* ruin their Christmas."

"Carstairs and his guys have probably gone home to their own families for Christmas," she argued.

He gave her the look that innocent assumption deserved.

She sighed at him. "Didn't you see how happy your mother was to see you looking healthy and happy?"

He closed his eyes for patience and tried to approach this from another direction. "Beazie, I know you want this to be the perfect family Christmas because you haven't had one since you were ten, but it's not. We've made the house look like it, but the Christmas capsule is broken, Bea. We're dealing with reality now. I don't want my parents in the middle of this."

She studied him with a curious detachment he wasn't used to seeing in her. Usually there was such strong emotion in everything she did.

"Are you sure that's it?" she asked.

"What do you mean?" he demanded.

"I mean, I think you don't really want your life back. You're going to live out the rest of it in martyrdom after your failure with Blaine. Or his failure with you. The great big-brother-cop was supposed to be able to fix everything and he couldn't, so you've just…retired."

BEAZIE STOOD HER GROUND as he came across the kitchen toward her. She probably didn't have the right to speak to him so candidly, but her instincts told her she was right.

She'd never seen him look this angry. She made herself keep eye contact, when all she really wanted to do was run. He stopped with a mere inch between them, his hands on his hips, his expression lethal.

"What makes you the great judge of character and motivation, when you didn't even know Blaine was married? Or crooked? Why do you feel qualified to judge *me?*"

"First of all," she said under her breath, "if your

parents don't know about Blaine, I wouldn't mention his being crooked at the top of your voice. And I'm not judging you, I'm simply telling you what I've observed because I know you.''

"No, you don't.''

"Yes, I do. Maybe you can make love with me and still not understand me, but it's different for me.''

"I understand you,'' he insisted, folding his arms. "I know that you never seem sure of your feelings for me from one minute to the next. You make love as though you're physically a part of me, then when it's over, you look at me as though you're waiting for me to rabbit like your stepfathers.''

She hated that he'd seen that. He was a gentle, generous lover and she did trust him. But old conditioning was hard to break.

"You're entitled to walk away anytime you want,'' she said, afraid he'd see how much she didn't want that. "We haven't made any promises. You don't owe me anything.''

She turned back to the coffee, but he grabbed her arm and gave it a small shake, probably to make sure she was listening.

"You sleep in my arms,'' he said, his eyes turbulent. "That's a promise if there ever was one.'' Then he dropped his hands from her as though he was too angry to trust himself to touch her another moment. "After we've had our coffee, I'm taking them to the inn. And I don't want them to suspect that we've had this conversation.''

"Then, maybe you should smile and try not to look so much like Herod."

He'd started back toward the toaster, but at the accusation that he resembled the Roman emperor, he stopped to turn and stare at her. *"Herod?"* he demanded.

She nodded. "The man who tried to kill Christmas. I'm taking this out to your parents. Hurry up with the muffins."

Beazie decided she was already in love with Alice and Barney Turner. She saw the maternal concern in Alice's eyes as she talked to Evan, asked about his work, about the mill project and the homeless shelter.

"Jackie told us how much time you've volunteered on it," Barney said. "That's a very fine thing."

Evan shrugged off the praise. "The budget to put it up was pretty small. A lot of volunteers have been involved."

"Jackie said you two were planning to get married before Christmas," Alice said, tiring of the work discussion. "Were you not going to tell me?"

"We were going to call you today," Evan replied, with a look in Beazie's direction that asked her to confirm that.

"That's right," Beazie said, playing the loving fiancée. "We...we had to confirm a date with Father Chabot first."

"What is it?" Alice asked.

"Now that you're here," Beazie replied quickly, "we can set it."

Alice shook her head regretfully. "I can't believe

Evan never brought you home. I'd have loved to meet you earlier.''

"Oh..." Beazie smilingly dismissed the past. "We were so on-again off-again, neither of us sure what we wanted. I worked all the time and he was always busy. I guess I just didn't realize how in love I was until he left to come here.''

"But that was a year ago," Barney noted with a frown.

Beazie shrugged. "I tend to be hardheaded."

"Amen," Evan said softly.

His mother gave him a scolding look. "We taught you to be a gentleman."

"Can I get you another muffin?" Beazie asked, getting to her feet as she watched Barney polish off the last bite.

Barney gestured her to sit down. "No, thank you. I'm fine.''

"More coffee?''

"No. Sit, girl. No need to wait on me, anyway. Alice never does.''

"What?" Alice turned to him in playful indignation. "I'm like your personal slave from the minute your feet hit the floor in the morning until you turn off the light at night. 'Allie, where's the paper?' 'Allie, have you seen my keys?' 'Allie, is there any more—'''

"I'm sure they get the picture." Barney stopped her with a long-suffering sigh. "If you wouldn't keep things where I can't find them...''

Beazie forgot her quarrel with Evan for a moment in her delight with his parents. Love for each other showed clearly in their eyes, but the playful accusations went on. She turned to Evan, smiling over their byplay.

He was momentarily distracted by affection for his parents, then seemed to remember his determination to have them out of the house when coffee was over.

"If you two can stop arguing long enough to listen to me," he said, interrupting them, "I think it might be a good idea if we—"

He was cut off again by the doorbell.

"Jeez, Louise!" he said, getting up to answer. "You'd think I'd put up an Open House sign or something."

Alice giggled and turned to Barney with a conspiratorial wink.

"I think we should have told him," he said in a low rumble, looking a little concerned. "Maybe even *asked* if it was all right with him—foreign as that concept of asking permission is to you."

Alice elbowed him. "He'll love it. Trust me."

"I trust you," Barney said. "But your average for being right is no better than anyone else's."

A woman's squeal came from the front door, followed by youthful shrieks of delight and a man's cheerful shout. "Evan! Hey, buddy! Good to see you!"

Whatever Evan responded was drowned out by the children's giggles.

Beazie wasn't sure what was going on, but she stood, guessing they were going to need more coffee. Before she could turn in the direction of the kitchen, however, Evan appeared with a towheaded little boy in each arm. One was slender with pixieish features and gangly legs. The other was younger, plumper, and a chatterbox.

"There's the surprise!" Alice said, coming to stand beside Beazie. "We were going to come together, but Clay worked until early this morning, and Dad and I wanted to be on the road by then. He gets restless, you know."

"*I* get restless?" Barney challenged.

One of the little guys in Evan's arms was talking excitedly about a near accident.

"An' there was ice an' we almost drove off the road into a fence!" He leaned out of Evan's arms to mime holding tightly to a steering wheel. When he noticed Beazie had been added to the audience, he revved up his performance a notch and made the sound of brakes screeching. Evan winced against the noise, as did the boy in his other arm. "Then Uncle Clay turned really hard and we didn't crash." He sounded almost disappointed.

Beazie's glance bounced off the pretty blond woman behind Evan and the nice-looking, dark-haired man at her side—apparently Uncle Clay. He was several inches shorter than Evan, but appeared to be thickly built beneath his camel-hair overcoat.

She recognized the woman from the picture Evan had shown her of Blaine and his family. Her heart bumped uncomfortably against her ribs.

This was Sheila.

"Who are you?" the boy asked Beazie, leaning out of Evan's arms toward her, the question one of interest rather than suspicion.

"I'm Beazie," she replied, reminding herself that these people had no idea she'd dated their father-husband-son. She forced herself to smile in a manner befitting Evan's fiancée. "I'm glad you weren't hurt," she said to the little boy, whose pale blue eyes looked directly into hers. "You must be Mark. Or Mattie?"

"Mattie," he replied, then pointed to his quieter older brother. "That's Mark." Then he pointed behind Evan. "And that's my mom. And that's Uncle Clay."

Sheila came around Evan to offer Beazie her hand. She was beautiful and gracious, and Beazie wondered why Blaine ever would have wanted another woman's company. But she made herself stop thinking about it, for fear the truth would appear in her eyes.

"I'm Sheila, Evan's sister-in-law," Sheila said.

Before Beazie could open her mouth, Alice came up to her. "Sheila, this is Beazie, Evan's fiancée."

Sheila gasped. "Fiancée?"

"They're getting married before Christmas."

"Oh my God!" Sheila threw her arms around Beazie and hugged her tightly. "You're getting married? I can't believe it! I thought he intended to spend his entire life being gorgeous and inscrutable."

"Gorgeous?" Clay asked in teasing disbelief. "I don't think he's gorgeous. Passably handsome, maybe, if you discount the fact that he's too tall, too fit, and too...too..."

"Smart?" Evan suggested helpfully. "Clever? Insightful?"

Clay came forward to shake his hand, a grin breaking through. "I was going to say difficult, but I am a guest in your home." Then he grew serious again. "You're really getting married?"

"He is!" Alice replied. "The mayor herself told us. Can you believe it? He says he was going to call us tomorrow."

"When's the wedding?" Sheila asked. "We can't stay past Christmas because my parents are coming to Boston the morning of the twenty-seventh."

Mattie hugged Evan noisily. "We're gonna stay with you until after Santa Claus comes!" he said, sparkling with excitement. "We get to have you and Santa Claus at the same time! Isn't that cool?"

Beazie saw whatever hope Evan held out that he could send his parents—and now his sister-in-law and nephews—to the inn go down in flames. His eyes seemed to melt as he hugged the child to him.

"How about that."

"We brought sleeping bags," Sheila said. "And Mom and I are going to buy food and fix everything. You two won't have to lift a finger."

"Okay. Well." Evan put the boys down. "Beazie, why don't you show Mom and Dad to their room, and Clay and I will go get everybody's bags."

"Come on, Grandpa!" The boys pulled Barney laboriously out of his chair.

"I should help…" He pointed toward Evan.

"We can handle it, Dad," Evan said. "Go on up. Have a nap or something. You must have gotten up early this morning to be here already."

When Barney complied, Evan grabbed Clay by the arm and led him outside.

IN THE PRIVACY OF THE DRIVEWAY, with the hatch of Clay's Blazer shielding them from view from the house, Evan told Clay the whole story of Beazie's arrival at the mill, her connection to Blaine, Carstairs's pursuit of her, and the suspicions Evan had but couldn't quite confirm.

"I'm going mildly nuts," Evan confided. "My parents and Sheila have no idea Blaine was involved in dirty deals, or that he was unfaithful to Sheila. I've got to get them out of here, in case Carstairs comes back, but if I insist they stay at the inn, they'll suspect something's up."

"That's always been your problem," Clay said, handing him a bag. It was made of pastel tapestry and was very, very heavy. "You never do anything simply. You can't just fall in love with a nice girl, you have to find a nice girl who's being chased by killers." Clay handed him a train case that matched the set, then peered over the top of the hatch to make sure they were still alone and asked quietly, "*Is* there really a wedding?"

"Eventually. Maybe."

Clay blinked. "Maybe?"

"Well, no, but yes."

"Ah. That clarifies it."

"I love her," Evan said, realizing it was impossible to explain something he didn't entirely understand. That had been Beazie's criticism—he didn't understand her. "She loves me. But we have issues.

And it's been a turbulent time and hard to focus. My friend's young daughter misunderstood a conversation with Beazie and told everyone we were getting married. That made sense to them, because I'd explained Beazie's presence here by saying she was an old girlfriend from Boston who couldn't live without me. And unfortunately, the folks met Jackie, my boss's wife, when they stopped for breakfast before coming to the house—everybody knows everybody here—and she told them we're getting married. So far, I haven't been able to straighten that out.''

Clay nodded with a half smile. "Now, issues I understand. Sheila and I have those.''

"How's that going? Did you ever ask her out?''

"Yeah. We went to dinner and a show.''

"Did you tell her how you feel?''

"No.''

Evan shifted his weight impatiently. "Why not?''

"Because she might tell me I'm an idiot and hit me with something.''

"Well, big deal. Somebody's doing that to you all the time.''

Clay braced a bag on the rim of the trunk while reaching farther inside for the boys' backpacks. But he still took a moment to give Evan a dirty look. "Could you save your stand-up routine for another time. This is my future we're talking about.''

"Then, have the guts to tell her the truth.''

Clay hooked the backpacks on one shoulder and got a firm grip on the bag. "Good advice from Mr. I'm-getting-married-maybe-yes-maybe-no-we're-not-even-really-engaged Braga!''

"Are you going to criticize," Evan asked, "or are you going to help me keep everyone safe?"

"If it was any other time," Clay said, "we could call some guys from the precinct. They'd still do anything for you. But it's Christmas."

"Right, I know. And I appreciate that, of course, but I've got my own guys."

"You do?"

"Yeah. They work with me."

Clay looked worried. "You mean plumbers? Repairmen?"

"Yeah. Don't underestimate them. They run every morning, they're all strong and tough."

"Actually, running sounds like a really good idea."

Evan winged him with the train case. "We're going to be fine. We just have to have a strategy."

"That's probably what Custer said."

"Clay…"

"Listen, I have to tell you one more thing before we go back inside." Clay rested his bag on the lip of the trunk. "I did find something in Gordon Hathaway's bank account."

"Yeah?"

"Two hundred thousand dollars," he said, a deep line between his eyebrows, "deposited on June eleventh, last year."

Evan's heart thumped. "The day after the accident. That means…" His eyes locked with Clay's as the truth hit home. "It's the money from Blaine's gym bag. So the car didn't catch fire as a result of the impact, if he was able to retrieve it."

"Hathaway probably set the fire. And the black Dodge Ram you thought you saw that was never found?"

Evan waited.

"Shows up on a list of things stolen from a Back Bay address."

"By whom?"

"Never turned up a perp. All I know is the owner was a woman named Claudia Boughton."

"You're kidding."

"Why? What does that mean?" Clay asked.

"She was Gordon Hathaway's ex."

Evan stood still a moment, absorbing all this information. He rubbed his forehead, where a headache was beginning to thump.

"Let me run this scenario by you," he said to Clay. "See if it makes any sense."

Clay sat on the rim of the trunk. "I'm listening."

"Okay. Hathaway was on the tape I told you about, where these guys are planning a hit."

"Right."

"He knew Blaine, he borrowed his ex-wife's truck to hit us, then had his ex buy Blaine's franchise to cover up the loss of the two hundred thousand. It's clear he had to be into loan sharks or something himself."

"Okay. Makes sense."

"What if *he* was the go-between for Blaine and the loan shark? What if Blaine was meeting him that day at the club, maybe to give him the money to pay off the loan sharks, but I found the money first and dragged him off?"

"Then...Hathaway saw you," Clay said, picking up the thread of possibilities, "and followed you. Took a parallel road and, aware that you now knew about the money...God...hit you at the intersection, hoping to kill both of you." Clay frowned. "But, wait. It doesn't make sense that he borrowed the truck to kill you if he was expecting Blaine to meet him there. He didn't know you were going to drag him away."

"Maybe he intended to get the money from Blaine, then kill him, anyway. If he intended to keep the money, he had to get rid of Blaine."

Evan was trembling inside, everything playing over in his mind with the new knowledge woven in...the strong possibility that he was not the reason Blaine was dead.

"Hathaway convinced the loan shark that the money burned up in the car," Evan went on, "and kept it for himself. Nobody knew. It was perfect."

"But why send you the tape? Why would he want you to know they'd plotted a murder that never took place?"

Evan considered, then shook his head. "I'm not sure, but I'd say revenge against the guys who offed him. Apparently he did something to tip them off that he'd stolen the money, because they killed him. He must have known I'd been a cop. Maybe he thought I could put it together."

Clay ran a hand over his face. "What do you want to do with this information?"

"There's nothing sure enough yet to give any-body, but I'm going to get it. You keep your eyes open, okay? When it comes to the crunch, we're sending everybody to the inn.'' At Clay's raised eyebrow, he added, ''The Yankee Inn. My boss's wife owns it. We'll leave some guys with them.''

Clay grinned, got to his feet and picked up the bag. ''Your plumbers and repairmen.''

''Don't scoff at my guys or I'll tell Sheila you're in love with her.'' Evan stepped back with the tapestry bags while Clay slammed the hatch closed and made a scornful sound.

''Go ahead. I'll tell your mom you're not really getting married.''

There was nothing to do but concede. ''We'll both keep our mouths shut, agreed?''

Clay nodded. ''Agreed.''

''You keep everyone entertained with your scintillating conversation, and I'll call my guys.''

BEAZIE CHOPPED GREEN ONIONS and radishes and added them to a bowl of lettuce with grated carrots and red cabbage. Right beside her, Sheila sliced tomatoes and chatted about how happy she was to be in Maple Hill, how thrilled the boys were to see their uncle again and what a wonderful thing it was to have family. Alice and Barney were napping, Clay and the boys were outside building snowmen, and Evan was making phone calls, inviting their friends over for a casual night of pizza and salad to meet his parents.

Beazie wanted to die. The last thing in the world she wanted was to have to look into Sheila's eyes, yet Sheila seemed determined to make a friend of her and to fill her in about Evan's wonderful family. She was just coming out of a long period of grief, she said, and was suddenly more aware of what she had than what she'd lost.

"The boys seem to really like Clay," Beazie said, hoping to divert the conversation from the topic of Blaine.

"He's very good with them." Sheila gave her a sidelong smile. "Treats them like his buddies, but he's also able to make them listen without a lot of fuss. I don't know what we'd have done without him. He used to come over with Evan after Blaine died, to mow my lawn, do small household repairs, help with the kids. Then, when Evan left, he continued to come." She sighed as she placed the tomatoes artfully around the edge of the salad. "It's becoming romantic," she said quietly, "but I'm not sure if I'm responding because I'm falling in love, or because I'm just so...grateful."

Beazie understood her confusion, but hated the thought of Sheila depriving herself of having Clay in her life. "If you're feeling romantic," she said, sprinkling the green onions on top of the salad, "it doesn't really matter why, does it? Gratitude engenders love. I mean, who *wouldn't* fall in love with a good man. Don't overthink it." It occurred to her that she should listen to her own advice.

Sheila nodded thoughtfully. "I know. You were smart enough to do that, weren't you? Evan's everybody's favorite person."

Beazie smiled, reaching for the plastic wrap to cover the bowl. "While I was helping Alice unpack, she told me you'd known Evan in Boston, and that when he left, you weren't ready to go. What made you decide to follow him out here? I mean...how did you know it was the right thing to do?''

Beazie put herself in that fictitious position and let herself work out how she might have felt, had she known him before. ''I guess I just finally came to my senses. I imagined the rest of my life without him and knew I'd be miserable. Nothing I was holding on to the old life for was making up for the loss of him beside me. So I came to him.''

''Wow,'' Sheila breathed longingly.

As Beazie turned to smile at Sheila, she saw Evan standing in the kitchen doorway. Judging by his expression, he'd heard her fantasy. He raised an eyebrow, a silent comment she couldn't quite interpret, except to know that she'd probably further confused an already entangled relationship.

''Everyone's coming,'' he reported. ''Six-thirty.'' He glanced at his watch. ''Anything I can do?''

''Just order the pizza,'' Beazie said.

Sheila put the covered salad bowl in the refrigerator. ''I can't believe you were able to collect all your friends at the last minute like that, this close to Christmas.''

''I just stressed the importance of...meeting my family,'' he said.

Beazie guessed the importance he'd stressed was the help he needed to keep his family safe. The Wonders were like a posse coming to one another's defense.

''Anything particular on the pizza?'' he asked.

"A small Canadian bacon and pineapple for the boys," Sheila said. "I like anything."

"Bea?"

"No anchovies," Beazie replied. "Anything else is great."

"Okay. Mom and Dad are going to pick up soda and beer. Anything else?"

"Hot pepper flakes and Parmesan. And napkins," Beazie said. "And probably paper plates and cups. I'm sure we don't have enough to go around. And something for dessert."

"Jackie and Mariah are bringing dessert. Is that it?"

"Yes, I think so."

He nodded. "Got it." He blew them a kiss and disappeared.

"You are *so* lucky," Sheila said, staring after Evan. "I used to wish I'd met him first."

Beazie leaned a hip on the counter, surprised by that revelation.

"I met Blaine in college and he was charming and clever, and I was so shy myself that his ease with people really impressed me. When he brought me home to meet his family, I found it hard to believe he and Evan were even related. I mean, the affection was there, but they were so different. I used to think that Evan was too serious, too private. Then I began to realize that he just…held his emotions close. Eventually I learned that Blaine could be freer with his feelings because they were more superficial."

Beazie did her best to conceal surprise. She'd

thought from what Evan had told her that Sheila had adored Blaine.

Sheila smiled wryly. "But that's not what we should be talking about when you're about to be married."

Afraid that Sheila might suspect any interest on her part, Beazie groped for the right response. Sheila, however, was eager to share.

"It's not that I want to tear Blaine down," she went on in visible anguish, "but I can't talk about him honestly to his family, because they're all so convinced he was a paragon. But...you didn't know him, so it's easier to talk to you about him. And I *need* to talk to someone, because if I'm ever going to move on, I have to get it out. If Evan loves you, you've got to be trustworthy. And you're the closest thing to a sister I'm ever going to have."

Beazie wasn't sure what made her suggest to Sheila that she go on. Partly, it was because Sheila considered her a sister, and Beazie had lived her entire life wishing desperately that she had one. And partly it soothed her guilt to know that Sheila had been unhappy with Blaine.

"He wasn't what he seemed," Sheila blurted, as though that had been stuffed inside her, and expelling it took much effort. "He wasn't abusive or mean, he was simply...I don't know...uninvolved, I guess. He loved his family, and he loved the boys, but I think if he'd had to make a choice between them and something he wanted, he'd have chosen what he wanted. He loved me in the beginning because I looked good on his arm and gave him two boys in a row—and that appealed to his masculinity. You know, he used to tease Evan about his tough-guy profession, but I think he was secretly jealous. Not that a man who sells insurance is any less a man than a cop is, but I think he thought so. Probably because he knew how thin the veneer of his character was. Blaine tried to surpass Evan by making more money, having more things.''

She poured herself another cup of coffee and heaved a sigh. ''Anyway, I finally asked Blaine to slow down a little. He worked all the time, nights and weekends, and we never saw him except when he came home to shower and sleep.'' She closed her eyes. ''He told me work fulfilled him. That if I needed company, I could get it elsewhere, as long as I was discreet and came home at night. But he wasn't slowing down.''

She opened her eyes to look into Beazie's, her demolished self-esteem visible there. ''I think if he hadn't died a week later, I eventually would have left him. Poor Blaine. If he'd gone to the game at Fenway Park that day instead of to the gym with Evan, everyone's life would be different today.''

Fenway Park! The tape had revealed a plan to get rid of the intended victim at Fenway Park. Blaine!

That possibility, and the knowledge that on some of the nights and weekends Sheila had thought Blaine was working, he'd probably been with her, served to make Beazie feel physically sick. This conversation wasn't doing as much for her conscience as she'd hoped.

Sheila opened the back door and drew a deep breath. Beazie quelled the urge to run out into the night and keep running, whether Carstairs was out there or not.

CHAPTER FIFTEEN

BART AND HALEY and the baby, Hank and Jackie and their four children, and Cam and Mariah and Brian and Ashley arrived en masse, just as the pizza truck pulled into the driveway.

Beazie and Sheila gathered up coats, hats and scarves and carried them upstairs, and Evan introduced everyone to his mother and father. His parents beamed, fussed over the children, told stories about him to his friends, while he managed to find seats for everyone. He congratulated himself on having asked every family to bring a pair of folding chairs.

Space was tight in the small room, but no one seemed to notice. His mother had always loved having a houseful of people, and his friends personified the always-room-for-one-more principle.

"You want me to take those coats up?" Evan heard Sheila ask Beazie.

Beazie shook her head. "I'll do it, if you'll put the pizza and salad on the nook table so we can serve buffet style."

"Right."

Sheila hurried off to the kitchen, and Beazie stood at the foot of the stairs, an armful of coats hugged to her as she watched the room filled with people talking and laughing. A small smile played around her lips.

He came up behind her and had to whisper in her ear to be heard. "What are you thinking?"

She drew a breath, the smile widening just a little. "That this is what a house should sound like," she said, indicating the crowd with the angle of her chin. "Laughter, men's rumbling conversation, women's eager voices, babies babbling, children saying "Mom, Mom, Mom" until they get somebody's attention."

Her smile waned as she spoke, and he couldn't equate the touching observation with the sudden sadness in her eyes.

"Then, why does that upset you?" he asked.

She gave him a reluctant look, then said quietly, "Can you come upstairs with me for a minute?"

"Sure." He followed her to his room, where she dropped the coats on the bed, then straightened them out somewhat. He couldn't tell if she was trying to prevent the garments from getting wrinkled, or avoid telling him whatever she wanted to tell him.

At last she faced him. Folding her arms defensively, she said, "They can't stay here."

He blinked in surprise. "Didn't we have this conversation, and weren't you on the other side?"

"I don't mean your mother and father," she corrected, looking away. "I mean Sheila and Clay and the boys."

"I thought we were all family and this was Christmas."

"You said it yourself. They don't know anything

about Blaine, and something could happen that'll ruin their Christmas. And they're not safe here, anyway. You should put them up at the inn.''

He thought he was beginning to understand. He'd been aware from the moment Clay and Sheila and the boys arrived that this could be difficult for Beazie, but he'd been distracted from it by what Clay had revealed.

"Sheila getting to you?" he asked gently.

She tipped her head back in exasperation. "She's taken a liking to me," she complained, her voice raspy with distress. "She's pouring her heart out to me about Blaine. Did you know they weren't happy?"

"I'd guessed," he admitted, "but I didn't know. She always put up a good front at family get-togethers and for my parents.''

"Well, she knows he was fooling around!" she said in a loud whisper, reaching around him to push the half-open bedroom door closed. It was now dark in the small room except for moonlight coming in through the window. "She just doesn't know he was fooling around with *me!* I mean, even though I never slept with him, he was fooling around on her with me! So she's telling me how sad and hurt she was because I'm the closest thing she has to a sister. A sister! Me!"

Her lips trembled dangerously, and he took hold of her arms. "Okay. Take it easy. First of all, you didn't know, remember? It wasn't your fault. He used you like he used everybody. And secondly, if you and I are coming together, and we're going to be looking at Sheila and Clay across a holiday table for the rest of our lives, we should probably come clean and try to resolve it.''

She shook off his hands. ''You're not listening to me,'' she complained. ''I can't do that to her. It's Christmas. This is your family.''

He jammed his hands in his pockets, having difficulty standing firm. ''So, you can tell me that I have to confront my problems with Blaine and explain things to the family, but you're somehow exempt from doing that?''

The determination in her eyes wobbled. Her chin went up a notch. ''That's different.''

''Because it's you rather than me?''

''Because you're trying to save yourself, I'm trying to save *them*.''

That was so blatantly self-serving and so unlike her that he had to smile.

She huffed and turned away from him. He turned her back and made himself be frank.

''You can't do it,'' he said, ''because your concept of family is some perfect, tightly connected unit that speaks with one voice and marches into the future with arms linked. Well, that isn't it at all. It's just people holding on to each other to try to make some headway. It's stumbling and falling and being selfish and unfair and sometimes just plain wrong. It's good people and misdirected people and aggravating people all mixed into a pot. And sometimes, there's even a bad one. But you don't get to decide you won't have anything to do with them just because it's hard

266 MAN WITH A MIRACLE

to cope. You have strings that connect you from way back."

"*You* have strings. They're your family. I just sort of wandered in by accident and messed everything up."

"You wandered in by accident," he said, taking her face in his hands, just beginning to understand this, "and somehow through all the insanity that surrounds you, gave me my life back. I know you love me, and that's made me determined to get those guys, help my family understand the truth about Blaine, and make a foundation for our life together."

She went into his arms and wrapped hers tightly around him. "What if it alienates them? What if...?"

"It won't. I know these people. Now, come on. We've got a houseful of guests. And I've got to talk to the guys."

She tried to push him toward the door. "You go ahead. I'm just going to curl into a fetal position under the bed and—"

He caught her hand and drew her after him as he pulled the door open.

Sheila stood on the threshhold, her face pale, her eyes wounded. Beazie expelled a quiet groan. "You heard."

"Yes," Sheila whispered. They stared at each other for several, miserable moments.

"I'm sorry," Sheila finally said. "I was...I was coming to ask you where to find a pizza cutter because there isn't one in the utensil drawer and I...heard you."

"Sheila." Evan put an arm around her shoulders

and one around Beazie. "I'm so sorry. Blaine told Beazie he was single, and she had no reason to believe otherwise."

Beazie caught her hand. "Please believe me," she said urgently. "We met at a party. He was there alone, no wedding ring, no…"

Sheila squeezed her hand. "You don't have to explain Blaine to me," she said. "It's all right. I'm sorry my confidences made you so uncomfortable."

"Only because I didn't want to hurt you."

There were tears in Beazie's eyes, and Sheila wrapped her arms around her. "You can't. I told you I'm moving forward. The past can't hurt me anymore." Sheila drew away, but kept an arm around Beazie as she looked up at Evan in concern. "Though from something else I overheard, I gather there's more of a problem than that?"

Evan's mother appeared behind them, her cheeks flushed, her eyes bright. "I love your friends!" she said as they all turned to face her. "What's the matter?" she asked, noting their grave expressions.

"Nothing," Evan said quickly. "We were just talking. How's it going down there?"

"Well, we're all starving," she said. "Are you coming down to host?"

"I'll be there in a minute. Meanwhile, can you help Bea and Sheila do that, while the guys and I have a brief meeting?" He started them down the stairs.

"A meeting?" his mother repeated, stopping to look back at him. "About what? This is a party."

"Just about work," Evan said, making a shooing

motion with his hand to encourage her to keep moving. "It'll only take a few minutes. Start without us."

"I put the pizza in the oven to keep it warm," Sheila said. "We'll have salads first and hold the pizza till you finish, but don't be too long."

Evan stopped Sheila at the bottom of the stairs and wrapped her in a hug. "You're an angel, Sheila Turner," he said, grateful that she hadn't tortured Beazie with what she'd learned. "He never deserved you. Clay does, though."

She kissed his cheek. "Thank you for putting him in my path. Now, let me get dinner moving before the troops begin to riot."

Sheila headed for the kitchen, but Beazie caught Evan's sleeve before he could get away. "What are you going to talk to the guys about?" she asked worriedly. "You're not planning heroics, are you?"

He kissed her quickly and grinned. "I don't plan them, they just come naturally to me."

When he tried to walk away again, she yanked him back. "Don't pretend my concern doesn't matter. If you're taking these guys on, I want to know what your plans are."

He stopped to give her a slow, lingering kiss. "So far, I have no plans. That's what the meeting's about. And stop worrying. This used to be my job."

"But it isn't anymore," she said, her eyes brimming with tears. "And I dreamed that you were shot three times."

"Dreams are not reality."

"I know, but it scared me, anyway. Evan…"

"Bea, come on. You've got to trust me to know

what I'm doing. I'll be right back." He pushed her toward the kitchen and went to collect Bart, Hank, Cam and Clay.

"WHY IN THE HELL didn't you tell us this before?" Cam asked.

They were gathered in the cold garage, surrounded by gardening tools and painting supplies. They sat on overturned boxes and buckets, and Evan stood in the middle of the group, explaining the plan he'd just assured Beazie he didn't have. The only thing he left out was the connection Blaine had to the whole mess.

"I wasn't sure what Beazie was up against, and what you weren't involved in couldn't hurt you. But now the weather's cleared, even in New York, and I'm sure they're going to be back. I'd thought if it was just Beazie and me, I could handle their return, but then my family decided it would be fun to surprise me for Christmas, and that puts a different light on it."

They nodded understanding.

"What do you want to do?" Hank asked.

"I'd like to send my parents, my sister-in-law and the kids, and Bea to the inn. Clay'll be there with them, but I'd like him to have a little backup."

They nodded again.

"How soon do you think they'll be back?"

"The way the weather improved today, I'd say late tonight or early in the morning."

"And what about you?" Cam asked.

"I'll be fine," Evan replied. "I was a cop, remember? I'm going to the shelter to wait for them to come back. I'm going to get them to admit everything in front of a reliable witness, then take 'em down.''

"And how are you going to know when they're coming?'' Bart asked.

"Randy's known about this from the beginning because he helped when Beazie collapsed in my office. I just called him, and he and a friend of his are going to stake out the edge of town and call when they see the red SUV.''

"You make it sound simple,'' Clay said. "But you know how those things go. There are variables you haven't even thought of. You can't wait alone.''

"I want you protecting the family.''

"Fine. But you're going to need help.''

"Cam, Clay and Bart will stay with the family,'' Hank said. "And I'll stay with you.''

"Why do you get to stay with him?'' Cam rose from an overturned box of floor tiles. "I'm his partner.''

"Because I'm in better shape. And I'm your boss.''

"Oh, stow it. You can't throw your weight around in personal matters.''

Hank stood to face him down. "We need more guys with the family. We're talking two old people, two little boys—''

"Careful who you call old,'' Barney said, walking into the garage from the kitchen. "I want to know what's going on,'' he said, "and I want in.''

Evan ran a hand over his face, wondering what it was like to have the freedom to do what you wanted without interference.

Cam invited Barney to sit on the box of tiles while everyone filled Barney in on their plan.

"Okay," Barney said. "Count me in to watch the family, and that'll free up one of you to go with Evan and Hank."

"Dad..." Evan began.

"Don't *Dad* me like you think I'm a couch potato and an old coot. I was in Vietnam for 18 months in my twenties. I have some training. And I've spent twenty of the past thirty-odd years as a swimming coach, and the past ten painting my house, mowing my lawn, patching my roof. I move with a kink, but when I get ahold of something, it doesn't get away."

There was a moment's silence, then Hank said, "I vote he's in."

It was quickly unanimous.

Barney gave Evan a superior lift of his eyebrow, then turned to Hank, who was refining their strategy.

THE PIZZA WAS GONE, the salad bowl empty and the younger children asleep, when Hank took over the meeting Jackie had intended to chair regarding the shelter, and explained instead about moving Evan's family to the inn.

Beazie, heart beginning to race, thought that was a sound idea. She couldn't believe it was all going to be over soon. She'd be rid of the threat that had shadowed her life for what felt like an eternity.

Evan caught her arm and drew her into the kitchen. It was cluttered with paper plates and cups, the sink filled with salad bowls and utensils.

"I think it's a good idea to send the family to the

inn," she said when he stopped her in the middle of the room. "I mean, those guys have to know where you live if they got the phone number from my call to Horie. And they'll probably go back to the shelter to find us. But if it's early in the morning…"

He put a finger to her lips to stop her. "I'd like you to go with them," he said. "Clay, my dad and Bart are going to make sure you're safe."

A round, ripe annoyance rose to the surface. "I'm not going with them. I want to stay with you and help you do this."

"No," he said simply.

She firmed her stance. "What do you mean, 'No,' in that pontifical tone? I'm staying. Carstairs wants *me*. I'm the danger. I'd…I'd…" She wasn't sure she could sell this, but she was going to try. "I'd be a danger to your parents and Sheila and the boys."

He knew precisely what she was doing and he smiled fractionally. "Nice try. You're going with them. I'll get your jacket." He tried to walk away, as though that settled it.

She caught his arm. "Don't. You can't make decisions for me, and frankly, if you think you'll be able to behave that way when we're married, I'm not sure I want to be your wife."

"Hopefully there won't be people threatening our lives when we're married," he said, removing her hand from his arm and kissing her knuckles. "Please, Bea. Get your jacket."

She went to the hook by the back door, grabbed her jacket and marched back to him. "All right, I'll go. But call Addie and tell her to put you back on her list, because you're an eligible bachelor again, buddy!''

She stormed out of the kitchen just as Bart walked in.

"Hooh!" Bart observed. "Not a happy camper."

"She wants to stay with me," Evan said, certain she was kidding about the bachelor remark. At least, he hoped so.

"We'll keep an eye on her," Bart promised.

"You'd better," Evan said. "She doesn't think very clearly when she's angry."

"Right. Everybody's ready to go. We're sending the wives and our kids to Gary and Parker's place. Jimmy and Glory are going over, too, just in case there's a problem. Chances are slim, but we want all bases covered."

"Good thinking."

Evan went out with Hank and Cam to wave off the small convoy.

Beazie sat in the back of his parents' car and refused to turn in his direction. He opened the rear door and leaned in, catching the front of her jacket when she would have moved away.

"I'm not talking to you!" she told him, her eyes hot and wounded.

"I didn't want to talk," he said, and used the fistful of coat to pull her to him. He kissed her until she struggled for air.

When he drew away, she socked his arm. He closed the door and waved his father on.

The cars headed down the driveway to the road—Clay and his father going to the inn, where Jackie had made arrangements for them, and Jackie and Haley driving Mariah and all the children to Gary and Parker's.

Evan, Hank and Cam stood in the driveway, watching the cars disappear.

"Do you remember a conversation we had a few weeks ago," Hank said, "where we predicted your demise at the hands of a woman?"

"Yeah."

"You insisted it wasn't going to happen," Cam happily reminded him.

"Yeah," he said.

Hank laughed. "When this is over, you owe all of us breakfast at the Barn."

They turned back to the house. "I seem to recall," Evan said, "that the winner of the bet had to buy everybody breakfast."

Hank clapped his shoulder. "You went down faster than any of us predicted. So we figure you owe *us*."

BEAZIE WAS BIDING HER TIME. Alice and Sheila shared a bed, and Beazie lay quietly atop the covers on a cot in the beautiful room decorated with wallpaper in a climbing ivy pattern. Though Alice and Sheila had changed into nightclothes, she'd remained fully dressed, shoes still on, hoping for an opportunity to get back to Evan. Clay and the boys shared the next room, while Barney sat out in the hall. Clay had taken the first watch and Barney relieved him at three a.m.

It was now almost five, and Beazie had run out of

ideas on how to escape without being stopped. She'd already checked the second-story window and found no convenient tree outside, no handy latticework to climb down.

Then she heard the very quiet ring of Clay's cell phone. He was up in a moment, and she heard the door to the hall being yanked open.

She scrambled quietly out of bed and went to the door to listen through the old-fashioned keyhole.

"...saw the red SUV," Clay was saying. "It was headed downtown. Randy wanted us to know. He's on his way in to help. You stay with the family, I'm going to the shelter. I'm low on gas, though. Can I take your car?"

"Sure."

Beazie heard Barney go into their room, presumably to find his keys, and saw her chance. She left the room on tiptoe, then ran down the hall to the stairs and raced across the empty lobby to the door and out into the night.

All the doors of Barney's station wagon were locked, but she tried the hatch door on the chance Evan and Clay had failed to lock up the previous morning when they'd unloaded bags. Yes!

It gave under her tug, and she climbed in and closed the door behind her.

CHAPTER SIXTEEN

EVAN HAD DONNED HIS WORK CLOTHES, turned on all the lights in the shelter and applied the last strip of the teapot border while standing on the kitchen counter. Randy had called to let him know that the red SUV was on its way in, and he was doing his best to look as though he'd come to work early and suspected nothing.

Cam hid in the broom closet, and Hank waited in the shadows of the common room, with its view of the street.

Evan tried to forget that Beazie had told him to consider himself an eligible bachelor again, and that she'd punched him after he'd kissed her. That had been temper at work, nothing more. Or so she hoped.

He rather liked having his house full of family and friends; liked the indulgent, affectionate way they looked at Beazie; liked her easy way with his nephews, his sister-in-law and his friends. For a man who'd tried hard to retire from the world for a while, he would have expected to be upset at finding himself in the thick of complex relationships again. Instead, he welcomed them. He was ready to put Blaine and the guilt behind him and move ahead. Having somewhere to put the blame for Blaine's and Gordon's deaths would give him a good start.

He could talk Beazie around; he knew he could.

"SUV pulling up," Hank's voice warned from the common room. "Heads up, guys."

Evan had left the front door unlocked, and heard it open now. Footsteps sounded, and he turned in feigned surprise to see Carstairs, the big guy Beazie thought might be Brick, and Ricky, the hard-case kid in the fleece-lined denim jacket.

Despite the grimness of the situation and all that was at stake, he had to make an effort not to laugh at their expressions. They were not happy. It must have been a bad couple of days on the road to and from Buffalo.

He was sure of that the next moment, when the big guy came and grabbed his ankle and yanked him off the counter. A year and a half of learning to protect his right thigh allowed him to land on his left side.

He expressed indignation as he got to his feet.

"We're very unhappy with you," Carstairs said, coming toward him with murder in his eyes. "Beatrice Deadham didn't go to Buffalo, did she?"

Good, he thought. *Name names. Give me details. Make this conversation worth something.*

He shrugged innocently. "She told me she was going to Buffalo."

The big guy punched him in the gut. Hot pain roiled in his stomach as he doubled over.

"No, she didn't," Carstairs said in a congenial voice, grabbing a fistful of Evan's hair and yanking his head up. The big guy grabbed his arms and pulled him back. "She came to you with the tape, didn't she. Because—and I didn't know this until I realized you'd stiffed us and I began to check on you—you're Turner's brother. And you used to be a cop."

So. No more point in pretending.

"That's right. Cambridge Division. We have good cops there—unlike South Boston, where you come from."

"Hey. I have a lifestyle to support that isn't going to happen on a captain's salary. I collared a loan shark a couple of years ago. He was out before I was finished with the paperwork, and I decided maybe we could help each other." Carstairs smiled cheerfully. "He provides me with a monthly supplement, and I see that no one notices him—or if they do, he isn't there when they go looking for him. It's worked well, and I'm not anxious to let it all go."

"You killed Hathaway just to gain a little extra money every month?" he asked.

"No. Hathaway brought us a few clients and that was a good thing, but we killed him because he also took a few things away, namely the boss's girlfriend. I guess all in all that really *was* a good thing. If Hathaway hadn't taken her to Barbados, we wouldn't have known that he had a condo, a boat and a Swiss bank account. He ticked her off by buying another woman a drink when he thought she was napping in the condo, so she came back to the boss and told him what she'd seen. Nobody takes from the boss."

Evan ran through the list of loan sharks he remembered from his days on the force. It was short. He needed a name.

"Pinky Davis is possessive about his women?" he fished.

"Not Pinky Davis," Brick corrected, tightening his grip. "Army Petulio."

Carstairs gave the big guy a shove that freed Evan's arms. "Idiot! You never say his name!" Suddenly suspicious, Carstairs tore Evan's shirt open, expecting to find a wire. He was momentarily surprised when he didn't see one.

That was all Evan needed. He hit Carstairs with a right cross, then dodged as Brick reached for him. As he struggled with Brick, Evan heard the ominous *click* of a bullet being forced into a chamber.

It brought both of them to a dead stop. Ricky took aim at Evan's head, but before he could fire, Cam brought him down with a chop to the back of his neck.

Then Carstairs was up, but Evan was busy with the much bigger Brick. He heard Hank's "Don't bat an eye. I'm a bad aim and you could linger a long time."

It finally took a stomach punch, then a knee to Brick's chin to bring him down.

Breathing heavily from the exertion, Evan turned to see Hank holding the gun on Carstairs, and Ricky still out cold.

"Chief?" Evan shouted.

John Walther, Chief of Maple Hill's small police force, emerged from the mudroom off the kitchen, gun drawn. "I heard it all," he said.

"All right!" Cam held a foot on Ricky. "What do we do now?"

"You do nothing, gentlemen," a new voice said. A pudgy, bald man with glasses walked into the room and waved a pistol at them. "Or I blow you away, one by one."

Evan recognized the voice. The speaker sounded as if he had a cold, just like Beazie had said. Murray. The one member of the group who hadn't appeared in the shelter the day of Carstairs's visit.

"And I've been to Buffalo in December," Murray added with a sneeze. "My cold has turned into pneumonia, and I'm a very angry man."

BEAZIE WOULD HAVE BEEN FINE had Mattie not left a stuffed toy that squeaked in the back of the car. She rolled on it, trying to free the foot she'd got stuck under the seat, and flinched as the loud *ooga* sound reverberated throughout the confined space of the car. She felt the wagon stop abruptly, then pull over and stop again.

"It's just me, Clay," she said, sitting up, disgusted with herself.

"Beazie!" he exclaimed, looking at her in shock over the back of his seat. "What are you doing?"

"I had to come," she replied defensively. "I dreamed that Evan was shot three times, and I'm sure if I'm here that I can prevent it from happening."

"Beazie," he said more quietly. "He's got good backup. And he's the best there is. He'll be fine. I'm taking you back to the—"

"No!" she shouted. "No, Clay. If you turn the car

around, I'll jump out of the back, I swear. Just keep going. Evan might need you right now.''

''Okay, but if he comes down on me for this, I'm letting you take the blame.''

''Fine.''

''You won't think so when it happens.''

It was just a short quarter mile to the shelter.

''The red SUV!'' Beazie said in a worried whisper as they pulled up behind it. ''They're here.''

''You wait in the car,'' Clay ordered.

''I won't,'' she said, reaching for the hatch handle.

''Beazie, if you don't stay in the car, I'm not going in.''

She subsided, sure Evan needed him. And she could escape the car the moment Clay was inside.

Clay leaped out and ran lightly up the walk. He'd just disappeared inside and she was climbing out the back, when she heard the shots. One…Two… Three…

Her heart fell to her shoes and she was rooted to the spot, unable to take a step. She remembered in cold detail the dream where she'd been stuck in ice and strong arms had embraced her, trying to free her. Then she'd heard the shots, and Evan had collapsed on top of her.

Something inside her screamed ''No!'' and kept screaming as she finally made her leaden limbs move. She broke into a run as she reached the side-walk.

''Please, please, please!'' she prayed as she swung the door open and stopped just inside the room. A

man lay on the floor, blood all over him, while another man bent over him.

The world went dark for an instant, and she heard
herself scream Evan's name. She tried to go to him,
but a rough arm came around her throat, tipping her
slightly backward and threatening to cut off her air.

She heard a weird and ominous *click,* and felt
something cold against her temple. "Everybody back
off or she's gone," someone threatened.

It was so strange. Her brain was whirling, and she
felt as if none of her limbs would move, yet she saw
and heard things as though she were watching a high-
definition television. Colors were brilliant. Sound
was pure.

She recognized the voice as belonging to the
young man who'd shot Gordon, the one the others
on the tape had called Ricky.

And she noticed when Evan got to his feet that he
wasn't the one who'd been shot. Clay lay on the
floor, his face pinched in pain, blood all over his
shoulder. Cam took Evan's place at his side, holding
a handkerchief to a shoulder wound. There were several bullet holes in the newly painted wall and Murray stared disconsolately into the empty cylinder of
his revolver.

She felt elation, then immediate guilt. Pressure
was applied to the gun held to her head, and she
realized she should probably spare a little concern
for her own life.

"There are four of us," Evan said, holding everyone back. "You can't get away."

"But I've got your lady, man. That beats numbers. Unless you want to see her dead at your feet."

Carstairs, Brick and Murray, all bruised and looking eager to be gone, gathered behind Ricky.

Evan was telling her to be calm; she could read it in his eyes. But the paralysis was leaving her and she was absolutely terrified. Now that she had so much to lose, death seemed an ignominious insult.

"Put your hand out!" Ricky said to Beazie. Then to Evan he said, "I want the tape she took from Hathaway. Now!"

So he *didn't* know it wasn't admissible evidence.

Evan turned to Hank, who stood slightly apart from him. The police chief tried to step forward, but exchanged a look with Hank and changed his mind.

"Do it," Hank said quietly to Evan, a curious significance she didn't understand underlying his words.

Ricky must have sensed it, too, because she felt more tension than strength in the arm that held her.

Evan put the tape in her hand. Then, in a movement so quick she didn't know what was happening until it was over, he yanked her toward him and pushed her to the ground. A shot rang out, and she turned and raised her head just in time to see Ricky crumple to the floor. Hank aimed his smoking pistol at the other three.

"Don't," he threatened simply.

The chief elbowed Hank aside and held his own gun on the men. "God, Hank, you guys are a bunch of cowboys! Backup's coming."

Evan helped her to her feet and wrapped his arms around her. She felt his heart beat hard against her chest. His embrace was tight enough to meld her arms to her torso. Then he held her away from him, gave her a look that suggested repercussions later and dropped to his knees beside Clay.

"How're you doing?" he asked worriedly.

"I'm okay," Clay said feebly. "I think it's just a flesh wound, but it hurts like hell."

A siren announced the arrival of the chief's backup and an ambulance.

IT WAS HOURS before Evan and Beazie and the family got home again. They spent an eternity at the police station giving reports, Evan spoke on the phone for some time with the District Attorney in Boston, then they'd all gone to the hospital, where Ricky was expected to recover to face charges and Clay was resisting the doctor's attempts to keep him for twenty-four hours' observation.

"I'm fine," he insisted, trying to reach for his coat. "I'm going home."

The doctor began to list all the reasons why it would be wise to stay, but Sheila silenced him with a raised hand and looked into Clay's eyes.

"Do you want to marry me?"

Clay's mouth fell open, but he didn't seem able to speak.

"Then, you'd better stay the night," she said, her eyes roving his face in a message of love no man could misinterpret. "I'll be by to pick you up in the morning."

"Okay," he said with sudden docility.

They all left the room as she kissed him.

REACTION WAS BEGINNING to set in as Evan tried to concentrate on driving home. All he could remember was Murray shooting at Clay as he walked into the kitchen unexpectedly, then Ricky holding a gun to Beazie's temple. It was a good thing Murray was a bad shot, and Hank a good one.

"I told you to stay at the inn," he said to Beazie. He hadn't wanted to discuss it now, because he still had to tell his parents and Sheila about Blaine's criminal activities and he was going to need all his reserves.

But his anger was expanding despite his efforts at control, and he had to release some of the pressure.

"You told me I had to go to the inn," she corrected, "you didn't say I had to stay there."

"Bea..." he warned.

"And you told me you didn't have a plan, that you didn't know what you were going to do, that you were going to be careful. Then Hank tells me at the hospital that you had this planned like a military operation. Then you take this awful chance while Ricky has a gun on you..."

"He had the gun on you! Because you didn't do what I asked!"

"Well, if people are going to hold guns on me for that, you'd better perfect that move where you yank me away, because it's going to happen a lot."

He had no response except "Wait till I get you home."

THE DAY WAS COLD and crisp, sunlight streaming through the living room windows, as Evan gathered his parents and Sheila around the fireplace. The boys, who'd managed to sleep the night through, had gone home with Hank to play with Rachel and Erica.

Beazie admired the way Evan explained the events that had brought her to Maple Hill, how they related to what had happened to him and Blaine that day, and how Blaine had "borrowed" the money. He left out the seedier details, and tried to make it sound as though Blaine had had every intention of paying the money back. He explained Beazie's connection by saying she'd been a friend of Blaine's.

His mother had been horrified, but Barney looked as though he'd seen things Alice had either ignored or refused to accept.

Barney rubbed gently between her shoulder blades. "Come on now, Allie. You knew he wasn't an angel. Smart and clever, yes, but he got away with whatever he could. And Evan was always getting him out of scrapes. You knew that."

She finally nodded and dissolved into tears. Evan went to kneel in front of her and put his arms around her.

"I'm not crying for him," she said, weeping into his shoulder. "I'm crying because you walked around with that burden all this time. That's awful! You should have told me."

"He just did," Barney said calmly. "What do you say we all try to get some sleep, and I'll take everybody to dinner tonight. Your friends, too, Evan. I liked them. That Breakfast Barn was a good place."

Alice held Evan away from her and said fiercely,

"If you don't promise me you're going to be happy from now on, I'm going to be very upset with you."

"I promise," he said.

"And we're going to get to go to this wedding before we have to go home?" She studied him closely. "There *is* a wedding. You didn't *forget* to tell the truth about that?"

"There is a wedding. Christmas Eve. I spoke to Father Chabot today." That was true; Evan had called him from the hospital.

"All right, then," she said, swallowing her tears. "This is going to be a good Christmas. Barney, let's go up. Sheila, honey, you look peaked. You should get some sleep." Then she said with sincere anguish, "I'm so sorry Blaine wasn't good to you."

"Don't think that," Sheila said briskly, standing. "We had a lot of happy times in the beginning, and he loved the boys. And I'm going to be happy now, with Clay."

"I'm glad." Alice got to her feet and hugged everyone, then she and Barney went upstairs.

The moment they were out of earshot, Sheila wrapped her arms around Evan and said quietly, "You're a bit of an angel yourself. You did that very skillfully. Thank you."

"Sure."

Sheila hugged Beazie next. "You're going to like this family. And I look forward to us having lots of good times together."

Beazie embraced her in return. "Me, too, Sheila."

Sheila went lightly up the stairs, and Beazie faced Evan. On the principle that the best defense was a good offense, she smiled and said, "Okay, you've got me home. Now what are you going to do with me?"

He didn't smile. "Don't toy with me, Beazie. I have never been as scared as I was when Ricky had a gun to your head, not even when the truck was coming at me."

That shook her attempt to get herself off lightly. "Okay, I'm sorry," she said, going to him and putting her hands at his waist. He didn't budge, but continued to frown at her. "But I was worried about you."

"I was a cop, for God's sake!"

"Well, that doesn't make you bullet-proof. And my dream was so prophetic. When I was running up the walk at the shelter and heard three shots, *I've* never been so scared." She moved her hands up to the back of his neck and linked them. "Don't think you can set the rules because you consider yourself the protector. Love makes women protective, too." She lowered her voice on the last few words, abandoning reason for feminine wiles. "Did you really talk to Father Chabot?" On the pretext of getting a better grip on him, she wriggled against him.

"Yes," he said. "I did." But his firm voice sounded somewhat strangled.

"You know, they've taken 'obey' out of the wedding vows." She nipped at his chin. "So you just have to accept that you're not always going to have things the way you want them."

HE WAS LOST, but he still had to make a point. "And you're going to have to accept," he said, scooping her up and carrying her over his shoulder to his office off the kitchen, "that having a husband is not like having a girlfriend. We'll have an equal partnership, but you will not ignore me or run off when you don't agree with me."

He dumped her in the middle of a futon he'd made up for them to use while his family visited. She sat up, disheveled and a little off balance. He took a certain satisfaction in that.

"And when I make reasonable requests," he said, "you won't refuse to comply simply because I'm a man and you're a woman and it's no longer politically correct for you to concede to me. We won't play those games."

She looked contrite. "I agree."

That made him suspicious. "Why?"

"Because you're right."

He put a knee on the bed, then placed a diagnostic hand to her forehead. "Okay, now I'm beginning to worry that you might have gotten hurt."

She caught his hand and pulled him down beside her until they were face-to-face, body-to-body in the middle of the bed.

"I'm fine," she giggled, snuggling into him. "I'm sorry. I knew you wouldn't like it, but I had to make sure you were all right."

He opened his mouth to remind her that he was better able to see to that than she was, when she stopped him with "I know, I know. You're bigger and stronger. I can't help it that I love you madly, that I'm under the control of a grand passion."

"Wow." He'd lost the anger and was drifting toward lust. "Grand passion. Does that come with clandestine meetings and torrid lovemaking?"

"I don't think anything clandestine can happen in your family," she said with a smile. "But the torrid lovemaking is a definite."

"Good," he said, lowering his lips to hers. "Let's have some."

THE OPENING OF THE Maple Hill Homeless Shelter attracted the members of the Massachusetts Board for the Homeless Foundation, many county officials and everyone in town who'd had anything to do with setting it up.

In the past three days, Beazie and Evan had been conscripted, along with their friends and families, to put up the shelter's tree, finish wrapping gifts, set up the room that would provide free clothing for residents and others in need and prepare the food for the night's event. Consequently, the shelter looked like a festive fantasyland with garlands and lights, and a large stack of gifts for the children near a brocade cathedral chair Jackie had brought to serve as Santa's throne.

When Evan learned that she had him in mind for the role, he balked. "Oh, Jackie, give me a break," he pleaded. "I won't know what to say. And this is a big deal for those little kids. They'll expect a credible Santa."

She patted his shoulder. He'd seen that look on her face before. She was going to get what she wanted.

"Evan, you don't have to listen to their requests," she said, "you just have to distribute presents. The blue tags are for boys, the pink tags for girls. If they do try to ask you for specific things, just tell them to listen to their parents, eat their vegetables and share their toys, and you'll do fine. Just don't make promises. Tell them Santa will do his best."

"Jackie…"

"I have a speech to give, Evan." She reached up to kiss his cheek. "Have fun with it." She handed him a heavy hanger, the clothing it held wrapped in butcher paper. The fur-trimmed red costume, no doubt. Beazie appeared with the pillow.

He gave her a severe look as she put it into his free arm. "You're a party to this?"

She smiled proudly. Despite her treachery, she looked delicious and slender in a green wool dress. The purple had been professionally washed out of her hair, and her own glorious red, though still only an inch and a half long, was charmingly funky.

With a flourish, she swept a red felt elf's hat with green trim and a green pom-pom from under her arm. "Not only that, but I'm going to be your elf. I can't think of anyone who represents to me the season of miracles more than you do."

She meant it with all her heart. It was right there in the bright blue eyes that gazed at his face with love and adoration. He felt himself dissolve into a puddle of surrender.

"Come on," she whispered, taking his arm. "I'll help you put the costume on."

"I like it better," he said, letting her lead him in

to one of the bathrooms, "when you help me take things *off*."

"Well, of course we'll have to do that first."

Evan locked the door behind them, but whatever he had hoped might develop there between the two of them was rendered moot when Hank rapped on the door and shouted, "Santa's on in five minutes!"

Beazie stuffed the pillow in, as Evan zipped up the front of the costume.

"How come Hank doesn't have to do this?" he asked resentfully.

"Because he's taking care of the visiting dignitaries, Bart and Haley are dealing with the press, and Cam and Mariah, and your parents, and Sheila and Clay are serving." The costume zipped up, she stood back to admire her work. "Not bad for a guy who really only weighs one-eighty." She fitted a scratchy beard and mustache on him, then topped off the outfit with a red hat. "You ready?"

He closed his eyes and prayed for inspiration. "If they ask me for things and I have to behave like a real Santa, we're sunk. I'm going to ruin all those needy children's faith in Santa, and it's going to be your fault."

She put on her hat and checked her reflection in the mirror. "You're not going to ruin anything. Come on."

Evan held his own with seven of the eight children moving into the new shelter. One little boy named David tugged at his beard and drew back wide-eyed when Evan yelled, "Ouch!" One chubby little girl in glasses looked disappointed at the gift-wrapped box he gave her and told him she'd asked for a horse.

"The shelter doesn't have a place for horses," he said, hoping she'd understand. "But if you try again next Christmas, we'll see what we can do."

The child looked into his eyes for one dangerous moment, then smiled. "Okay," she said. "See you next year."

As she walked away, he turned to Beazie with a "Whew!" of relief. She winked at him, then pointed to the last child in line.

It was another little girl, thin and small in a red jumper over a white shirt. The clothes were big for her, probably hand-me-downs. She had black eyes, glossy black hair and a shy smile, and as she approached, she beckoned him to lean down to her.

He did.

"I have something for Jesus," she said.

He sat back in surprise, uncertain how to react to that. There was an inner strength about her, despite the fact that she couldn't be more than six or seven years old.

"But...I'm Santa," he said.

She came closer, seeming to conquer her shyness. "I know. You bring toys to all the good children. But you and Jesus always come out together when it's Christmas, 'cept I don't get to see Him. So, I figure you must be friends. I thought if I gave this to you, you could give it to Him."

At the risk of hopelessly entangling religious and secular concepts, he agreed, thinking that accepting the child's generosity was important.

"Uh...okay. What is it?"

She held out something palm-size, wrapped in tissue. "My mom and I made a whole bunch of these to sell to make some money to buy the babies something for Christmas." She pointed to the sidelines, where a slender woman stood with a baby in her arms and one of the toddlers who'd just come through his line. "You can look at it."

Before he could do that, she leaned trustingly into him and undid the bow around the tissue. The paper fell open to reveal what appeared to be a wooden ball and scraps of fabric. Then he realized he was looking at an angel ornament. Features had been painted on the ball for a face, a circle of glittery fabric served as a dress and gossamer ribbon made the wings.

He'd seen several of these on the shelter's tree, but this one was less finely made—the little angel leaning against him had helped.

She smiled into his face. "I prayed and prayed for us to have a place to stay instead of the car." She shrugged bony little shoulders. "And here we are. Father Chabot says miracles always happen, but a lot of them come at Christmas. Will you tell Jesus this is from Missy, and that I said thank-you?"

Evan opened his mouth to assure her that he would, and found that he had no voice. He cleared his throat and tried again. "I will. And I'm sure it'll make Him very happy."

One large box remained in the stack, and Father Chabot came to help Missy pull it aside. Her mother and siblings crowded around as she opened it.

All around the room, children were squealing in delight, and windup toys filled the place with noise.

Pie and coffee was served to the adults, and Evan took the opportunity to escape into the bathroom, change out of his Santa suit and fulfill his promise.

Beazie was waiting for him at the shelter's front door. She was wearing her coat and carrying his. She held it open for him, then hooked her arm in his when they stepped outside. The night air was crisp and cold.

"So, not only a very convincing Santa, but a confidant of Jesus, as well," she teased, squeezing his arm.

He laughed softly. "She had that a little mixed up, but I'm sure God understands."

"I'm sure He does," she agreed. "He gave me more than I deserve this Christmas. And only He knows how mixed up I've sometimes been."

It was a very short distance from the shelter to the front lawn of St. Anthony's Church next door. Evan went to the Nativity figures he and Beazie had repainted, her touches of beading and gold braid picked out by the streetlight nearby.

He knelt down in the snow, Beazie beside him. He'd learned so much in the past few weeks, and his throat was tight with emotion as he realized the tremendous gift he'd been given, and the future that awaited him, filled with all the treasures he'd been so sure he'd forfeited when Blaine died.

He offered his own prayer of thanks, Beazie's arm wrapped in his. Then he reached into his pocket for the bead-and-fabric angel and placed it in the manger beside the cherubic figure of Jesus.

"That's from Missy," he whispered. "She says thank you for the shelter."

Beazie put her hand on the figure's little foot. "I'm Beazie," she said in a soft but strong voice. "Thank you for Evan."

SILHOUETTE®
SUPERROMANCE™

AVAILABLE FROM 19TH DECEMBER 2003

ON HER GUARD Beverly Barton

The Protectors

Secret service agent Nikos Pandarus has never been able to resist Ellen Denby but he can never truly have her. For she will become a target for his enemies. Yet, now that Ellen is in his arms once more he's sworn to protect her. But will their passion come at too high a price?

LYDIA LANE Judith Bowen

Girlfriends

Lydia Lane didn't take the Girlfriends challenge too seriously. But then first love Sam Pereira finds her! One-time bad boy Sam is now a successful lawyer and single father, and Lydia knows she could fall for him all over again…and for his little girl.

CODE OF HONOUR Kathryn Shay

City Heat

Lieutenant Jake Scarlatta knows Chelsea Whitmore, one of the best firefighters on his team, needs his help. But helping the woman he is falling for to clear her name means implicating one of his men. Will Jake choose misplaced loyalty over love?

THE TARGET Kay David

The Guardians

Hannah Crosby wants marriage and children—but Quinn McNichol can't forget the dangers they face each day as members of the bomb squad. What if one of them doesn't come home one night? And now it seems as if a bomber is trying to help them answer that question…

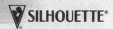

SILHOUETTE® SENSATION™

*proudly presents
a brand-new series from*

KYLIE BRANT

THE TREMAINE TRADITION

**Where undercover assignments lead
to unexpected pleasures...**

Alias Smith and Jones
January 2004

Entrapment
April 2004

Truth or Lies
July 2004

*Look out for more from Kylie Brant.
Coming soon!*

0104/SH/LC79

FREE

2 BOOKS
AND A SURPRISE GIFT!

We would like to take this opportunity to thank you for reading this Silhouette® book by offering you the chance to take TWO more specially selected titles from the Superromance™ series absolutely FREE! We're also making this offer to introduce you to the benefits of the Reader Service™—

- ★ FREE home delivery
- ★ FREE monthly Newsletter
- ★ FREE gifts and competitions
- ★ Exclusive Reader Service discount
- ★ Books available before they're in the shops

Accepting these FREE books and gift places you under no obligation to buy; you may cancel at any time, even after receiving your free shipment. Simply complete your details below and return the entire page to the address below. **You don't even need a stamp!**

YES! Please send me 2 free Superromance books and a surprise gift. I understand that unless you hear from me, I will receive 4 superb new titles every month for just £3.49 each, postage and packing free. I am under no obligation to purchase any books and may cancel my subscription at any time. The free books and gift will be mine to keep in any case.

U3ZEC

Ms/Mrs/Miss/Mr ....Initials...

BLOCK CAPITALS PLEASE

Surname...

Address...

....

....Postcode ....

Send this whole page to:
UK: FREEPOST CN81, Croydon, CR9 3WZ
EIRE: PO Box 4546, Kilcock, County Kildare (stamp required)

Offer valid in UK and Eire only and not available to current Reader Service subscribers to this series. We reserve the right to refuse an application and applicants must be aged 18 years or over. Only one application per household. Terms and prices subject to change without notice. Offer expires 31st March 2004. As a result of this application, you may receive offers from Harlequin Mills & Boon and other carefully selected companies. If you would prefer not to share in this opportunity please write to The Data Manager at the address above.

Silhouette® is a registered trademark used under licence.
Superromance™ is being used as a trademark.